IN HIS CORNER

A FIGHTER ROMANCE

SKARA GRAY

READER REVIEWS

NEW extended & fully edited version published October 2023! +5000 more words.

Praise for this fighter romance from over two million readers!

In His Corner by Skara Gray

"This was such an amazing story with its tantalizing promises of more to come. I loved the heat and chemistry between the main characters. A job well done, I can't wait to move onto the next enthralling story that you create." - Emily B.

"This book was sooooo good! The characters, the emotions, the suspense was everything! I enjoyed it so much. I can't wait for you to blow up on here. You deserve it." - P. B.

"This book really affected my soul and heart with all kinds of emotion. I'm still speechless after reading it in a day, minute by minute till the end. I remember when I started Thai-boxing to get through my daily life and now I am reading a book about it. I have no words. I can't explain it. It just feels so right to read it. It was so specially written and I loved their story together. Rhett and Ava, such beautiful people." - Annah E.

"I miss this book so much! Can we get like a bonus chapter when Ava was still in school or something? Anyway it's a great book and each update and chapter was amazing. Love the complexity of the plot and the realistic characters!!! Congrats on finishing yet another great book." - Dawn W.

Enjoy a sneak peak of my next fighter romance at the end of this book, *Against The Ropes*. Happy reading!

Website: skaragray.com
Instagram: @skaragray
Wattpad: @skaragray

Dedicated to the millions of readers who fell in love with this story and encouraged me to keep writing.

EXPLICIT CONTENT FOR 18+

I mark this original piece of work as mature and appropriate for audiences 18+ due to sexual scenes, cursing, and limited violence. I am always open to feedback about all aspects of my work but please keep this in mind.

GET A FREE BOOK!

Join Skara Gray's Mailing List to get a FREE book as well as news on upcoming releases and exclusive bonus chapters!

OTHER BOOKS BY SKARA GRAY

Fighter Series

Against The Ropes: A fighter romance

Below The Belt: A fighter romance

Standalone

Seeing Red: A billionaire romance

Sold To The Boss: A narcos romance

IN HIS CORNER

Rhett Jaggar is Boston's hottest underground fighter. He has the body and the winning streak to prove it. He trains like a mad man, with more discipline than a monk. But even he can't keep his attention in the ring when a brunette distraction shows up in his boxing gym.

Ava Young had it all. The fancy house on a hill, a successful businessman father, an adorably decorated off campus apartment, and a group of fun-loving college friends. That is, until her father's company is exposed for embezzling. She has no place to turn but her childhood best friend's couch and a new, strange life filled with underground fighters. Including the intimidatingly sexy, Rhett Jaggar.

These two opposites may come to find that they have more in common than they realize...but will it be a harmless attraction or end in a dangerous addiction?

Read as a standalone fighter romance. Part of a series of standalone fighter romances including *Against The Ropes* and *Below The Belt*. Complete at 75,000 words.

COVER ART

Cover image is professionally created with proper image licensing.

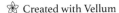 Created with Vellum

1

RHETT

The music blares loudly, nearly in sync with the discordant rounds of punching taking place in the gym. I fall into the familiar rhythm of the speed bag, moving my hands so quickly it's like they're not moving at all. *Thud, thud, thud, thud.* The noise makes me miss my days on the streets when the *thuds* came from ribs and cheekbones rather than stuffed leather, but I'd been adhering to a strait-laced lifestyle over the past few years in more ways than one. Too much money at stake in the ring to get caught up with the cops these days.

"Hey, Rhett, why don't you cut yourself a break for a minute and come over here to meet a new fighter I've been telling ya about." My coach, Barry, waves me over with a nod of his bald head as he rests his weathered forearms on the worn blue ropes.

I head towards him on the other side of the gym, running a fresh towel down my neck and shoulders. I don't like meeting new people, especially new fighters. Barry is always trying to get me to take on a mentor role but these new guys are usually fucking pricks that are in need of some quality ass beating and a slice of humble pie.

"Rhett, this is Eric. We're gonna start him off on the lower circuit soon, he's a heavyweight like you." Barry slaps the kid on the back. Eric is grinning from ear to ear like some cocky motherfucker. Is he really flexing his biceps at me right now? I could kick his ass. Easily. This guy is all bulk and no agility. I feel the familiar itch of a punch in my fists, the adrenaline spiking through my fingers.

"Hey man, how's it going? Wanna spar a bit? See how long the veteran can last?" Eric cocks his neck like some wild animal and despite myself, I let out a deep laugh. The sound is rich and full but laced with sarcasm. If he thinks my age will have any impact on my stamina he's not nearly as familiar with my track record as he should be.

"Hey now boy, settle down," Barry chides. "Rhett's got a lot of money on the line Friday night, can't have him wasting his precious time beating your ass." Barry throws me a wink and I smirk. At least Coach Barry still knows what's up.

I turn to head back to my punching bag, a fresh wave of annoyance to work out on the leather, when I hear arguing.

"Shelly, don't touch that! Stop messing around. I'm serious. Let's go." I hear a sweet, frustrated feminine voice coming from behind Eric and it stands out crystal clear among the standard clamor of the gym since a female voice in this place is about as foreign as manners.

"Oh my god, Ava, lighten up. We're here with Eric, it's cool." Another girl's tinny voice chimes in before I'm finally able to see the two female figures making their way through a maze of punching bags.

"Who are they?" I cross my arms over my bare chest and turn toward Coach Barry. This kind of shit in the gym is nothing but a distraction. I don't need all my sparring partners to lose their focus over some ass. What I need is some actual competition in the ring, especially with my mounting annoyance at Eric whose smug look seems to be permanently stained on his boyish face.

"Ah, they're with me. We just came by to check out the place, thought they might like to take a look." Eric throws a glance over his shoulder at the two girls who are still whispering angrily at one another. They're largely hidden by one of the larger punching bag sets.

"They should leave. Easy distraction. I gotta get back to training." I run a hand through my sweaty hair in annoyance and make my way back to my bag. I already know I won't be able to take out all my frustration on the bag alone today. Hopefully Barry will come through with a worthy sparring partner so I can actually exhaust myself to the point of sleeping through the night.

I deftly hop into an open ring, a move that feels as natural as walking. I turn back towards Eric and Coach Barry. The girls have come out from behind the punching bags and are standing near Eric. One of the girls has straight blonde hair and her thin, tanned arm is draped possessively over Eric's bulky shoulder. The other girl is standing off to the side, fiddling with her phone. She clearly looks uncomfortable and annoyed to be here. I wonder if she even notices all the eyes now descending on her. She's fucking stunning with long, light brown hair and curves for days. For a long minute, I can't take my eyes off her. She finally glances up for a moment and looks in my direction before the other blonde girl lets her know that they're leaving. Good. I need to get my head back in the ring for my fight tomorrow. I already have enough pressure on my shoulders as is. The bets placed on tomorrow's fight are high and I can't afford any mistakes. Turns out the people who love you when you make money are the same as the ones who want to kill you when you don't.

"Coach! Send me a sparring partner," I yell out towards Coach Barry, making quick eye contact with the sexy-as-hell girl brunette one more time before the intruding group exits the gym. "A legit one!" I bounce lightly on my calves, the addicting feeling of fighting energy coursing through me.

After a few more hours of sparring, my arms are sore as I pull my leather jacket tighter around my waist. The weather is finally starting to turn and the cool night air licks against my damp neck. But even though my arms are sore from a full day of training I'm still wired. My limbs are strung so tight, I'm just waiting for the snap. It's something I work to avoid in vain. I hate that I'm still so awake, walking down an all-too familiar alley, straight toward *Blue Moons*. I fucking hate these shitty dive bars. They bring me back to nights of drug-induced fights and seemingly endless stupors. I might still be fucked up, but I don't want to go back to *that* place. Ever. But every fighter knows that sex before a fight is good for performance in the ring. And right now, I'm looking for an easy lay. Finding women has never been an issue for me. Maintaining interest and making sure those women don't get attached? Those are issues I deal with often. Good thing about *Blue Moons* is these girls know the deal. They fuck with fighters often and don't expect sweet text messages or follow-up dinners in return. And as shitty as it may be, I know that no matter what girl I end up taking home tonight, I won't be able to get the gorgeous brunette from the gym out of my mind. The way her waist pinched in and her hips flared out. Her full lips and breasts. Something about her was sexy and innocent at once, seeing as she was clearly uncomfortable in a gym full of fighting men. I'm not used to shy women like that. They don't tend to mix with my lifestyle.

But I also know those women are trouble because they expect commitment. And the only thing I've ever been committed to is the ring.

2

AVA

"Shelly, I just don't want to go. It's not my scene *and* it's illegal."

"Ava, the cops are like the biggest supporters of this stuff. They are totally in the loop and have money on the line. It's not getting busted." I hate it when Shelly just recites exactly what Eric says with a sense of haughtiness as if she truly knows the information firsthand. As if she actually has any idea what she's talking about. I'm usually suspect of most of Shelly's flings but Eric is a different kind of trouble. And after everything I've been through recently, I'm not exactly keen on getting involved in his "underground fighting" lifestyle. A lifestyle I didn't even know existed until last week.

Two weeks ago, I was a college senior at a posh private school pursuing a degree in marketing. Now, thanks to a ridiculously tragic serving of fate, I'm a college-dropout, *technically* homeless, and beyond penniless thanks to my lying, cheating, completely-faking-his-entire-life father. I also may be officially friendless aside from Shelly, considering my college friends and the guy I'd been casually dating, Jacob, have yet to reach out to me after what I call *the reckoning*. A literal scene from hell, it's when the cops came to find me at my dorm to inform me that my father had been arrested for fraud and that all of my accounts were now frozen. If not seized for everything they'd been worth. Which, I'm now realizing being on the other side of life, were worth a hell of a lot of money. The likes of which I'm not going to see anytime soon.

So the last thing I need in my crumbling life right now is to engage with anything risky or unknown when I'm still reeling from the loss of everything I've ever had.

This includes grappling with Shelly's latest and eccentric dating choices.

To be fair, Shelly was the only person there for me when my whole life fell apart before my very eyes. We have been friends since childhood, always incredibly different but somehow in sync. We met in elementary school and hit it off even though we never hung out in the same social circles. I went off to private college and she went to cosmetology school, working in various high-end salons around Boston. When I called her telling her I needed a place to stay, she didn't even question me about it. Which is more than I can say for anyone else in my life, including my greedy and nosy network of aunts, uncles, and cousins who were only concerned with the dollar signs flashing before their eyes.

So maybe I could just do this one thing, this one time, for her. Even if it is scary and illegal and insane. Just the thought makes my stomach knot.

"Okay fine. But I'm not going to any parties after the fight. I don't know these people."

"Ava, stop being such a snob! Meet new people, it's fun." Shelly bounds over to me, twirling the ends of my long hair playfully. "Can I pick out your outfit?"

"No." More like *absolutely not.* I am already agreeing to go to an underground illegal boxing fight; there is no way I'll also be caught dead in one of Shelly's outfits. She can rock the off-duty model look with strappy, slinky dresses, but I cannot. If I try to pull off her style I just look downright outrageous, my chest and hips much fuller than her slender, waif-life physique.

Besides, my goal right now is blending in and not attracting any unnecessary attention. I've had enough attention over the past few weeks to last me this lifetime and into the next.

"Fine, fine, I won't push it. Let's leave at 7:00 PM. It'll be fun I promise!" She gives me a quick peck on the cheek before running into her bedroom, likely to try on seven variations of sparkly short skirts and tank tops. I can't help but smile a bit to myself. As frustrating as Shelly can be she is always happy and positive, never harboring on painful moments from the past.

—

The underground arena is fairly dark with lights surrounding the ring. There are metal chairs close to the ring itself and long metal benches further out. I'm surprised at how close our seats are, but it seems like Eric has decent potential for this fighting stuff so I guess the coach we met with the other day at the gym wants him up close and taking notes. We find our way to our seats, only the second row back from the ring. I keep my eyes on the floor, desperate to get away from the overt looks and catcalls from several other fans finding their seats. I'm certain the catcalls are mainly directed at Shelly, whose blonde hair stands out brightly under the spotlights dancing above the arena. After chancing a quick look around, I'm certain that I am in fact *the* most conservatively dressed woman in the whole arena. I'm wearing my favorite light blue denim jeans and a long-sleeved cream ribbed sweater that hardly shows any cleavage. Even so, I find myself self-consciously pulling up on the neckline.

"Okay, so you remember that guy in the gym the other day? The one that seemed all pissed at us being there and whatever?" Shelly knees me to get my attention, already bouncing excitedly in her seat like a child at a show. Meanwhile, I'm practically terrified, wondering if sitting this close to the ring will mean we get any blood or sweat on us. *Okay brain, shut down that gross mental image.*

"Yeah..." My voice trails off as I recall the ridiculously strong, dark-haired fighter who seemed more than a little annoyed at our presence in the gym. I couldn't blame him really. I knew when we stepped foot in there that it wasn't a great idea. But I hadn't been able to see him up close. Still, even from a distance he seemed like he was built to inflict some serious damage.

"Okay, well that guy was Rhett Jaggar. And he's like a *really* big deal in the underground. Eric's gonna be like him someday." Shelly turns to look at Eric affectionately before turning back to me. I can't help but smile a little sheepishly to myself. Eric is all beefy muscle and cocky attitude. That fighter, this Rhett or whoever he was, seemed like a real slick killer. I know next to nothing about fighting but even I'd place a bet that Eric will never be anything like this supposed fighting legend.

"He's fighting tonight and there's a lot of money riding on him. If he loses, it'll be real bad. But everyone is sure he will win. He gets a fat percentage of the winning pot too. I don't know how much exactly but Eric just said it's at least six figures. Can you believe that, Ava? Six figures for one night?! Apparently the guy has unending amounts of energy. He's undefeated this year." Shelly's eyes are practically glittering as if she's loved boxing her entire life. The way she's rattling off stats about some stranger, no doubt just repeating verbatim whatever Eric told her. But Shelly is always like this with her new boyfriends. She instantly becomes obsessed with whatever they do, whether it's abstract painting or street racing. And then there was that one guy in a motorcycle gang guy...

"Basically what I'm saying is, we snagged up-close seats to one of the hottest fights of the season!" She slaps my thigh playfully and I can't help but laugh. I can name about a dozen places I'd rather be right now, including organizing my new tiny bedroom in Shelly's apartment or going to the grocery store. Despite this, I try to let myself absorb some of her genuine excitement. I glance nervously down at my phone, willing it to buzz with a response from one of my college friends or Jacob. Even a dreaded "K" which is usually text speak for "screw off" would be better than radio silence at this point.

"Hey, Earth to Ava," Shelly grabs my phone from my lap, "please let up on this Jacob loser. If he's not willing to stick around when shit hits the fan then he's not worth it. Besides, based on the pics you've shown me, he looks like he has a real stick up his ass." I groan at her and reach for my phone, part of me hating to admit she's right while the other part is still desperate for him to text me back. We had only been dating for about six or seven months when the whole scandal went down about my father and the entire event was more than humiliating. My guess is that he's embarrassed to have anything to do with me which isn't a great sign of character but can I really blame him? I can hardly think back to that night without a full body shiver. Maybe I'm just craving a little connection to my past life and his lack of a text response is giving me a sinking feeling in my stomach that there are no connections left. Nothing but a blunt sever like a lost limb, quick and painful.

The lights in the arena start to dim even further and the noise deepens with intensity, a sense of something carnal brewing in the air. I can feel the tension building in the space as it strums through my body, making me nervously cross and re-cross my legs. I can't get over the feeling that I'm doing something wrong. It's an adrenaline rush that brings a heat to my face. I hate the thought of getting in trouble. I always have.

"Ladies and gentlemen!" An announcer booms out over a microphone. "Welcome to the fight, or rather *fights*, you've all been waiting for. Most of you are regulars but let's review a few rules for this evening. First, no weapons or guns in this ring, real men fight with their fists only."

Um, what did he just say?! That's an actual rule that needs to be stated? I grip Shelly's hand in fear but she only pats the back of it while staring excitedly ahead, not a drop of concern in her eager expression.

"Second, we are fighting to win, not fighting to kill. Although we all know things do happen..." The announcer's upper lip curls in a wicked smile and I literally feel goose-bumps break out over my entire body. I truly cannot believe I actually agreed to come here.

"Lastly, no rigging of any kind is allowed. We gamble honestly here, my friends." The arena breaks out in a crushing wave of laughter and cheering at the irony of honest yet illegal gambling. I can't help but notice that this also seems like the only rule that the audience is actually concerned with truly upholding and it makes my stomach clench with nausea.

"Alright, enough with the rules and the chit-chat. Let's bring out one of our first fighters of the night. This fighter hails from Chicago. It's his first time in this tournament, so let's give him a warm Boston welcome. Come on out Zax, the Demon, Cade!" The entire arena breaks out in a discordant bellow of boos and expletives. I nearly cover my ears in horror. The crowd is shouting insults so nasty and scandalous I've never even heard them before. How can people even think of such vile things...

"Okay, okay be nice," the announcer jokingly chides. Zax, the Demon, Cade cracks his neck back and forth in his respective corner of the ring, nodding fervently at his coach who seems to be passing along some last-minute instructions. He looks wild, like an animal released for a hunt.

"And now, the man, the myth, the legend...the one you all came here tonight to see. Come on out Rhett, the Reaper, Jaggar!" I clutch my neck in shock as the arena breaks out in a deafening cheer. I wonder how truly underground and secret this place even is if people are comfortable making this much noise. I feel like I'm in the middle of an audible earthquake, the sound reverberating through my body.

"Oh em gee, it's him, it's him!" Shelly grabs my arm enthusiastically and directs my attention, along with the attention of the entire arena, towards the massively strong, tanned figure approaching the ring. His head is covered in a dark red silk cape. He walks with a sense of severity that completely contrasts his opponent's jaunty, cocky sprint to the ring. Rhett is not playing or pandering to the crowd. He almost seems like he doesn't even notice anyone else is here, like the audience just blends into the furniture and architecture of the arena itself. I'm not sure if I'm more shocked by how much these people love and worship him or the fact that he seems completely unaffected by it.

The cheering continues as he slips off his red cape and bounces lightly on his heels in his corner of the ring. I hate the way my mouth pops open a bit at seeing his bare abdomen up close. He's ripped. Like completely and utterly shredded in a way I've never seen before in real life. I don't think I've ever used the word "shredded" to describe a man before, even in my own head. His strong muscles are covered in a patchwork of various tattoos with none of them being too big to hide his olive-toned skin underneath. His hair is dark and slightly damp and even from here I can see his jaw ticking ominously. I am entirely aroused and terrified at once and I resent myself for it. This is violence. This is illegal and dirty. So why do I imagine myself licking between the defined lines of his ab muscles? Those things look like they're chiseled straight from stone. I clear my throat, mentally chastising myself, and look down at the floor for a moment to regain control of my fraying female hormones. I feel my cheeks start to warm again.

"Holy. Shit." Shelly grabs my arm, whispering in my ear. "I mean, have you ever seen a man so strong? He's sexy as hell. Even your prude self can't deny that!"

"I mean yes. He is...attractive." I let out a nervous laugh, more like a pent-up huff of air, as my eyes fixate on him. He scans the audience with dark, detached eyes. "And for the record, I'm not prude."

"Attractive?! Ava, please. The preppy college boys you've dated like Jacob are *attractive* at best. That man in there is molten hot lava sex on a stick." I'm about to protest that her description makes no sense when his dark scanning eyes land on mine. Since we're so close to the ring, there's enough light cast on us for him to see me fairly clearly. I feel my heart thundering in my chest and a fresh wave of pink flush starts to creep up my neck, over the collar of my sweater. It may be my overactive imagination but I swear I see his eyebrows rise a little higher onto his forehead, either in annoyance or surprise. It's hard to tell with him. We maintain eye contact until he lazily pulls his gaze away and focuses squarely on his opponent.

"Was he uh...did you feel like he was looking at me?" I whisper quietly to Shelly, desperate for some form of validation that *that* just happened.

"Um yeah, captain obvious. He practically fucked you with his eyes, Ava! Maybe he's into your whole preppy school girl vibe! Kudos to you for rocking that outfit, I wouldn't have figured it would be his type." She wiggles her blonde eyebrows suggestively at me and I can't help but laugh quietly at her words, her obsession with men and sex always trickling over to me when she isn't single. But I'm certain he hadn't been *fucking* me with his eyes or whatever. He looked faintly surprised, even a bit disinterested. But definitely not lustful.

"Okay you crazy Rhett fans, settle down and settle in! Round one starts now!" The announcer's voice rings out crisply over the darkened arena, blanketing the space in suspense. *Holy crap, round one?!* How long is this thing going to last? I feel my stomach churn as the first blow of flesh against bone is heard throughout the arena, wrapping my waist securely with my arm in a desperate attempt to not throw up.

3

RHETT

Fucking hell. My eyes must be playing tricks on me. The arena lights can fuck with you when you're in the center of the ring. But even though I didn't get as solid of a look as I would've liked, I swear the brunette beauty from the gym is *here*. In the underground. At my high-stakes fight. I didn't think I'd mind seeing that pretty face anywhere, but somehow seeing her so up close in a place as violent and corrupt as this feels wrong. Like it doesn't fit. I can't get those full pink lips out of my head as I turn away from her and towards my piece of shit "opponent" Zax. His cockiness and stance alone tell me this fight is going to be a warm-up. It's what the audience wants. They get off on me knocking out fighter after fighter until the last fight when I actually get an opponent more worthy of my time. But I have never been into fighting for the drama and the spectacle. I just fucking love fighting. No audience necessary. Sometimes I wonder why people even like watching me so much since I hardly do any antics or crowd-pleasing maneuvers. Except knockouts but those are always for me, not for them.

I breeze through the first three fighters, hardly breaking a sweat. By the time the third guy comes around, I actually do dance around him a little and let him get a few punches in just to drag out the process a bit longer for the crowd. Coach Barry won't appreciate that but my investors will. Once he's out I finally chance a look around the crowd and make eye contact with my brunette beauty again. She looks like she's about to vomit. The thought makes me smirk, wondering how in the hell such a goodie-two-shoes girl ends up in a place like this on a Friday night. She should be away from here with some finance pretty boy at a nice restaurant, asking her boring questions about what she likes to do in her free time. I wonder what it'd be like just to watch those pretty pink lips move in response. Then I briefly imagine those pink lips moving over my dick but I forcefully stop my mind from going there while I'm in the ring.

"Okay, arena! We are ready for our final fight, the fight where your bets matter, the fight you've all been waiting for. Rhett, the Reaper, Jaggar, our crowd favorite, against a truly worthy opponent...Falcon Brawler!" The crowd breaks out in a mix of screams and boos, the loud cacophony raking through the entire space. The audience is looking towards Falcon, his large burly figure slowly approaching the ring. This motherfucker is dirty, inside and outside the ring. Once I committed to underground boxing full-time I quit any bullshit fighting outside the ring. Not this one. He's not above sending his henchmen to beat up other fighters, or even their girlfriends and wives, before a big fight. He's known for threatening opponents into throwing the match. I can't wait to break his wide, garish face in. Before I turn to face him, I see my brunette beauty, her eyes fixedly on me while everyone else is looking to Falcon. I only manage to tear my eyes away when Falcon is directly across from me.

When the announcer rings the bell, I see Falcon lumber forward, trying to fake an attack. He's definitely the hardest opponent of the night, hence the high-stakes bet on this particular fight. He's one of the only fighters who's beaten me before in my younger years. But I was hungover during that fight, back when I hadn't fully committed to the ring yet. Years ago I swore to myself that I'd never let anything as stupid as alcohol keep me from winning again.

I move in quickly, getting in a few hard and tight jabs to his abdomen. As he defends and recoils, I bounce out quickly, knowing I'm faster and more agile than him but also that he's the kind of boxer who likes to trap his opponent underneath him. I move in for him again but he gets a strong uppercut to my jaw and I can taste the familiar metallic tang of blood between my teeth. He quickly assaults my abdomen, knocking the air from my lungs and I stumble back onto the ropes. *Fuck,* it hurts. Doesn't matter how many times you get hit, the pain never stops. I'm nearly positive he's broken a rib. Definitely not my first broken rib but it's always a bitch. I quickly twist away and out of reach before he bulldozes at me and ends up slamming chest first into the ropes. I come up behind him and lock his arms behind his head before jabbing a few hard hits into his kidneys. I let him fall forward into the ropes and back away, gripping my side and desperately gasping for a few precious breaths. Falcon turns around slowly, his eyes slightly glazed over. I stand to my full 6'4" height, fighting to ignore the throbbing pain in my side as I rush towards him to land a final round of lightning-fast punches. He lands a clobbered fist to the right side of my face before he finally goes down and I can feel the familiar pressure of an oncoming black eye. I hardly even hear the deafening screams of the crowd, my hearing, and vision starting to blur as if I'm underwater. I fucking know this feeling. It's that moment before the blackout from the pain I've been putting off with coursing amounts of adrenaline. The last two things I remember are the announcer lifting my arm high in the air and a pair of pretty, golden eyes looking like they're about to cry before the edges around my vision go fuzzy and black and I feel the mat rise up and swallow me with it.

4

AVA

I feel the buzz of nerves and energy course violently through my body after this insane night. It's like the high of the fight is now within me. Seeing Rhett land smooth punch after punch, watching his long muscular arms connect perfectly with the opponent, his rippled torso twisting and contorting, every muscle a line cut from stone. I've never really seen anything like it. A baseball game with my dad or college sporting events didn't even remotely compare to this. I definitely can't say I *enjoyed* it, but undoubtedly it was an experience I wouldn't easily forget.

As the crowd starts to rustle and move towards the exits, a wave of incoherent shouting mixing with too-loud music now blaring through the underground arena speakers, I look back at the ring to see Rhett bloodied and gasping for breath, hitting the mat after winning the fight like some fallen warrior after battle. He still looks strong, even in pain, but his naturally tan face now looks ashen. I notice the stress lines pulling around his eyes and I don't move from my chair despite the surging crowd around me.

"Ava! The fight's over, let's go." Shelly pushes gently at the small of my back forcing me toward the aisle.

"Uh...is he okay? Should someone call a doctor or something?"

"Who Rhett? Sweetheart, relax. That man is flying high, trust me. He just made a lot of important people a lot richer tonight. Including himself. Just a little blackout from the broken rib pain. The dude's been beat up way worse than this and still won. Look, the medic is already in the ring, he'll be better in no time. No need to get your panties in a knot."

Double ew. I do not like the idea of burly, boyish Eric thinking about my panties. Even in a metaphoric capacity. I turn back to the ring and Rhett is now sitting upright, his forearms resting on his bent knees, his head hung low between his long outstretched legs. The medic tries unsuccessfully to push away a slew of fans, crowding in on Rhett and shaking his coach's hand. Another two medics set the massive, limp body of Falcon on a stretcher. If I wasn't able to see the subtle rising and falling of his barrel-chest, I'd be pretty certain he was dead.

"Listen, Ava, we're going to a bar. Don't protest okay? Everyone goes. We won't stay long I promise. Like, an hour max. Plus, you could use a drink, your face is paler than a ghost!"

To Shelly's surprise, I don't protest. I'm too in shock, my thoughts still replaying what I'd just witnessed in the ring. I let Shelly and Eric guide me towards the exit, trying to avoid the roaming eyes and hands of random men as we meander and shove our way through the slowly thinning crowd out into the brisk evening.

The bar is fairly packed when we arrive but less crowded than the arena. I'm grateful for the fresh night air and the

welcome cool weather against my overheated skin. I feel
wired, my nerves on edge from the fight. I want to go for a
run or a swim or *something*. Anything to help dull this
strange sensation of adrenaline attacking my body. Instead,
Shelly pushes a pink fruity cocktail into my hand and I
decide I'll have to go with alcohol as my release for the time
being. I drink it quickly, too quickly, and feel the light
familiar buzz of tipsiness. Chalk it up to being a twenty-two-
year-old lightweight. I stand near Shelly as she ogles over
Eric and his arrogant comments about being the next Rhett
Jaggar. I don't think *anyone* could be the next Rhett, but at
least Eric has some ambition I guess. I block out the conversation as I scan the rest of the bar, my eyes widening at the
group of beautiful, scantily-clad women surveying the
crowd like they're on a lethal hunting mission, waiting to
strike.

"Who are they?" I nudge Shelly's side and we turn our
heads in the girls' direction.

"Oh. Those are the ring bunnies." Shelly's voice comes
out cold and annoyed. She's clearly seen them before.

"Gotta give them credit, I'd freeze to death in anything
less than jeans and a jacket." I laugh lightly into her side and
watch a scowl cross over her face but she doesn't protest.
These *ring bunnies* are practically wearing lingerie during
early fall in Boston. And they don't even look the least bit
uncomfortable doing it. I find myself a little in awe of them.

"Well, you're always cold, even in the summer." Shelly
takes a sip from her second drink and looks back at me. "A
ring bunny is basically a groupie. They stick around after
the fights and try to saddle up to one of the fighters. Of
course with Rhett being the winning fighter tonight, they
are out in full swing." She wraps her arm tighter around
Eric, and I try not to laugh out loud since none of the ring

bunnies are even looking in his direction, nor is he looking at them. Shelly definitely has some serious trust issues from past relationships. She just falls too hard too fast, usually for the wrong guys. Hopefully that won't be the same story with Eric. I order another drink and watch as the beautiful women primp themselves in small pocket mirrors and saunter over to high-top tables scattered throughout the bar. But by the time I finish my drink, I've grown wary of the whole scene, ready to be safely tucked into bed with my comfortable flannel pajamas and a Netflix show.

Even the confident ring bunnies start to look antsy since Rhett appears to be a no show. Part of me was hoping he would come to the bar, just so I could see him outside of the ring or the gym, up close. He seems non-human in my mind right now, replaying the rounds of fighting he just endured. But the other half of me is relieved he didn't show. Blood and violence makes me queasy enough, I'm not sure I can stomach seeing his various bruises and cuts up close and personal. Especially since watching him take each hit in the last round made my stomach roil, wondering why the heck anyone would voluntarily put themselves in that position. A flinch snaps across my shoulders just thinking about it.

"Okay bestie, time to go home." Shelly sidles up next to me and playfully knocks her slender hip into mine. *Thanks goodness.* I'm so tired and worn out from the chaos and strangeness of this night. All I want is a hot shower and my bed. I let Shelly wrap her arm around me as we make our way toward Eric's car.

But later that night as I'm snuggled comfortably into my new twin bed at Shelly's, I see Rhett's strong, tattooed arms behind my eyelids, his dark scorching eyes desperately seeking out mine among the crowd as if he's looking for answers that only I can answer.

5

AVA

I'm hungover. Not quite wasted, totally miserable, hungover, but certainly pounding headache worthy. I groan out loud and roll myself off the small twin sized toward the ground, leaning my head back dramatically. After a few minutes, I head to the kitchen, in desperate search of where Shelly keeps the Tylenol. Since I've only been here for two weeks I still don't know where everything is. The realization makes me yearn for my modern off-campus apartment and my very recent past life where my biggest concerns were upcoming exams or what to wear to a fraternity party with Jacob. Now I had looming college debt, an entirely uncertain future, and a shadow of a social life that was a bit too close to illegal underground fighting for my taste.

"Looking for Tylenol?" Shelly comes up behind me, her straight blonde hair in total disarray. I smile weakly at her as she takes a medicine bottle down from a cabinet by the refrigerator before pulling out a carton of orange juice.

"Shell, I need a job." I slump down onto one of her bar stools, holding my pounding head in my hands.

"Okay well, one thing at a time. Tylenol first, job second." She slides me a full glass of orange juice. "Eric said that Coach Barry is looking for a gym assistant. Not like for fighting stuff but more like back of house work. You know, folding towels, keeping up with the supplies list, making sure the equipment is replaced when needed. Administrative type things. I guess I just assumed they'd look for a guy but I mean, why couldn't you do the job? You're more organized and punctual than anyone else I know."

"Um, Shelly, no. We barely survived a fifteen-minute visit to the gym. I cannot work there." I had been studying marketing in college. Yes, I am organized but there is no way that trait alone would be enough to bridge the distance between my world and a fighting gym. I'm not trying to be overly picky considering my shit hand at the moment, but what Shelly is suggesting is simply not a viable job option. Even in my currently desperate situation.

"Look Ava, jobs are slim pickings right now. And the way I see it, you need one fast. Plus you need to get your mind off of all that shit with your dad and school. This phase is temporary, I promise. The faster you get working, the faster you make money and the sooner you get back to your life. I'm sure at some point within the next year a job will open up at the salon, but it will be a few months before Kara is trained enough to leave her front desk rotation." Shelly gives me a pointed glare and I can't help but admit that many of her points are valid. At this point, I have about five-hundred dollars to my name. Plus, beyond the money, which I very much need for the first time in my privileged life, I'm also in dire need of routine and structure again until I can figure out my next steps.

"Okay, I'll think about it." *I'll also be scouring literally every online job board for alternative options,* but I kept this inner dialogue to myself. My tone comes out accurately doubtful so I don't get her hopes up, but the reality of my situation hits me. I've never had a *job* before. I'd only ever interned at my dad's office or worked on various college committees. What did I really know about an honest day's work? I was a college girl. I had planned on finishing my four-year degree and having my pick of marketing agencies to choose from. I thought my job decisions would come down to factors like what city I wanted to live in or whether I liked the company's mission statement. Not whether or not I felt physically safe surrounded by brawling underground boxers.

But those plans abandoned me like something caught on fire, dropping me out of the clear blue sky when the facade of my dad's life blew up. His entire company had been a scam. Behind the smoke and mirrors, he had no money to his name, and the supposed money he'd been using to pay for my degree was all loan money he'd taken out in my name. So now I have two years of unexpected college debt, no savings, and a father who has basically lied about his entire life and career. Since my mom died when I was just two years old, he had always been my rock. My whole family. I felt like I was falling without any idea of when I'd hit the ground. Shelly had been my only saving grace when all this shit hit the fan.

—

The next day I find myself standing outside the boxing gym entrance, nervously running my fingers through my hair. I stare anxiously at the brass door handle. *Only a few months. Then I'll be safely working the front desk at Shelly's salon, or better yet, somehow back to school to finish my degree.* Eric told Coach Barry I was interested in the gym assistant position and he agreed to an interview. I know I should be grateful. I know I need to nail this interview, although I have no idea what the requirements for doing that will be. Coach Barry is probably taking pity on me by even giving me this interview in the first place. I take a deep breath and block out the avalanche of unhelpful thoughts that threaten to restrain me from taking forward action. Shelly was right. The faster I move forward and start putting away some money, the faster I can get on with my life. Harping and crying over what happened won't get me anywhere. Except puffy-eyed and a few pounds lighter which has done me little to no good.

I hold my breath and walk into the gym with as much confidence as I can muster and scan the space for Coach Barry's bald head. Thankfully he's standing near the entrance and offers me a warm smile.

"It's Ava, right? Nice to see you again. Follow me this way and we can head back into my office before taking a more formal tour of the gym." He waves me over and I follow a few paces behind him as we weave our way through various rings where boxers are warming up or sparring with one another. I try to avoid the curious glances and occasional whistles. Luckily Coach Barry ignores them as well, although the tight look on his face indicates he doesn't exactly appreciate the impolite behavior from his fighters. He ushers me into his office which sits like an elevated loft in one corner of the gym, open on two sides but accessible by a short flight of stairs.

"So Ava, thanks so much for coming by. I'm sure this isn't your most popular job location," he laughs lightly to himself before continuing, "but we really are looking for someone to start as soon as possible with how fast the gym's growing and the number of new fighters we are bringing in house.

We used to have some of the newer guys help out with things around here, but now they're too busy training." He stops talking and clasps his hands on his desk, his expression friendly. "Do you have any work experience, Ava?"

I find myself feeling fractionally less nervous because of his kind blue eyes, faint lines crinkling at the corners as he smiles. I clear my throat before answering. "Well, I interned at a logistics firm last summer so I'm familiar with maintaining various tasks and order lists. I'm also a generally organized, type-A person and I used to be the treasurer for the student marketing committee at my college."

"Oh, fantastic. Yes, that should work." Coach Barry gives me another warm smile. I feel like he can almost intuit that I must be in some seriously dire straits to be looking for a job at his boxing gym when I so clearly don't fit into this environment at all.

"Okay, so the main job responsibilities will be helping me with supply lists, taking note of any new equipment we need, and making sure to get those orders filled. Also folding towels. Don't worry, our janitorial staff washes the dirty ones." He looks at me a little apologetically and I try to keep a grimace from showing on my face. "Occasionally I may need you to help coordinate the logistics of various fighting events. Only the sanctioned ones. I'll handle any... others." It's like he's read my mind, or more like he read the obviously concerned expression that flashed across my face at the mention of "fighting events." I may have agreed to attend an illegal underground fight but I certainly won't be partaking in arranging one.

"So, some of the fights are...sanctioned?" I twirl my hands in my lap. No need to try and pretend I have any idea about how this world works. "Does that mean they're legal."

"It does." Coach Barry nods encouragingly. "We're actually trying to move the majority of our business into the sanctioned realm. But the unsanctioned fights...well there's just no beating the money that comes from the bets. But," he holds up a reassuring hand, "you won't ever have to do anything related to those. That's for me to handle."

I nod slowly a few times, absorbing this information. "So, you won't need me to engage in any sparring or boxing related duties?" I try my hand at a joke since the interview isn't bombing horrendously as I'd expected coming in here. I don't actually think I will completely hate most of the job tasks Coach Barry listed out. Aside from all the towel folding.

"Haha no, no. Wouldn't subject you to that. And if any of my boys give you even an ounce of trouble you let me know and I'll set 'em straight. Between you and me, most are all bark and no bite." He offers a friendly wink and I nod my head gratefully as he leads me out of the office loft to take a quick tour of the facilities. Which includes the laundry room area and a small women's locker room that looks as if it's never been used.

During the tour I find myself scanning the gym for Rhett before I can stop myself, remembering my first visit a few days ago. I have no idea how long it takes a broken rib to heal or when he'll even be back in the gym. Part of me starts to wonder whether he's really that impressive up close, or if the adrenaline from the fight had muddied my memory. I shake my head to mentally clear my thoughts and remind myself to focus and listen to Coach Barry as he points out various pieces of gym equipment and shows me where the towels are stocked. *Damn, that's a lot of towels to fold.*

"Well Ava, it was great meeting you again. When can you start?" It takes me a moment of shock before I can actually respond. I got the job? I got my first real job! Granted it's light years away from any job I ever expected to have but still, it will come with a much needed paycheck.

"Wow, um thank you! I can start as soon as you need me." I shake his proffered hand, my eyes still wide with surprise.

"Fantastic, the gym will be lucky to have you. Why don't you come back tomorrow after lunch and we can go through some new hire forms and then you can officially start the day after."

"Absolutely, I'll be here." I give Coach Barry a quick wave as I head out of the gym and into the afternoon sunshine. I feel a small sense of accomplishment bloom in my chest, accompanied by a sense of relief. In the last few weeks, between losing my life in college, my beautiful sleek apartment, and in many ways my father, I'd felt like everything was just happening *to* me. But finally, as small as this win might have seemed to me before, it's still something I can own. I crank up the radio in my car and take the long way back to Shelly's apartment, finally feeling a tiny bit like my former self again.

6

RHETT

I t's only been three weeks since my last fight and my broken rib, but I'm itching to get back to the gym. Besides, I'm so used to having a broken rib at one point or another that pain from healing isn't as jarring for me anymore. Still hurts like a bitch but at least it's one that I know. I initially promised myself that I'd stick to circuits and strength training and abstain from any sparring for a few more weeks but I can already feel that restless adrenaline that inevitably comes from having to sit still for too long.

I head into the gym late, around eleven AM, the usual workout grind well underway when I arrive.

"Rhett! The man. You rich as hell yet or what?" Marcus comes up and slaps me on the shoulder. He's one of the few fighters I actually can tolerate.

"It's not about getting rich, it's about winning." A cocky smile pulls at the corners of my lips, my tone uncharacteristically playful. The truth is, I've become well-off financially from fighting, especially compared to the shit-hole where I was born and raised. My standard rate is a 20% cut of the bets placed on me in the underground, which can turn out to be a hell of a lot of money when the big fights bring in one, even two million in bets. I started out moving from foster home to foster home, fighting for food stamps, and stealing from corner stores. That past hustle makes my contemporary two-bedroom townhome in an affluent Boston neighborhood feel like a goddamn palace. I'm more comfortable than I ever imagined I'd be and have everything I could ever need. But despite that, financial security hasn't change how much I want the next fight.

Today I need to check in with Coach Barry about my next big round. I have to capitalize on this winning streak and career high while I can before I face the inevitable retirement of any underground fighter approaching their mid-thirties.

"You sure you're good to be back here, Rhett? Don't get me wrong, you fought like a champ, but you also blacked out at the end like a little girl. Been there myself from the rib pain. Don't push it."

"Didn't realize you got your medical degree, doc." I run a hand through my hair, hating the fact that I can't spar right now. It would be fun to put Marcus in his place. "I'm all good, just going to ease back in."

"Okay boss man, I trust you." Marcus playfully puts up his hands in mock surrender.

"Where's Coach?" I scan the crowded gym, looking for that glistening bald head of Coach Barry's under the bright incandescent lights.

"Probably in the back, working with Eric." *Fucking Eric.* That new prick Coach introduced me to a month ago. Definitely not a fan of that one. I give Marcus a quick nod and make my way toward the sparring rings in the back. I'm in the the narrow aisle between two rings when I notice a slender waist and perfectly round ass making its way up the stairs to Coach's loft office. *Who the hell is she?* When she turns at the top of the stairs, I realize exactly who it is. *Her.* The too-pretty brunette good-girl who keeps randomly showing up in my space.

I've definitely thought about her on more than one occasion while I was locked up healing at home, nursing whiskey and Vicodin for the pain. But I sure as hell never expected to actually see her again. And this is the last thing I need right now. The gym is my place of peace, of worship. I know that makes no sense to most of the world but this is the only place I can clear my mind and just be. With her here, that'll be...difficult to say the least.

She trots genially back down the metal loft stairs, a stack of papers in her slender arms. I finally spot Coach leaning on the lower ropes of the back ring. After I allow myself a few shameless seconds of watching her perfectly full breasts bounce as she descends the stairs, I turn my attention fully toward Coach. *Yeah. This was gonna be a hard 'no' from me.*

"Coach—"

"Rhett! Feeling better? I hope you're not planning on trying to convince me you're ready to fight again anytime soon?"

"What is she doing here?" I keep my voice low and stern so he knows exactly the kind of mood her presence here has put me in. I know I don't need to elaborate on who I'm referring to since *she's* the only female in the gym.

"Oh Ava? She works here now. She helps me with supplies ordering and restocking. Been a real life saver to be honest."

Ava. Even her name suits her. Sexy and sweet and feminine.

"Hire someone else." My response is flat and cold leaving no room for alternative options.

"Rhett, I'm not going to do that. She needs the job and she's good at it."

"How can you expect these motherfuckers to focus with her walking around? I need some decent attempt at quality to train with. You know that." I grip the ropes tighter, staring directly at the mat floor.

"These motherfuckers or you?" Coach Barry flashes a teasing grin, his eyes crinkling in that fatherly way of his before his expression gets more serious. "Look, I know it's not the most ideal setup to have an attractive young woman surrounded by trained fighters...and a few of the guys did give her a little trouble at first, but she's really helpful and you know how short-staffed I am. I keep an eye out for her and if it gets bad, well, we'll figure it out. But so far, so good."

I don't even bother to respond. I can tell by the expression on Coach's face that he already views Ava as some daughterly figure or whatever bullshit. Too bad there's no way any other red-blooded male in this place views her as anything remotely close to a daughter figure.

I head into the locker room, hoisting my duffle bag up higher on my shoulder. I can't tell if I'm more pissed at the thought of Ava being a distraction for other guys in the gym or the fact that my own focus is at risk wherever she's concerned. As I turn the corner of the hallway into the locker room I see her coming out of the supply closet. She has her head down, studiously looking over a list on her clipboard. She rolls her full bottom lip between her teeth, a look of intense concentration marking her pretty features. I'm so close to her that I can see a faint dusting of freckles over the bridge of her nose and I immediately get turned on right then and there. *Fuck me* if freckles on such a sexy woman aren't the biggest turn on ever.

"What are you doing here." My question comes out as a statement and her shoulders jump a little in surprise. Her eyes widen and her cheeks start begin flush as she scans my face. She doesn't respond.

"I said, what are you doing here." I move in closer, dropping my duffle bag to the floor.

"I, um, had to check on the medical supplies. You know, stitches and gauze and some weird superglue stuff that apparently can seal pretty deep skin gashes..." Now she's babbling, glancing nervously between her checklist and me, clearly thrown off guard by my presence. *Good, hope it scares her away.*

"Ava. Why are you in this gym at all?"

"How do you know my name?"

"Answer my question, Ava."

"I work here."

"Well quit."

"Excuse me?" Her face goes from doe-eyed to haughty in a quick second. *Oh, this good girl has a fiery side?* Interesting.

"I said quit. Get a new job. Go work somewhere where you won't be more of a distraction than a help. I'm not trying to be a dick, but it's the truth. Coach Barry is just too nice to say it."

She narrows her honey-colored eyes at me and crosses her arms over her ample chest, briefly drawing my gaze lower.

"If you must know, I need this job. Believe me, this is not my first choice either. But I'm not going anywhere. At least for the time being." Her voice is frustrated but sincere which makes me think that this girl must be in some sort of serious trouble if she needs a job so badly she's willing folding hundreds of towels in a boxing gym for underground fighters. The thought makes me soften my tone just slightly.

"Fine." I pick up my duffle bag without turning back to her and head further into the locker room before speaking over my shoulder, "but you're going to regret it."

7

AVA

I feel my legs shaking slightly as I stare at Rhett's broad back as he retreats deeper into the locker room. *What in the hell was that?* I pull my cell phone from the back pocket of my jeans and text Shelly.

> Ava @ 12:30 PM: Rhett Jaggar is a total asshole.

> Shelly @ 12:32 PM: Woah, need the details. What happened? Is he back at the gym already? Eric said he shouldn't be sparring yet.

> Ava @ 12:33 PM: Yes and he told me to quit! Literally just walked right up to me and said it. Who does he think he is?

> Shelly @ 12:34 PM: Well...he is Rhett Jaggar :D but I'm sorry he was an ass to you.

I let out a frustrated groan at Shelly's response and an eye roll at her mention of Eric saying Rhett shouldn't be back in the gym yet. Despite his majorly asshole attitude, the guy didn't even look like he had so much as a scratch on him. Even with a partially broken rib, I'd bet he can still easily kick Eric's ass.

And even though right now I'm really wishing it wasn't true, Rhett was even more insanely handsome and intimidating up close than he'd been in the ring. His dark hair looked a bit longer, curling slightly at the ends around his neck. His eyes were just as black and impenetrable, smoldering but impossible to tell why or if he's just angry. Maybe that's what makes him such a legendary fighter. The guy is permanently looking to start a fight with anyone. Including the new supply girl who desperately needs this job!

Part of me wants to bring up the incident with Coach Barry but I don't know gym politics well enough yet. The last thing I want to do is look like a tattletale. Like I can't handle myself in this environment. Clearly I am not the *ideal* candidate to help run a boxing gym, but despite that I know I've been helping Coach Barry a lot over the past few weeks and I've been busting my ass to prove myself. Getting up extra early, making sure Coach Barry has enough food and coffee and supplies ordered on time so he can dedicate every minute to the boxers' training. I don't even condone this whole underground, paid-for-violence world and yet I show up because I have to. Even some days, want to. The taste of independence after my entire life was ripped out from under me is rewarding. So the *last* thing I need is for some big-headed jerk reminding me just how out of place I still am.

I head outside the gym for some fresh air, enjoying the cool breeze against my warmed skin. I pull my phone out of the back pocket of my jeans and my eyes go wide when I see a missed call from Jacob. I also notice yet another voicemail notification from my dad but I'm not ready to go there yet.

Maybe I'll never be ready. But definitely not going to address that today.

I dial Jacob back, tapping my foot anxiously. It's the first contact any of my college friends have made with me since the incident went down almost six weeks ago. My heart starts to sink at the thought that it may have been nothing more than an accidental dial.

"Ava?" Jacob answers on the second ring and I hesitate before responding. I don't even know what to say. I feel a small but painful crack in my chest at the familiarity of his voice as he says my name.

"Um, hi, Jacob. You haven't been responding to any of my texts for weeks." I know I sound accusatory but I want answers. He wasn't my official boyfriend or anything, and I was more than fine with that at the time, but we had definitely been close. We went to themed parties together, had sex most weekends. Being with him was fun and casual, part of my college social life. Hanging out with him had felt so normal just over a month ago and now, despite the familiarity of his voice, I feel like I'm addressing a stranger. Without the shared context of college life, what do we really have in common anymore?

"Look Ava, I'm sorry. I really am. It's just, you know, finals and then with baseball training and…" His voice trails off and I hear him sigh deeply. "Look Ava, I miss you. We all do. And I'm sorry we haven't been more supportive. The whole thing was just so…epic. It was all people could talk about and I didn't want to be caught up in that. I mean the cops even came to my parent's house. Questioning me because of my association with you. My dad's a lawyer, Ava. He basically banned me from talking to you. I mean, you know I can't risk anything that could kick me off the team."

Baseball had always been Jacob's number one obsession,

something I previously found admirable and am now finding pretty damn shallow. I lean up against the exterior concrete wall of the gym, tilting my head upward to feel the warmth of the sun on my face. I try to suppress the memories of my own police interview, a group of four grown men drilling me with questions about my father and his business. The fact that they thought I might somehow be involved, have aided in the coverup, makes my stomach feel sick all over again.

"It's okay, I understand." My voice is aloof, distant. I mean I do and I don't. I'm not interested in being anyone's victim but I also don't care to hear a former friend-with-benefits calling me about all his college boy problems that pale in comparison to my real-world catastrophe. The comfort I've been seeking from a friend just isn't there. It's all about him. I shouldn't have expected anything different.

"Look, just give it a few more weeks. Then, come back to campus. Like I said, we all really miss you. Just let it all blow over and then people will be onto the next dramatic event." His voice is hardly convincing but I nod anyway, not really agreeing.

"Yeah, maybe." My voice is flat but I try to keep my tone neutral. The truth is, I have no idea when I'll even be able to come back to campus. I have to sort out my loans and assess the new financial reality of my options before even thinking about taking on more debt.

"Talk soon? I'll be better about texting back, I promise." I cringe at the whiney tone in his voice, now sounding childish and desperate compared to the men I've been surrounded by for the past several weeks at the gym. Not that fighters are my new type, but at least they own their actions. Jacob is just looking for any easy out, for no one to be mad at him.

"Sure, Jacob. Talk soon." I hang up and square my shoulders before heading back into the gym. This whole thing will blow over. Well, maybe *blow over* is too benign for the gravity of what happened, but it will pass. My life *will* go on.

I hover over my dad's new voicemail, considering listening to it before tucking my phone securely in my jeans and shaking those thoughts away. I grip the front door handle of the gym and stride back in with as much confidence as I can muster. Nobody is going to save me this time. I'm on my own. And that asshole, Rhett, is just going to have to suck it up and deal with me working here.

8

AVA

Over the next few weeks, Rhett avoided me at the gym like I'm practically radioactive. Fine by me. The other boxers are friendlier, sometimes asking me out on dates or trying to show off when I'm around, but true to Coach's word, they pretty much stay in line.

These guys are completely focused on their training and it's been pretty admirable, if not humbling, watching them work, day in and day out. I still don't understand choosing fighting over a less violent sport, but the characteristic attributes of any athlete are the same. Extreme discipline, repetition, and mental focus. It's attractive and intoxicating in a way I still don't fully understand and certainly haven't admitted to anyone out loud. Seeing their dedication pushes me to work harder and get better, even if my current work is just administrative tasks and towel folding. I'm really starting to understand the value of work, even though helping out at this boxing gym is nowhere near my dream job. Although if I'm being honest with myself, I'm not really sure what that dream job would be anymore.

I glance up to see Rhett at the punching bag. His moves are calmer and steadier than the younger fighters, yet more forceful. Even a newbie like me can spot the difference that years of experience makes. I don't like him one bit, but it's hard not to watch him. His body moves like a machine, exerting just the right amount of energy and force in every motion. Even though Rhett's arrogance and pride grates on my nerves, his physical ability is still downright impressive. And annoyingly hot. I feel my back pocket vibrate and pull out my phone to see a new text from Shelly.

> Shelly @ 2:15 PM: Did you make up your mind yet?? Please say yes! He's cute, I swear.

Shelly has been busting my butt about going out on a date and I roll my eyes toward the heavens. But then again, my unwelcome lustful staring at Rhett's strong back might mean that a date is exactly what I need right now. It's been a few months since I've had sex, and clearly the drought is getting to me.

My last time had been with Jacob. Sex with him was fun, at times even hot. But not all-consuming, nerve-racking like I imagined it to be when I was younger. My gaze wonders lower to Rhett's strong and lean hips, the way his torso flexes with every punch. What would it be like to have sex with a man like *that*? The feeling of strong, calloused hands on my soft skin, the smell of sweat mingling with the sounds of sex. No, not just sex, but *fucking*. I flush as the word flashes through my mind. Something about the two, sex versus fucking, seems inherently distinct when looking at a man like Rhett Jaggar even though I don't have much experience to draw from...

My sexual reverie is interrupted by another buzz from

phone.

> Shelly @ 2:19 PM: Earth to Ava! This guy is a catch. If you don't want to go that's fine, but I don't want to leave him hanging.

I run my hand through my hair and quickly skirt away from view of Rhett. I send Shelly a response before I can change my mind.

> Ava @ 2:20 PM: Fine, I'll go. But you know I hate blind dates.

Shelly responds with a slew of excited emojis and a flurry of nerves fill my stomach. I'm just not good on blind dates. I like being social just fine, at least before my life imploded, but all of my relationships have always stemmed from friendships. Hence, Jacob being a friends-with-benefits situation that likely would've ended up with us as boyfriend and girlfriend had everything not gone down the way it had. Dating just feels...so adult. Meeting someone for the first time while sharing an intimate dinner and trying desperately to avoid awkward silences? Not my cup of tea. Shelly, of course, is a master at it, the consummate extrovert. But if the guy is as cute as she says he is and a nice enough person, what's the harm in spending one evening of my life with him?

I quickly head to the back of the gym to finish folding clean towels so I can head home a little early. If I'm going to somehow manage this date successfully, I'll need some extra time to get ready. And maybe a few pre-game drinks for liquid courage.

Aside from Rhett's coldness, I've actually enjoyed working at the gym. Coach Barry is kind and helpful, never pushy. I get a lot of time to myself, where I can put my headphones in and just think as I take stock of the medical supply closet or make sure the janitorial staff is paid on time or while I fold the never-ending pile of clean towels. I've started to save a decent amount, especially since Shelly has me paying way less than my fair share of rent, and I'm starting to make a small dent in the debt I've recently acquired. It won't be enough forever, but the freedom and independence it's given me makes me see myself a little differently. Like I don't need my dad to swoop in and take care of me like he always used to do. Which is a good thing since that offer is no longer even remotely on the table.

By the time I finish folding, the gym is pretty much cleared out. So much for leaving early. I glance down at my phone, nervous about the time but I realize I still have a solid two hours before I'm supposed to be at the restaurant. I can make that work.

I hear one loud speed bag still going a mile a minute, the thuds keeping a perfect rhythm. I know it's Rhett without even seeing him. The other fighters aren't nearly as steady or methodical. I grab my purse and keys and head toward the front door. A few feet from the exit, I spin around on my heel and head right back in the direction of the *thud, thud, thud* of the speed bag.

"Rhett." I stand behind him, getting another painfully glorious view of his broad muscular back. Rivulets of sweat run down between his shoulder blades and I lick my lips without meaning to. Stupid sexy man. *Stay focused, Ava.*

He turns around slowly, his dark eyebrows raising up higher onto his forehead in surprise. "Yes?" He rests one hand on the speed bag, his profile facing in my direction, giving me a delicious look at his insane obliques. I let out a small pent-up breath, not wanting my voice to come across as nervous as I feel.

"Look did I...did I ever do something to piss you off? You know, around the gym? It's clear that you're not a fan of having me here but I've been working hard and I really need this job. I kinda like it too." I'm surprised at my own honesty. But if I'm going to continue working here for the foreseeable future, it'd be nice to a least know if there is a specific reason why the gym's premier fighter has a chip on his shoulder when it comes to me.

"Ava, it's fine. I know Coach appreciates everything you've been doing for the gym." He looks me right in the eye as he says it, his jaw tight. I swallow hard, unable to say anything else as his eyes wander down the length of my body, shamelessly checking me out. I let him take his time, his eyes working back up from my toes to my legs, pausing a little longer on my hips and breasts before finally landing back on my face.

I clear my throat and mumble a barely audible, "okay, thanks," before turning on my heel and power walking towards the exit. If that's what getting a semi-compliment from Rhett feels like, I can't even imagine what other *nice* things from Rhett would do to me. Thank goodness I have date tonight. Clearly I need the distraction.

—

Later that night I join Shelly in our small living room, plopping down next to her with a heavy pour of red wine in hand, tucking my feet underneath my legs on the couch. I'm dressed and ready for my blind date, hoping the wine will calm my nerves. I can only admit to myself that most of my nervous jitters are from flashbacks of Rhett's insane body and the way he'd looked me up and down like a man who was *hungry*. But it's also highly likely that I'd been projecting, my own lust making me see things in his dark, taut expression that weren't really there.

"Ava, your dad has called me at least four times today." Shelly keeps her tone soft, knowing not to push me on this but also knowing I have to address him at some point.

"Can we talk about this later? As in, not right before I'm about to go on a freaking blind date?"

"Okay, okay fair enough!" Shelly's face instantly becomes brighter and more excited as she joins me on the couch. "He's the brother of a girl I work with at the salon. And he's a real, working man. Not one of those college frat boys, you're so used to." I roll my eyes, Jacob's face popping unbidden into my head at the mention of frat boys. "You're so freaking hot, Ava, and you don't even use it to your advantage enough, it's such a waste." Shelly shakes her head dramatically and pats my leg.

"You know, many men used to be college frat boys, and other than having a job, I'm not sure they've actually changed. " *There is no way Rhett had been a frat boy. He probably didn't even go to college.* I try to push down the intruding thought, not wanting to voice it to Shelly. Rhett couldn't be more opposite of my type. Aside from the way he looks, I'm sure I'd find nothing I like about him at all. Not to mention he barely tolerates me.

"Just give him a chance. And have fun! If you hate it, I'll find you another date. Simple as that!" Shelly wiggles her blonde eyebrows at me suggestively. When Shelly is in a relationship I always become her pet dating project, setting me up with her idea of eligible bachelors left and right.

I take a deep breath and check my phone. I request an Uber and stand up, setting the wine glass on the kitchen counter before slipping on my heels. I can do this. Maybe he'll even be great.

9

AVA

I keep pulling up the too-small tank I borrowed from Shelly. I should've stuck to the safe predictability of my own wardrobe instead of trying to wear one of Shelly's more exciting tops. Mainly because my boobs are at least three cup sizes bigger than hers. The top makes me me look like some trying-too-hard cartoon character. When my pulling at the fabric of the shirt makes no attempt to stretch it farther over my chest, I try to awkwardly cross my arms over myself. Thank goodness for my long hair at least. I can pull it around to the front for some much-needed coverage. Walking into a bar filled with off-duty underground fighters wearing skintight clothes suddenly feels like walking into a lion's den draped in raw meat.

"Oh my god, Ava, stop fidgeting so much, we're almost at the door. You look great, just try and relax. Maybe, get laid even." Shelly throws me her signature wink, earning a horrified look on my end, before flipping her blonde hair and swinging the heavy wooden front door of the bar open like a performer taking the stage.

I follow her inside, relieved for the warmth since Boston fall is nipping at late summer's heels. The bar is vibrating with laughter and drunkenness. Maybe a few loose punches considering the crowd. The amber lights cast a strangely cozy vibe against the wooden walls and natural slab countertops. The requisite pin-up girl posters and bar lights adorn the walls, giving a sense of familiarity and casualness. Of course, I've already lost Shelly to the crowd of testosterone and vibrant ring bunnies that mingle about naturally in the dimly lit space.

I continue to scan the bar, not really looking at the décor or the lights. If I'm being honest, I'm really looking for *him.* After my less than stellar date last night, my plan of distracting myself from Rhett's hotness with a new love interest has seriously backfired. My date had been cute and sensible but stiff as a board. He only seemed interested in talking about himself, his stable job in finance, if he talked at all. Part of me left the dinner feeling like he'd been put up to the date versus really wanting to be there. I'd left even more frustrated than I'd gone in, images of Rhett's strong body flashing through my head even though I barely know the surly underground legend.

Maybe it's just sex that I want? The raw, sweaty kind that I've never had but only have heard about from friends and in books. Shelly mentioned to me on the way over that apparently Rhett isn't the partying type and the rumor is he'll be another no-show tonight. She mentioned something about a wild past but I didn't want to ask her to elaborate for fear of looking too interested. The less I know about him the better. Maybe the fact that he doesn't like to party much anymore is nice. Okay maybe not *nice*, nothing about Rhett Jaggar seems *nice,* but relatable at least. The loud showman types are always too much for me. They suck all of the air out of the room. Like Eric.

As I continue to scan the bar on the tiptoes of my boots as nonchalantly as possible, I feel a strong hand slide down the middle of my back.

"Hey there precious, can I help you find what you're looking for?" Hot breath feathers across my neck. Anyone who knows me knows I don't appreciate being snuck up on. I mean, who does? I turn jerkily to the side, putting a face to the voice behind me. I try to slide my back away from his hand as subtly as possible. It doesn't work.

"Well aren't you a pretty little thing. What's your name?"

I haven't seen this guy at the gym before but I can tell from his build that he's a heavyweight. One of the beefier ones with muscles that look like industrial rope tied in thick, overlapping knots.

"Distracted by my arms, sweetheart?" I look away from unnamed beefy guy's arms and into his mouse-brown eyes. He wears a smirk like it's tattooed on his lips and he can't stop blatantly staring at my chest, barely attempting to make eye contact. *Gross.*

"Hi sorry, I'm actually kind of looking for someone." I mean I hadn't planned on approaching Rhett if he was here, but I'm desperate for an excuse to get this creep off my back. *Literally.* I try again to scoot away but beefy guy's hand on my lower back turns into a rough grip around my waist, his fingers digging into my exposed skin.

"Hey now, don't get so squirmy on me. I'm Mitch. Why don't you tell me your name and who you're looking for? Maybe I can help you find them?" His offer is anything but friendly. Mitch and I are standing near the entrance of the bar, separated from the rest of the crowd a bit too much for my liking.

"I'm looking for Rhett." I keep my voice flat and firm and stare Mitch right in the eye as I say it. For some reason, I feel like I can use Rhett's name as a weapon or some sort of shield. He's known in this world, and from what little I've seen, very few fighters want to mess with him outside of the ring unless they have some sort of death wish. I sure as hell hope it will work on Mitch because I left my pepper spray in Shelly's car and this guy doesn't seem like the type who's used to taking 'no' for an answer.

"What the fuck do you want with Rhett? Hey Rhett!" Before I can even attempt to answer to his first question, Mitch addresses the loud, rowdy bar like he's calling someone to a fight. And not just someone but *Rhett.* My heart rate spikes as I try to keep my breathing under control. There's nothing I dread more than a scene.

"Yo Rhett, where you at? Some pretty piece of ass says she's looking for you!" Mitch cracks his head to the left and right, flexing his gripped hand on the pinch of my waist. Shelly's borrowed top begins riding up again, and I cringe at our skin-to-skin contact. A path starts to clear from the back left corner of the bar as fighters and ring bunnies scoot in closer to one another, creating a clear pathway for an approaching figure.

I hold my breath as Rhett emerges from the quieting crowd. He is wearing dark black denim jeans and a white t-shirt stretched tightly across his broad shoulders. The hint of an ink trail peeks out on the side of his neck where his black, zip-up hoodie had fallen. He appears dangerous as all get out, sexy, and annoyed as hell. *Well shit, don't let me piss off two fighters tonight!* I feel a pink stain of embarrassment spread across the apples of my cheeks as my poorly laid plan comes to an epic fail.

What the heck am I going to say now? We've all but said a

few sentences to one another at the gym and now I'm telling random men in bars that I'm looking for Rhett as if I have a right to him or something?

"This bitch yours?" I flinch at the harshness with which Mitch says the word *bitch*.

"Don't call me that." My voice is quiet but firm. I can hear my heart beating wildly at the base of my throat. I'm afraid but I'm not going to let some random jerk at a bar call me a *bitch*.

"I'll call you what I want to call you unless you tell me your fucking name." Mitch growls near my ear. "I asked if she's fucking yours?"

Rhett isn't looking at me. He keeps his eyes focused on Mitch, but in a way that looks as if he's seeing right through him. Almost like he's already imagined Mitch's meaty body pinned against the wood-paneled wall behind the bar.

"Yeah, she's mine." Rhett's voice is low and threatening. He still doesn't look at me when he says it. My stomach does a somersault gymnastics flip. I feel hot and cold at the same time. Partially like a totally embarrassed loser but also incredibly turned on by hearing those words come out of his mouth. Even if it's not true. "And if you call her a bitch again, I'll knock you out."

I almost faint at the gravel in Rhett's voice.

I feel Mitch's hand drop from my back, a tense air settling over the bar. Mitch lets out a half snort, obviously a mask for his nerves. But even faced with the threat of a knockout by Rhett Jaggar himself, the asshole still won't quit.

"Guess even Rhett Jaggar gets pussy-whipped from time to time, huh?" Mitch's voice sounds like a desperate snarl, but Rhett doesn't take the bait. Part of me wishes he had.

"Come here, baby." Rhett extends a long arm towards

me and I freeze for a moment. I look into his dark, unreadable brown eyes and I swear he quickly rolls them in annoyance.

Get it together, Ava! Just move past this mess you created as painlessly as possible. At least the guy is giving you an out.

I chastise myself as I move toward Rhett. I can't help the shiver that snaps down my spine replaying the word, "baby," from his lips as he offered me his hand. He pulls me into his chest and wraps a strong, commanding arm around my waist. And while the recently discovered sexy-hungry girl inside of me could've swooned at the realization of being tucked securely into Rhett's side, his movements are rough and jerky, like he's in a rush. We make our way back through the crowd, Rhett carving out the path he'd taken earlier without seeming to notice the ease with which he does it. Using his free arm, he pushes a heavy steel door open and the cool outside air washes over my flushed skin. I welcome the breeze at first, cooling my overheated cheeks. We're standing on a small back patio area where groups of smokers gather in dispersed circles.

Once outside, Rhett lightly pushes me off of him. He takes a cigarette from his back pocket and lights the end of it, the amber glowing orange in front of his face. It's deathly silent as he takes a full and steady inhale, not glancing at me once during the entire motion. I run my hands down my cold bare arms and tap my high-heeled boots trying to think of something to say to ease the awkwardness of the situation.

Thank you? I'm sorry? I wasn't really looking for you, that guy was just creeping me out?

"You'd be less cold if you had an actual jacket." Rhett finally breaks the silence before taking another long pull on his cigarette, the end pulsing with a glow. He still won't look directly at me which starts to grate on my nerves.

"Well, I usually do always have a jacket with me. It is Boston after all. But I didn't exactly pick my own outfit this evening." I chew on the inside of my cheek for a moment before blundering on. "Besides, if I had it my way, I'd be in my comfy sweats snuggled into bed right now watching a movie I've probably already seen, so there's no need for you to be so critical." I come off sounding more offended than I intend but my embarrassment has turned defensive. Despite Rhett helping me get away from Mitch, he's clearly still a grade-A asshole and I just need to accept it.

I let out a small sigh and turn to head back inside. His arm juts out lightning fast, a large palm landing lightly on my hip from behind, halting my progress toward the door to head back inside. It's the only time he's touched me so gently, so intentionally, and to be fair it's barely a touch at all. But I feel it. *Everywhere.* Like a heat searing through me.

I stare down at his strong, calloused hand resting above the waistband of my dark blue jeans, trying to make sense of our skin to skin contact. For a moment I feel as if I'm outside of my own body. When I turn back to glance up at him, he has a faint smirk on his sinfully full lips. The closest thing I've seen to a smile. He removes his hand from my hip to shrug off his black hoodie and holds it out for me to take. I quickly put it on, avoiding direct eye contact. He must think I'm a freak for how much I just reacted to his simple touch.

"Thanks for the hoodie. And for getting me away from that creep." I pull the black fabric around my torso, essentially swallowing myself in it.

"Hell, I didn't even get to do any damage. It's been a while since I've had a fight outside the ring. To be honest, I'm itching for one."

"So, why didn't you? You could've taken him." I cringe inwardly at myself for such a stupid, albeit accurate, line. I wasn't even trying to flatter him, it's just the truth.

"You were standing too close. Didn't want your pretty little face to get mixed up in it." He takes another long drag of his cigarette, this time keeping direct eye contact with me through the small cloud of smoke as he exhales. "And I can't control myself very well outside of the ring. Been an issue for me in the past."

"You think I'm pretty?" My voice is a surprised whisper and I inwardly roundhouse kicked myself for my lack of a filter! Clearly this evening I have no control over my stupid mouth or body.

"You one of those girls who's always looking for a compliment?"

"What? No." My genuine response seems to appease him.

"Every man in that bar would bend you over this railing. Especially when you decide to wear clothes so tight I can see the outline of your lace bra. For a girl who blushes every five minutes, it's an interesting choice, Ava." He tosses his cigarette butt to the ground and stomps it out with a black leather boot. My head is spinning like I'm drunk. And I hadn't even had a chance to order anything from the bar yet.

"Would you?" I square my shoulders, a sense of brazenness and burning curiosity boldening me.

"Would I what?" Rhett steps closer, his eyes slightly squinted.

"Bend me," I swallow hard past the lump in my throat, "over this railing?" My voice nearly expires on the last words but I force them out. *Would I even want that?*

But immediately after I say it, I wish the outside deck flooring would open wide and swallow me whole. I look away from him, running a trembling finger on the railing's cold, metal surface. Rhett looks up from his ashen cigarette butt, his brows furrowed over a pair of gleaming dark eyes. His tongue darts out to lick his lower lip and I try and fail not to notice.

"No." His response is like a splash of cold water to the face. To my entire overheated body. My mouth pops open before I can stop it. I can't even play off a cool reaction to his outright rejection. He moves in impossibly closer, resting his palms on the metal railing on either side of my waist, not quite touching me. He leans down to whisper harshly in my ear.

"No, I wouldn't fuck you at this dive bar. I wouldn't fuck you at all. Not because I don't want to. Jesus Christ, Ava, I do. But no matter how sexy and pretty you are, you're still a good girl. And I don't get mixed up with good girls. Never been my type." He pauses for a moment, his eyes slightly hooded and fixated on my lips. "Haven't had to turn one down as sweet as you though."

My breath gets caught in my throat as he leans in further and plants a soft kiss on my neck, right beneath my ear. It's so tender, so delicate, so out of character with the strong, confusing fighter standing over me. But it barely softens the sting of his rejection.

"Maybe you're making assumptions about me." *Did I just blurt that out loud?*

Rhett releases a deep, gravelly chuckle, a sound that makes my stomach perform an Olympics-worthy tumbling routine.

"I'm taking you home, Ava. Let's go." He pushes himself off of the metal railing, putting a healthy distance between us again. I let out a frustrated sigh as I follow him back through the crowded bar, forcing myself to accept that this man, who has the self-control to train for hours and weeks on end, will likely have no problem continuing to control himself around me.

I'm not his type. Time to let my ridiculously futile crush go for good.

10

RHETT

I move through the crowded bar, knowing Ava is right behind me even without looking back or holding onto her. This girl is truly driving me crazy. I need to get her the hell out of this bar and away from these dirtbag guys before one of them really makes a move.

At least at the gym, the boxers have their training to focus on. But here at the bar it's all about two things: booze and women. And despite the appealing array of ring bunnies making their way throughout the bar, Ava stands out among the rest. It's hard to put a finger on exactly what it is about her, but it's definitely more than just her beauty. And I'm currently torn in half between being drawn to it and annoyed by it.

When she asked me if I'd bend her over that patio railing? *Was that some sort of joke? An insane experiment to test my willpower?* Now I can't get the mental image out of my head. Her skin-tight, dark-washed jeans, her perfect ass high in the air as I run my hand underneath her too-small tank top along the center of her back, her breasts pushing against the rail and spilling out over the front of her shirt...

"Ava!" A shrill female voice calls out to Ava from the bar, and I notice the skinny blonde-haired girl who I first saw with Ava at the gym a few months back. Ava comes around to stand beside me, her breasts lightly brushing up against the outside of my arm and I move away quickly before I damn near change my mind and take her right back out to that patio rail.

"Where have you been? I've been looking for you! We're doing shots." The blonde girl jumps up and down excitedly, clapping her hands together. I peek a glance down at Ava and her expression looks wary and uncertain.

"I was actually about to take Ava home." I give Ava's friend a tight smile, her overly bubbly and bossy nature getting on my nerves.

"Nope, not a chance." She shakes her head from left to right dramatically. Probably already tipsy. "Ava is having fun tonight. We're staying out and we're doing shots. You're welcome to join in if you'd like." She braces one hand on her skinny hip and reaches for Ava with the other.

"One shot." Ava sounds somewhere between resigned and apathetic but I can't tell which. I *do* know that I won't be able to leave this place knowing Ava is still here among a den of horny fighters, taking shots with this not-so-low-key blonde chick.

Ava looks over her shoulder at me, something like a question mark in her honey-colored eyes as she lets her friend pull her toward the bar. I keep eye contact with her as I move to the far end of the bar, posting up at a small high-top table against the wall.

"Hey Rhett, long time no see. How are you feeling tonight? Surprised to see you out." A ring bunny, I think her name is Amber, sidles up next to me and rests her forearm on my shoulder. I shrug flippantly in return, trying to give a hint without being overly harsh. Too bad she either doesn't get it or doesn't take it.

"Can I get you a drink?" Her voice is overly sensual and I try to trap down the annoyance on my face. I focus on keeping my eye on Ava, her slender back coming in and out of my line of sight as various patrons make their way to the bar.

"Whiskey neat, thanks." Too bad I won't be drinking any of it, but I'll pretend to nurse it for appearance's sake. I lean back in my stool and pull my hoodie back up over my head. I swear it smells faintly of her, sweet and citrusy after she handed it back to me before joining her friend.

If I can't have Ava tonight, I'll just have to settle for my hand in the shower with thoughts of her insane body and sweet innocent lips moaning my name.

I resign myself to the night, oddly satisfied watching Ava from afar, enjoying our few moments of eye contact here and there and relieved that she doesn't try to keep up with her blonde friend shot-for-shot. I swirl my untouched whiskey and engage in a few meaningless conversations with various ring bunnies, their overly made-up faces and fake breasts blurring together. But I know I won't be able to leave this bar until I saw Ava safely tucked into a cab or an Uber. And most importantly, without any other man joining her.

11

AVA

I can't remove the slight scowl from my face. I'm almost done getting ready and I just can't get into the idea of going on this date tonight. My last date had been a dud, but that hadn't deterred Shelly one bit. Of course she had another *eligible bachelor* waiting in the wings. My dress is black and ends just above my knees. My hair is styled down in soft loose waves that fall past my shoulders. I try harder than normal with my makeup which is still minimal at best, but at least I'm wearing mascara. I attempt to fix my scowl with some lip-gloss but it only makes my distaste appear more prominent. I'm sure this *Dave* is a fine guy with his strait-laced job and sensible attire that Shelly showed me from his Facebook profile photos, but I still can't seem to quell the flow dread and nerves in my belly.

I don't know what I expected to happen between Rhett and me after the bar incident, but it turned out to be a whole lot of the status quo. He avoided me the next day at the gym after chatting it up with several ring bunnies at the bar, and hardly spoke another full sentence to me after that night. I try to convince myself to stop letting it bother me. To stop thinking about it altogether. The guy is a jerk after all, despite helping me out of a dicey situation with that heathen Mitch, there's really nothing else we have in common.

I take a deep breath and square my shoulders in the bathroom mirror. Hopefully this date will help me get my mind off of my stupid, rambling thoughts of Rhett. After all I've been through, I really need to stop behaving like a teenage girl with a pointless crush. I'm not even sure if crush is the word for it really. More like fascination? Curiosity? Whatever it is, it's going nowhere quick and certainly won't help me with the forward progress I've been trying to make in my life.

I give my hair a quick tousle, running my fingers through the curls, and bend over to strap on my favorite pair of black heels. Rarely is a girl lucky enough to find a cute, sexy, and comfortable pair of shoes. It feels nice not to have to borrow a pair of shoes from Shelly for once. I gather a few personal items to put in my sparkly black clutch, and give myself a final once-over before heading out the door.

The restaurant is cute and cozy with a long dark bar that wraps itself in a semi-circle into the back right corner. Small circular tables with lightly glowing centerpieces cast the room in a romantic glow. Couples lean across the small space of the tables as if they can't get close enough to one another. Just walking in here would make anyone feel some butterflies. Anyone but me. Instead I feel like I have a knot in my throat. *What if this Dave stands me up? What are we even going to talk about?*

"Um hi, are you Ava?" A deep voice behind me causes me to turn around on my heels. Standing there is Dave, looking reassuringly just like his Facebook profile photos.

"Hi, Dave! Yes, I'm Ava, great to meet you." He embraces

me in a slightly awkward hug but I find myself getting less nervous since he is clearly a little nervous too. And cute. He rests a light hand on my lower back and steers me toward the bar.

"I made our reservation at the bar, I thought it'd be more fun. Hope that's okay?" Dave throughs me a shy smile and I notice one deep dimple. *Okay, Ava, we can do this. Maybe this won't be an awkward disaster after all.*

We spend the next half hour exchanging pleasantries and trying to break the ice. Honestly, it's flowing pretty smoothly and I find myself leaning into the date more easily than I expected. Dave is cute and nice with a good, almost shy sense of humor. He has a respectable job at a technology company doing something I still don't quite understand but it sounds important and interesting enough. He has two older sisters and a dog named Lucky and recently moved to Boston from Michigan after college. I find myself nodding and giggling intermittently as Dave tells me about some story from college involving his roommate when I hear a too-loud, sultry female laugh from across the restaurant. It's overtly sexy and seemingly out of place among the whispery, quiet vibe of the restaurant. I swivel in the barstool, turning my head over my shoulder toward the sound.

Sitting in one of the small tables on the opposite back corner of the restaurant is a leggy platinum blonde whose bright hair glows amidst the darker aesthetic of the space. She is leaning over the short length of the table, rhythmically running her fingernails along a strong, tense forearm. I feel a chill break out over my neck and back. As I follow that tense forearm up, I see a strong jawline, lightly dusted with a five-o'-clock shadow. He's looking down into an untouched dark amber drink.

He would order a whiskey neat. My chill turns to a warm

flush as the reality of the situation settles in. Rhett Jaggar is here. In this restaurant. *And he's on a date.*

I turn back to Dave, offering him a tight smile as I try to mask my distraction. *Is that really Rhett? Or is my overactive mind making me see things?* I desperately want to turn back around but I know that would be rude and Dave already looks a bit antsy at my obvious shift in attention.

"Ava, are you okay? Something not good with the food?"

"Oh, no, no! Everything is great, really. I'm, uh, just going to go to the ladies room, I'll be right back." I lightly tap his forearm with my hand in an attempt to keep him from feeling too skeptical about my sudden change in demeanor. I slide off the barstool as elegantly as possible in my short dress and quickly moved towards the bathroom. Or at least, my best guess at where I think the bathroom is since I don't take the time to ask a waiter. I end up in the back of the restaurant, pushing a heavy door open only to find myself outside on a small cement stoop. The floor is littered with abandoned cigarette butts, likely the go-to break spot for all the servers.

I run my hands up and down my shivering arms, kicking absently at a few cigarette butts with the pointed toe of my heel. *Okay Ava, focus on Dave. Nice, stable, handsome Dave who actually wants to be here with you on this lovely date--*

"You do this to all your dates?" I spin around, startled by the sound of another voice. Rhett is leaning against the heavy metal door, both hands in the front pockets of his dark jeans.

"What?" I practically splutter as I try to play it cool. "Uh, Rhett, what are you doing here?" I cross my arms over my breasts, my questions smashing up against one another between my stammering and my teeth chattering.

"Saw you practically run away from the bar. Wanted to

check on you." He pushes himself off the wall, moving only an inch closer to me but somehow I suddenly feel his presence everywhere.

"Why?"

"Your date say something to piss you off?" Rhett ignores my question, his dark eyes serious.

"No," I stand up straighter, hoping he can't see the slight trembling in my legs, "did yours?" I smirk lightly but it's forced and I see the faintest amusement dance around his eyes at my question.

"She's not my date. It's a business dinner." Rhett drags his bear of a hand along his unshaven jaw and I track the movement. I can't help the disbelieving laugh that bubbles from me, the cold air cutting it short.

"Business dinner? What does that even mean?" *What kind of business dinner involves a boxer and a beautiful blonde other than the business of sex?*

Rhett just stares at me, his mouth opening and closing once, stopping himself from saying whatever it is that he planned to respond. I drop my cold hands to my sides.

"Well, I better go back in. Just needed a bit of fresh air. Enjoy your...business dinner." My lips pull into a tight, close-lipped smile and I push lightly past him to head back into the restaurant. I adjust the hem of my dress, grateful for the gust of warmth that washes over me when I head back inside. Even though I shouldn't, I tousle my hair, swaying my hips and walking as confidently as I can muster back to the bar. And even though I'm fully facing Dave, my entire body is focused on the fact that Rhett is only a few feet behind me as we both walk back to our respective dinner dates, watching my ass walk away from him toward another man.

12

RHETT

I stop punching the speed bag when I realize the rest of the gym has gone quiet. Too quiet. I turn over my right shoulder to see that nearly every other guy in the gym is distracted by something at the gym's entrance. Wiping a towel over my face and bare chest I turn in the direction that they are looking. And *fuck me.*

Ava is taking inventory at the front of gym, like her usual morning routine, but everything else about her is anything but usual. The sweet, preppy Ava is now wearing short, ripped Daisy Dukes that do nothing to hide her perky, round ass as she bends down to check the weight equipment on the lower racks. Her lower bare back is fully exposed thanks to a barely-there crop top. She has her long, light brown hair in a high ponytail, revealing her perfectly smooth chest and neck. I feel my traitorous dick harden instantly just looking at her. I also feel the familiar urge to punch someone squarely in the face: in this case that *someone* happens to be every other male fighter currently ogling Ava's feminine body like they're about to eat their first meal after a long fast.

"Princess, you trying to tempt me? Because it's working."
I notice Roy inch his way too close to her, his bare chest
almost touching hers as she stands up straight, her trusty
clipboard still in hand. I notice her nervously scan the gym,
her eyes finding mine for such a short moment so full of
tension and intensity that I wonder if I imagined it. Then I
watch as she puts a confident mask on her face, her glossed,
naturally bee-stung lips curving into a full-toothed smile. If
I wasn't sure before, I am certain now that she's doing this to
mess with me. And it's working.

"Afraid not, Roy." She pats his arm lightly. "Sorry to
distract you though." She returns back to her inventory list,
Roy looking anything but discouraged. I can feel tension
radiating all the way down through my legs, and I notice I've
already assumed a fighting stance. *What's Ava's endgame
here? Why the fuck is she doing this?* I suspect it must have
something to do with her seeing me with that blonde the
other night, her strait-laced date exactly the type of corpo-
rate guy with soft hands that I'd expect a girl like Ava to be
dating. But after she'd worn that tight black dress and heels,
how could she possibly think I'd been able to have any
other woman but her on my mind the rest of the night?

And now if she think this is some clever or cute way to
get under my skin, she has no idea she's kicking a hornet's
nest in this gym.

"Listen, baby. Ignore Roy. Let me take you out tonight."
The newest boxer, Sampson, wedges himself in between
Roy and Ava, essentially giving Roy his back. I've seen and
finished enough fights to know a punch is about thirty
seconds away from being thrown.

I'm striding across the gym before I fully realize I'm even
moving. It's like my legs just move toward Ava of their own
volition.

"Hey, douche, back the fuck up. You don't even have rights in this gym yet." Roy forcefully yanks Sampson around, bringing them face-to-face. Sampson has a few inches on Roy, but Roy is built like a military tank. And unlike Sampson who is an elite, gym-trained young athlete, Roy is a barroom brawler through and through.

"Pretty sure I don't need rights to hit on a piece of ass. Back off Roy, she doesn't want your dick--" Roy's fist connects with Sampson's jaw before the sentence is even fully out of Sampson's mouth. My vision is rimmed in a haze, the words "piece of ass" replaying in an angry loop in my head. In a second I'm on Sampson, taking one or two blows to the back from Roy before he realizes that I have inserted myself into the fight. Yeah, both of these fuckers are dead to me. I don't stop punching and jabbing until I hear a small feminine cry shriek out, recognizing it as Ava's.

13

AVA

I don't know how he made his way so fast. One moment I saw him all the way over on the other side of the large renovated warehouse space of the gym, and the next he's right in between Roy and Sampson, only a few inches away from me.

Roy is forcefully shoved backwards by Rhett and Roy's bulky arm swings out wildly behind him, accidentally throwing me into a bay of metal lockers against the wall. I feel the cold metal of an open locker door cut into the apple of my cheek and let out a small yelp. It doesn't hurt as much as shock. Immediately Rhett stops his assault on the still squirming Sampson, his large knuckled fist in midair and his tanned muscular torso breathing heavily. Our eyes connect and I wonder what he's thinking. I see his gaze scan the side of my face cut by the locker, that strong jaw clenching impossibly harder. His normally unreadable and hard eyes are wild, almost animal. The way he's looking at me now looks like he's more angry with me than with the brawling fighters. But perhaps even more potently, like he's also angry with himself.

Rhett hops up off the floor with a surprising amount ease and grace as if he hadn't just been bloodily pounding two massive men. The other fighters in the gym are whistling and hollering, clearly enjoying the commotion. I notice Coach Barry cut his way through the crowd, slapping and scolding different fighters who reluctantly amble away and head back toward their training stations. I've never seen Rhett lose his cool like that outside of the ring. Ever. His tan skin is slick with sweat and his upper lip has swelled slightly from the fight. Without saying a word he grabs my elbow firmly, but with a gentleness that I imagine takes great effort on his part, and starts leading me toward the locker room. I nearly stumble trying to keep up with him, his long legs taking huge strides.

"Rhett, what in the hell do you think--" Coach Barry steps in front of Rhett's path, nearly getting himself knocked out of the way.

"Not now, Coach." Rhett brusquely pushes past him without glancing back. I look back briefly to see Coach's face turn a bright pink, a deep scowl marring his expression as he looks between Rhett's retreating back and the crowd of fighters.

"Rhett...Rhett! Slow down. Please." He doesn't. Instead, he forcefully throughs open the locker room door, his large hand still firmly wrapped around my elbow.

14

RHETT

S till holding her by the elbow, I pull her into the men's locker room, knocking loudly on the wall that leads to the showers to make sure no other guys are inside. The last thing I need are any more Ava admirers, let alone naked ones. After she plops herself down on one of the cold metal benches I run both of my hands through my hair to try and stop them from shaking.

"I'm sorry." Ava's voice is a whisper, suddenly quieter than her earlier protesting. I don't respond right away as I pace back and forth still trying to calm myself. "I never expected a fight to happen, honestly. I shouldn't have been so flippant with my response to Roy, I guess. I really wasn't trying to bait anyone. I mean I probably even lost my job because of this. Did you see Coach Barry's face? He looked livid."

"Don't worry about Coach." I stop pacing to grab a first aid kit from one of the open lockers. I pull the other metal bench closer, sitting in front of Ava without looking directly at her. I open the first aid kit and find an alcohol wipe and some gauze.

"What are you doing?" Ava's voice is strained and nervous but I still avoid looking her in the eye.

"Stop talking." I grab the wipe and run it gently across her cheek, hating with every fiber in my being that she's cut and bleeding. Thankfully she doesn't protest as she flinches at the cold sting of the alcohol and manages to sit still long enough for me to finish cleaning the wound before blotting it with some gauze. I attach a small piece of tape, focusing all of my energy on addressing the cut and not on what just took place out in the gym. When I was finish, I quickly run another alcohol wipe over my own cut knuckles and stand up to throw the used items away.

"Why'd you dress like this, Ava?" The edge in my voice is harsh even to my own ears but I'm pretty certain I already know the answer: to get under my skin. For being on a "date" with another woman which truly was nothing more than a *meeting* Coach encouraged me to go on because he thinks my fighting is too tight these past few weeks. In the world of fighting, that's code for telling me I need to get laid. But I want to hear Ava say it. Hear her say that she wants my attention. That at least some part of her posh, too-pretty self wants my calloused hands and swearing lips on her. Even if it's wrong for a man like me to even dream of having a girl so innocent and perfect.

"I can wear what I want, Rhett." Wrong answer. Not that it isn't true. I'd never dare tell a woman what she can and can't wear. But unfortunately this gym is full of horny bastards, including my traitorous self, who can't be left unaffected by her sudden change in attire. Ava crosses her arms over her ample chest and squares me with a look of defiance, clearly trying to assert itself above her wave of nerves.

"What is sweetheart, Daddy didn't give you enough attention?" I see her eyes widen a fraction and her cheeks flush with anger or embarrassment, I can't tell. But before I can take it back, she stands up from the bench and slaps me square across the face.

Neither of us move. For a moment we are both frozen aside from our chests heaving with labored, uneven breaths. Her honey eyes are wild and huge like a deer in the head-lights and I can tell that she's just as surprised by her slap as I am. I feel the sting of her palm against my right cheek and I don't know if it's because I'm so far beyond fucked up, but the harshness and earnestness of that slap has turned me on even more.

But that sensation is mirrored with me feeling like a piece of shit because I obviously struck a nerve. I guess my brunette angel does have daddy issues. Some serious ones. I suddenly feel a blind rage toward whatever man did this to her, my palms tingling with that need to punch.

Her eyes look like they are beginning to water but she furiously blinks away any tears before before they can fall.

"Ava, I'm sorry. Shitty thing for me to say." She just stares at me for a long moment, letting me see the full extent of the hurt and surprise on her face. Then she turns on her heel quickly, storming out of the locker room while giving me another glorious view of her ass in those ridiculously short denim shorts.

I've always known I'm an asshole, but I feel it more in than moment than I ever have.

15

RHETT

I have no idea what I'm going to say when I get to her apartment. I don't do apologies. I'm beyond out of my comfort zone here but I know from the look in her eyes after she slapped me that I struck a dangerous nerve with my "Daddy attention" comment. And while I know just how much of an asshole I can be when provoked, I can't just leave her like that. Teary-eyed and red-faced, so angry with me her slender limbs were shaking. It also got me thinking and wondering a little too much about the piece of shit dad that made Ava feel this way. And despite trying to deny it, I want to know more. A lot more.

I got her apartment address from Coach Barry who looked like he wanted to strangle the air out of my lungs back at the gym. Not that he'd be able to get me in a choke-hold if his life depended on it.

"Rhett, what in the hell was that? You promised me, no fighting outside the ring! And where is my goddamned gym assistant?"

"I didn't start the fight. Relax. I need Ava's home

address." I started rummaging through papers behind his desk, looking for one of her pay stubs or hire forms.

"Rhett! Stop fucking with me. What are you doing--"

"Just give me her fucking address, Coach! Please. We can talk about the rest later." Coach flinched slightly at my threatening tone and reached in his drawer for a piece of paper.

"Here." He slid it towards me with regret written all over his face and I took down the address before sliding it back to him.

"Thanks." I started heading down the steps from his office to the main floor of the gym. "Oh, and Coach? Put Roy and Sampson through the wringer today." He gave me a tight nod, hopefully putting the pieces together on what had actually gone down, and I made my way out of the gym without looking at any of the other fighters despite their curios stares.

Ava's apartment is on the rougher side of town. The building has faded shingles and motel-style wraparound balconies on each of the three floors. I make my way to the top floor and find her apartment number before rapping my knuckles a few times. Shit, I don't even have a way of knowing if she's even home right now.

I hear the door latch slide open to reveal Ava standing in the doorway. She's wearing a plain white t-shirt and athletic shorts. Her hair is damp and hanging over her shoulders like she just took a shower. She doesn't have a stitch of makeup on her face and it's painfully clear from her red-rimmed eyes that she's been crying. Because of me. But her expression is stoic which is somehow both sexy and admirable at the same time. She looks so young and beautiful, holding her chin up just a little higher than normal. I desperately want to kiss her, the thought flashing dangerously in my head before I can stop it, but I clench and unclench my fists at my sides to keep myself from reaching for her.

"Hi." Is all I'm able to manage for the moment.

"Hi." Her tone is clipped and laced with suspicion as she rests one of her perfectly curved hips against the doorframe.

I'm about to apologize when I look past her head and see a bunch of furniture kit parts strewn all over the small carpeted floor of the living room. Whatever she's trying to build doesn't look like it's going too well.

"You building something?"

"Um, yes. A desk."

"Need any help?"

"No."

"You sure? Looks like you need some help."

"Rhett, why are you here?"

Instead of answering, I gently push past her and into the small space of the apartment. It's fairly dark inside since the sky is overcast and there is only one floor lamp in the corner throwing light over the various desk pieces messily scattered on the floor. Without saying another word, I kneel down and start assembling the leg hardware.

"Rhett, what are you doing? I don't need your help." Her voice is soft, almost like she's given up but doesn't want to. Or maybe like a small, quiet part of her is grateful that I'm here and doesn't want me to leave. More likely that's my own wishful thinking. She sighs lightly when I don't make any attempts to stop assembling and comes down to sit next to me, crossing her legs and looking over my shoulder as I work on the various components of the desk. It isn't too complicated but she's managed to thread a few of the screws in the wrong places so that takes a bit of extra time to fix. I don't even mind the work. Always been a better doer than a talker. Somehow I feel calmer being near her. She watches me silently for several minutes.

Suddenly my stomach growls and it hits me that I haven't eaten since this morning. And I've already packed in a full day of training plus an unexpected one-on-two brawl.

"Let me get you something to eat." Ava gets up off the floor and makes her way to the kitchen. I get up from the floor as well, stretching my sore legs a little, that annoying pain I've learned to live with flaring in my lower back. I stand up the desk and slide the single drawer into the shelf tray with a satisfying click. Then I head over to the kitchen which is open to the living room on one side.

"Hmm, not too many options." Ava laughs nervously, staring into her fridge. I walk around to stand behind her, looking at the practically empty white shelves. A yogurt, a few beers, a bag of carrots, and a container of mustard. How can anyone make a decent meal with this?

"Do you live here alone?"

16

AVA

He sounds annoyed with me. Again. What is it about me that constantly puts him on edge? Or maybe it's simply the fact that he'd fought off several fighters today, built my desk pretty much from scratch, and is therefore understandably starving and all I have to offer him is a sad handful of baby carrots and a yogurt. Shelly and I haven't quite mastered the whole art of fully adulting yet. We are doing our best, okay?

I don't miss the edge in his voice when he says the word, "alone."

"No, Shelly lives here too. It's her apartment actually. I just moved in a few months ago temporarily." My tongue darts out nervously across my bottom lip, wondering if I've said too much, hoping he doesn't ask me more about it. "But she's usually at Eric's. So I often have the place to myself."

"Her boyfriend?" He crosses his arms over his broad chest, his thick corded veins wrapping around each forearm, criss-crossing his patchwork tattoos. My mouth suddenly goes dry realizing this massively strong man is in our suddenly comically small kitchen, being awfully domestic and concerned about my living situation. *Why is something about that sort of...hot?*

Before I can confirm his question, he's closing the refrigerator door and the outside of his rock solid bicep grazes against mine.

"You need food, Ava. I'll be back." He runs a large tanned hand through his already tousled hair and makes his way back to the front door. He leaves so quickly I don't even have a chance to ask him where he's going. I stare at where his back just was, my front door now closed and my new desk fully built, my jaw ajar.

Forty minutes later, Rhett is back in my small kitchen with his arms full of various grocery bags. I start to protest but he just ignores me, giving me his broad back. He begins to unpack each bag, placing items in the fridge and in the cupboards above the stove. Resigned to him not putting up with any of my protesting, I help him put the items away and my stomach is doing all sorts of gymnastic flips having him so close and personal in my space. It's hard to piece together this Rhett with the trained near-killer in the gym. The man in the ring. The fighter the underground flocks to see.

But then it hits me that he probably just feels bad about his rude "daddy attention" jab earlier and this is simply his form of repentance. Heck, Coach Barry probably even put him up to it. And I hate the thought that he's pitying me. I shouldn't have let him see how much that comment affected me.

"I'll pay you for the groceries."

"Don't be ridiculous."

"How is that ridiculous? I'm not a charity case."

"I know that. I've never treated you like a charity case."

"You are right now."

"No. Right now I'm feeding you because you have no food in your apartment. I'm also feeding myself because I'm fucking starving." He pauses for a moment and turns to face me directly. "You like your pasta with red sauce or olive oil?" He raises his dark eyebrows up higher onto his forehead as if to say, *are you going to keep pushing me on this or just let me cook?*

"Rhett sauce."

"What?" His face morphs from confusion to a masculine smirk at my stupidly embarrassing word mixup.

"Uh, red sauce. I meant red sauce." I clear my throat nervously, averting my eyes.

"Same." I can still see his satisfied grin from the corner of my eye. He starts getting out various ingredients for pasta and red sauce. I'm surprised when he begins to quickly and expertly dice tomatoes and holy hell if watching him do *that* in my kitchen isn't somehow the hottest thing I've ever seen.

"Thank you for your help with the desk." My words are tense as I stand across from him, my small kitchen island separating us as he moves between cutting up vegetables and the stovetop. Somehow the silence feels so...domestic, too normal. Like we cook dinner together all the time. Not like we've hardly ever spent any real time together outside of the gym. Even there, he barely speaks to me.

"Why did you wear those shorts today at the gym?" His voice is low, a trace of gentleness. It's the second time he's asked me today. He doesn't look up at me, keeping his eyes focused on the food he's prepping.

"Why do you care?"

"Ava."

"What?"

"It's...distracting. At the gym. I need my sparring partners focused. Plus it's...unlike you."

"And how would you know what *is* and *isn't* like me?"

"You're a good girl, Ava. You don't seek out blatant attention from men, especially not from the kind of men at the gym. You pride yourself on being effective at your job despite the fact that you're clearly going through some personal shit. I just don't know what it is." His dark eyes finally flash up to mine, one brow cockily raised as if to say, *tell me I'm wrong.* And even though he's nearly dead on with his assessment, I don't like him telling me he can read me like an open book.

"Stop saying I'm a good girl, whatever that means. You hardly know me."

"Ava," he sighs deeply, the sound settling like a weighted pit in my stomach, "can't you tell that I'm trying to get to know you?"

"Why? You clearly don't like me and you go out of your way to ignore me, unless you're telling me to get another job away from the gym. Or if you're criticizing my clothes as if *I'm* somehow at fault for those disgusting fighters not being able control themselves?"

Rhett puts the dicing knife down and plants both of his large palms on the kitchen island counter, squaring his intimidating shoulders.

"Well first off, I'm not criticizing how you dressed today for the sake of being a dick. I'm telling you because you could have seriously gotten hurt. You're like a lamb in a lion's den at that gym. Second, you clearly have no fucking idea *why* I avoid you at the gym."

I straighten my back and cross my arms over my chest. "Well clearly you don't have issues avoiding other women. Would the woman from your date be okay with the fact that you're here in my apartment, cooking me food?"

Rhett just glares at me, his jaw working. I can tell my

question isn't one he expected. For a moment it appears like he's going to say something but doesn't. Instead, he turns his back to me and starts plating our pasta and sauce into two separate bowls. I keep shifting from foot to foot, my confidence and sass waning with each minute of silence on his end.

"Eat." His tone is surprisingly soft again as he slides me a steaming bowl of pasta. It smells delicious. He comes around the side of the island and sits down on the stool next to mine. We start to eat in silence. I realize how hungry I am and have to actively keep myself from inhaling the food. I'd already come to terms with the fact that Rhett is strong and sexy and intimidating and completely unavailable but does he also have to be so good at cooking? Very unfair to my spasming and irrational female hormones.

"My *date's* name is Kelsey. She's...a friend. And for the record, Coach set that up. Not me."

"Okay."

"Okay?"

"Yeah, whatever." My attempt at sounding unbothered ends up making me sound even more childish and jealous.

"Since when do you care who I go on dates with anyway?" He turns toward me and I can feel the heat radiating from his body. I hate that my cheeks are starting to pink at his close proximity.

"I don't," my voice trails off, "I just don't get what it is about me that bothers you so much, but not other women I've seen you with."

"Bothers me?" Rhett barks out an incredulous laugh with an understanding that I don't grasp. "That's what you think? That you *bother* me? Jesus, Ava, that doesn't even scratch the surface." His words sound more like he's talking to himself or the room. He pauses before looking back up, directly at me. "Look with Kelsey...the woman I was on a date with or whatever...sex is important for a fight. It's a technicality. Keeps you loose in the ring. That's all that was about." He runs a hand through his hair, almost like he's irritated or even embarrassed. "Make sense?"

The only thing that *makes sense* is the thought of a blonde and beautiful Kelsey with her long legs wrapped around Rhett's waist. The mental image makes me shockingly annoyed. Really, really annoyed. I stand abruptly, taking my empty bowl over to the sink. If that's his way of trying to make me less irritated, he's failed. Miserably.

"I still don't think you quite get it, Ava." Rhett comes up behind me, his voice like a dark warning purr as his arms brace on the counter on either side of the sink, trapping me in.

"I get it just fine. I'm glad Kelsey is able to meet your *needs*. Thanks for the TMI." He smells so good standing over me, I want to turn around and lick his neck which is a thought I've certainly never had about a man before.

"See that's the thing. She didn't. Recently, no one has. I've been wound up so fucking tight these past few months, even Coach told me to get laid. It's not good to go into a fight like this. Especially with so much money on the line." He bends his head closer to my ear, his warm breath fanning out over my neck. I feel a shiver break out from the top of my head all the way down to my toes.

"I didn't fuck her."

"Such a gentleman."

"Never said I was."

"Why didn't you?"

"You really need to ask me that, Ava?" He slides a strong hand around my hip and pulls my ass flush up against his front. I can feel how hard he is, digging into my lower back.

"You said you didn't want me. That first time I saw you at the bar." My voice is practically a whisper, painfully hoarse. I can hear the blood pounding in my ears, matching my racing heartbeat.

"I never said I didn't want you. I said I *wouldn't* have you. Two very different things." He places a gentle, feather-light kiss underneath my ear in the exact same spot he'd kissed after rejecting me at the bar and I let my head fall back against his chest.

"What about now?" I try my best for seductress. A role that definitely doesn't come naturally to me. Rhett lets out a deep chuckle that makes my sex clench.

"Now? Now you're driving me fucking insane. But I still won't have you."

"Why not?" My voice comes out as a whine and I regret how desperate it sounds but I don't stop myself. "Just screw me like Coach wants you to and get on with your big fight. Isn't that how it works?" Rhett quickly flips me around so that I'm facing him. He cups my entire face in one hand, tipping my chin up to look at him. His hold is firm enough that I can't look away but gentle so as not to hurt. I know the damage he can do with those hands, the restraint he's using on them now. He uses his other hand to trail up and down the bare skin of my torso under my shirt.

"Ava. I can't have you just once. I won't fuck you for the sake of a fight. That won't be enough. So that means I can't have you at all. I'm not good for you. So please," he lowers his head, a few wayward dark waves falling over his forehead, "stop tempting me. Having you and then having you hate me would be worse than not having you at all." He sounds like he's begging and the thought of a man like Rhett Jaggar pleading nearly brings *me* to my knees.

"Why would I hate you?"

"Because you're a boyfriend type of girl. And I don't do that shit. Ever. I eat, sleep, and breathe fighting. I even fuck to fight. You would hate me when I left you and I don't want you to hate me. I'm selfish like that." He smirks at his last sentence but it doesn't meet his dark eyes. His words are sincere which pisses me off even more. How would he even know what I want? Maybe I don't want a boyfriend! Maybe I just want him to throw me down on my bed and take out both of our frustrations!

Before I think it through, I lean up and kiss him. I've never been the first to make a move before but I don't care. He stays still for a moment, so deathly still he's not even moving his lips as his hand digs deeper into my waist until I'm sure it will leave a mark.

Finally, he moves his lips over mine, violently returning my kiss, his teeth pulling at my lower lip until I involuntarily let out a small whimper. He winds his fist into my hair and pulls my head upward, arching my back and curving my body more tightly into his. I've never been kissed like this before, so desperately and angrily, an intoxicating mix of punishment and pleasure. And Rhett.

17

RHETT

Well, I'm fucked. I always knew it'd be bad if I kissed her. I knew her lips would be soft and plump and downright addicting. But I had no idea they'd be this good. She's so silky and smells like vanilla. I want to lift her up onto the counter by her ass and see if her other set of lips tastes as good as these but I force myself to stop. I have to. I pull away from her, our breathing heavy. Her cheeks are flushed pink and her lips a sexy shade of just-kissed red. With her hair tousled from my pulling and her back up against the counter for support, she's quite literally the sexiest thing I've ever seen. And that means I need to leave. Now.

I stare at her confused, flushed face for a long moment before calling on all of the self-discipline I have left in my body and heading for the door. I built her desk. I bought her groceries. I made her dinner. Even if leaving her breathless and without explanation is a dick move, I can at least reassure myself with the fact that I've done a few decent things to make up for my shitty actions earlier today. But I know from the look on her face that she will definitely hate me after this. Probably for the best so she keeps herself away from me, but that doesn't mean it doesn't take the wind from my gut like one hell of a sucker punch.

"I have to go. Ava I--" I cut myself off before even trying to explain. How do you tell a sweet, sexy girl who is obviously into you that you want her so much you can't have her? That you are in danger of becoming damn near obsessed with her but know you don't deserve her? That there is no way you could ever make a girl like her happy? It doesn't even make sense in my own head let alone spoken out loud. Not unless I tell her everything. And hell would have to freeze over before I did that.

I head out her front door and move quickly down the three flights of apartment stairs, effectively preventing myself from going back inside and doing all the things I really want to do to her. All the things I'll never let myself do.

18

AVA

I have successfully managed to get Shelly off my back. She finally stopped asking me "what's wrong" and has been tiptoeing around the apartment, worried she might set me off. After Rhett left my apartment a few days ago, I feel like an electric wire that might snap, the heat and intensity from Rhett's kiss contrasted by how quickly he'd left the apartment. No, not left, *fled*. Regret streaking across his too-handsome face. Our kiss hadn't even lasted very long but it was different. More potent and desperate than any kiss I'd experienced before. His whiplash reactions to me are so confusing and frustrating, leaving me to wonder if I should just pretend the whole thing never even happened. Too bad that was proving to be an impossible feat.

I decided to take a few days off work. Coach Barry actually came by the apartment to check in on me and I was grateful and relieved that he wasn't planning on firing me after the fight that broke out. But he was understandably less than happy about the whole event. I may have initially been less than thrilled about working at the gym, and still can't see it as a longterm position, but I definitely don't want to lose my job. I've come to really like Coach Barry and his mentorship. The kindness he's shown me, the chance he took on a girl who needed the job more than he could ever know. Even though it isn't my fault two of his fighters decided to lose their rational minds over a pair of too-short shorts, I still feel embarrassed and ashamed about the whole event.

And of course it had been to get under Rhett's skin. Trying to deny that, even in the privacy of my own mind, is futile. My attempt to make a man, who could probably get any woman to go to bed with him, jealous. I shake my head at the shortsighted foolishness of it, vowing to not make that same mistake again.

I reluctantly agree to go to another underground fight tonight, only because it is Eric's first and Shelly is a nervous wreck. She has been such a good friend to me, taking me in and basically picking up all the pieces of my past life, so I know I have to do this for her even if it means being faced with so many reminders of Rhett. Let alone that there is a good chance he will actually be there. I push all of those thoughts out of mind because I'm about to go do the only thing that can potentially make me even more nervous than the thought of seeing Rhett: seeing my father.

He has consistently been calling Shelly trying to get in touch with me, and the few days off from work forces me to slow down for a moment and face the fact that I have some majorly unresolved issues with my dad. I decide to make the forty-five minute drive to see him in person because trying to talk through such serious things over the phone feels daunting and damn near impossible. As much as he's hurt me, lied to me and risked my future, I still miss him. I want to see his face, feel his bear hug around me, know that he feels sorry for everything that's happened.

He's the only blood family I have and I want him in my life, even if healing fully will take many, many years. Maybe forever.

I grip the steering wheel so tightly my knuckles turn white. I wonder how this whole conversation will go down. A growing part of me also hopes his wife won't be there. Lydia isn't the stepmom from hell or anything, but I really need to just be with my dad for a moment, like when I was a young girl and it was just the two of us against the world.

I pull up to the rundown hotel where my father relocated after our home was seized. A 6,000 square foot McMansion with a large backyard where I spent summers playing and swimming with friends. I had trusted my father completely. I was ignorant about his financial firm being a total scam. My mother passed away when I was a young girl so my father had been my whole life, my hero. To see him now, staying in this rundown place and me crashing at Shelly's...it's a reality I never could have imagined.

I sit awkwardly in the small lobby, the place smelling of must and cigarette smoke. I send my father a quick text and fidget in place. I haven't seen him since *that* night. The night my life was flipped upside down and I left my perfectly decorated off-campus apartment, escorted by a police officer, to my childhood home. The lawn had been lit up with police lights, the entire neighborhood out on the street. News reporters started taking over the lawn, women in tight A-line skirts rushing up the perfectly manicured hill, their cameramen trailing close behind. It was like the scene of a bad movie. And my father was the villain.

Now, it's quiet. Too quiet. I thought the chaos and embarrassment of that night would be the worst moment of my life. But sitting in this rundown apartment lobby, waiting for my father who I always revered as the smartest man in the world, to come down and shamefully see me...this moment is worse.

"Hi, honey." I turn to see him at the familiar sound of his voice. I can't conceal the look of sadness and shock on my face. His hair has grown out and is a bit scraggly. He's wearing a worn polo and khaki shorts, nothing like the polished businessman I'm used to.

"Hi, Dad." My voice cracks and I can't keep my eyes from welling up with tears. You'd think after crying so much there wouldn't be any more left.

"Let's head up to my room, where we can talk." He keeps his head down low, a tinge of pink embarrassment blanketing his cheeks. As angry as I am that he lied to me for so many years, my heart breaks at the sight of him.

The room is small but thankfully clean. Well, aside from the empty bottles of alcohol I see scattered throughout the room. I know my father likes to drink, he always has at various work parties and social events, but something feels different about him drinking here. Alone.

"Where's Lydia?" I look around the room for any signs of his wife; a purse or a jacket. Her coveted cosmetics on the bathroom counter. None of it is here.

"Um honey, why don't you sit down. Can I get you something to drink?" He looks into the mini-fridge, throwing me a sad, closed-lip smile.

"A water would be good."

"Great. Here ya go, hon." He hands me a small water bottle and pulls out the chair opposite mine. I spin the cap of the water bottle nervously, dragging the rough ridged plastic against my finger. Finally, he breaks the awkward silence.

"Lydia and I...well, we aren't doing so good right now. She met me at the height of my success and you know...she might not be willing to stick around during this bad luck spell." I snap my head up at his words. They bring my anger back to the surface; anger at his refusal to admit his responsibility in all of this. He's acting as if it's something that happened to him versus something he did, not only to himself but to everyone else around him.

"Dad, you can't blame Lydia. You lied to her. You lied to all of us. To me." My words are harsh but I won't keep them in. It's the truth.

"I know baby, I know. Look I didn't invite you here to talk about how badly I messed up. I can't tell you how sorry I am." I see tears well in his eyes and he reaches for my hand. I let him take it in his but I sit rock still.

"How are you? Shelly's been treating you well? Are you able to take your college classes online?"

I flinch before taking a deep, calming breath. "I dropped out, Dad. I got a job at a local gym. I'm trying to save up enough money to even make a dent in paying back the student loans. Who knows when I will be able to go back to school." I don't say it out loud but it isn't just about the money. Plenty of kids take out massive loans to go to school. But I just know I need more time between what happened and me going back. I was the news story of the century on campus. Everyone gossiping about the financial fraud that is my father. The thought makes my body break out in chills.

I see my father drop his head in sadness or resignation. I'm not sure which. He looks back up at me with desperate, tired eyes. "Well, I'm proud of you for getting a job." I don't know whether to agree with him or be angry. I simply nod in response, not trusting the words that might slip past my lips.

"You look lovely, Ava. A little thin." He gives me a smile

that is a shadow of the megawatt grin he used to wear and I feel like I'm talking to the ghost of someone I once knew.

"Well you know I'm not the best chef. Neither is Shelly. But I'm learning." A fleeting mental image of Rhett in my kitchen making me pasta comes to mind and I shove it back down just as quickly.

"Honey..." My father pulls his hand away from mine and suddenly looks a bit nervous. I sit up straighter in response. "I wanted to invite you to something. Well, more like ask if you're willing to come..." His voice trails off again, the uncertainty in it making me edgy. I don't move an inch. Whatever he wants to ask for, he's going to have to come right out and say it.

"Ava. I know it doesn't look like it right now, but I am trying to get better. I really am. And my lawyer, he's been telling me how I have to start by improving myself. For my perception in court. They aren't going to go easy on me, sweetheart. I really burned a lot of powerful people. I mean it happens in business, you know? Everyone loves you when they're winning, but they hate you even more when they lose." His voice quivers and I think again of Rhett, of all the people betting on his fights in the underground. Money, a thing that had always given me peace and pleasure and opportunity, now sits leaden in my gut like a poison.

"I've been going to an AA group. I mean I've always loved to drink but I just didn't realize how bad it was until all the music stopped. And now...it's just me...and it's too easy to reach for the alcohol. But I want to beat it! I want the court to see me as a redeemed man. I think maybe my addiction is why I wasn't able to keep the business going, why I let it slip from my grasp." He swallows hard, dragging his palms against the thighs of his shorts. "Tomorrow my AA group is hosting a family day. It's nothing fancy, just bad fruit punch and awkward small talk." He laughs nervously and darts his eyes between the table and me.

I feel utterly torn. My father is my only blood and he's struggling. He wants my support. Need its. Of course, I want to see him healthy and on the other side of his addictions.

But I hate the voice in my head telling me that he's only doing this for the court. For the *perception* of being a redeemed man. He's being selfish. He doesn't actually care to stop drinking. He wants to lessen his impending jail sentence. Likely at the advice of his lawyer. But I stop the thought in its tracks. Because dealing with the reality of my father going to prison just isn't something I'm ready to fully face yet. Maybe ever.

"I'll think about it, Dad. I want to come...but I need some time to decide." It's the best that I can offer. And it's the truth. I want to be there for him. But after everything, I just don't know if I can. I don't know how much more I can care and still expect to survive intact. I'm already just barely keeping it together. Just barely crawling myself forward.

"That's fair honey. I appreciate that." I can see the sadness in his eyes but he doesn't push me on it. Clearly, he's lost his *never-take-anything-but-yes for an answer* attitude. I stand up to leave, not sure what more there is to say.

"Text me the details?" I turn back to him, my hand on the hotel room door. I feel like if I don't leave soon, my chest will crack in half and I won't be able to stop the onslaught of threatening tears.

"Of course. I'll do that, honey. And thank you again. Even just for considering. I love you, Ava. Anything I've done...any mistakes I've made, it doesn't change that, you know?"

"I know, Dad. I love you too." I turn to leave before he can say anything else and power walk outside to my car. The only thing more depressing than his hotel room is the idea of bawling my eyes out in the musty lobby.

Once safely in the driver's seat, I let myself go. The tears and the wailing sound like something foreign outside of my own body but I need it. I've been distracting myself by putting one foot in front of the other. Dropping myself into Shelly's life, getting a new job, surrounding myself with scary and sexy fighters who make no sense to me. None of this makes any sense! This isn't how my life was supposed to go. I know there's a growing new strength inside of me but seeing my father so broken is too much.

After a solid cry, I feel better. Not good, but numb. And numb is better than the overwhelming sadness that feeling nothing keeps at bay. I tell myself that I'll decide tomorrow morning about going to the AA meeting with my Dad. Tonight, I'm going to distract myself by supporting Shelly during Eric's first underground fight, putting as much distance as possible between my present reality and my past life.

19

RHETT

I'm not fighting tonight. Even if my rib is fully healed, which Coach and I continue to disagree about, this circuit isn't up to my standards. These guys are far less predictable for bettors, making it more fun but also lower stakes. My matches are never low stakes these days. A small part of me envies it.

"Well, well, isn't it a real treat seeing you at a match in actual clothing? You clean up pretty good, Rhett." Coach Barry slaps me playfully on the back and I snort at his dumb comment. I'm wearing a black button-up shirt, rolled up to my elbows, and a dark pair of slacks. Definitely not my usual ring attire since I'm typically only at underground events when I'm sweating under the hot spotlights above the ring.

"Figured I'd try something different." I give him a tight nod and don't miss the fact that he seems genuinely happy I decided to come. Coach and I have a bond, never openly stated or easy to nail down. But it's there, something like family. If he really needs me, I'm there. Works both ways.

Eric is fighting his first few rounds tonight in this underground circuit and I have to admit that I won't mind seeing his obnoxious face get squarely punched in a few times. But the real reason I'm here is for Ava. I don't know for sure if she's be coming, but considering her best friend's man will be in the ring for the first time, I figure the chances of her making an appearance are pretty high. High enough at least that I managed to comb my hair and make myself presentable, even if Coach thinks it's a gesture of support for him. I could've just gone back to her apartment or gotten her number like a normal person. Tried to explain to her why I left in a such a rush the other day after feeling her lips against mine. I could've asked her not to hate me. Begged her. But I want to see her in person. Read her body language, take note of the expression on her perfect fucking face when she sees me. I just want to be near her again. Even though I try to ignore her in the gym for the sake of my own sanity, her absence over the past few days has weighed on me more than I care to admit.

Our seats are at the very front of the arena and Coach stands up to go check on some of the fighters in the prepping rooms backstage. I use the opportunity to scan for Ava in the crowd. She and her friend should be sitting nearby. I glance between the crowd and my phone before finally spotting her. She's wearing a dark red dress, showing off her lovely curves without showing too much skin. The fact that the fabric goes all the way up to the base of her neck and covers her arms only makes the dress even sexier. She hasn't noticed me yet as she and Shelly navigate the growing crowd, making their way toward the ring.

I turn to face the front, aiming for nonchalance. Ava and her thin blonde friend start making their way to their seats in the very front row and that's when Ava finally makes eye contact with me. Her face looks surprised at seeing me so close to her seat and I notice her checking out my outfit with an adorably confused look. She gives me a long stare before taking the seat directly in front of mine without saying a word.

"Hey, Rhett. How are you?" The blonde, Shelly I think is her name, turns in her seat with a sassy look on her face but I can tell she's masking some serious pre-fight nerves.

"Good, thanks." I give her a curt nod and focus my gaze on the back of Ava's head willing her to turn around, her shiny auburn hair straighter than I've seen it before. I'm reminded of just how good it feels wrapped around my fist.

"That's good." Shelly taps her heel against the concrete floor and releases an unnaturally loud sigh. "I'm nervous. Like so fucking nervous. I don't know if it's worse sitting here watching, or being the one in the ring. What do you think?" She giggles like a hyena and even though I find the sound grating as hell, I want to do or say something to help calm her down.

"Eric will be fine. He's gotten a lot better, and he loves to fight. Loves to perform. That's what matters most. If a guy has skills but doesn't want to be in the ring...well then, that's when you should be nervous."

Shelly smiles back at me gratefully and it's the first time she doesn't look like she has some complaint or demand on the tip of her tongue. The arena speakers start to blare painfully loudly with rap music, signaling the doors have opened for general public seating. I lean back in my seat, still keeping my eyes squarely on Ava who refused to move an inch during my brief exchange with Shelly.

As the music grows louder, I lean forward. I can smell the back of Ava's neck and it's driving me insane.

"Are you as nervous?" Ava's shoulders jump at my words in her ear and she starts to turn her head back towards me but then snaps it decidedly forward, once again facing the ring.

"No." She folds her arms over her chest.

"What about now?" I lightly kiss her in that spot beneath her ear that she likes so much. I'm leaning in casually, making it look like we are just talking so that no one else can see exactly where my mouth is. Goosebumps break out over the sliver of exposed porcelain skin on her upper neck.

"What do you want, Rhett?" Her voice is breathy, barely audible over the music.

"I'm sorry, Ava. I didn't mean to leave mixed signals." I lean in further so my lips are nearly at her cheek and decide to go for earnest. "I am so fucking attracted to you, it's insane. I want you in my bed, in the locker room, anywhere I can have you. But I have a fucked up past. I have an addictive personality and sometimes when I give into one craving, it opens up the urge for others. Does that make any sense?" My voice is a loud whisper, wanting only her to hear my words but still needing to compete with the blaring music.

"Couldn't we just try?" She turns to me, her lips nearly connecting with mine. Her eyes are eager but guarded. There's an intoxicating mix of innocence and womanhood in her expression that has my blood rushing.

"Maybe. I want to. Find me after the match." I search her eyes for any signs of regret or apprehension. She pauses a moment before nodding and I feel a genuine smile pull against my lips. At least I will have an opportunity to be honest with her before getting her alone, and hopefully I'll be able to give into my need for her without calling on the demons from my past. Demons I never want her to see.

20

AVA

I keep hearing Rhett's words on a loop in my ear and I want to run my hands up and down my arms to quell the full-body chills that have taken over me. Apparently, Rhett rarely even comes to matches as a spectator, and seeing him sitting right behind my seat next to Shelly, dressed in a black, button-down shirt, just about did my female hormones in. I remind myself that I'm here for Shelly. Here to support my best friend. But now all I can do is think about the sexy as sin man behind me. The one who asked me to find him after the match. The one who admitted just how attracted to me he is. I almost forget that we are about to watch Eric get his face pummeled in when Shelly's clammy hand reaches over and grasps mine.

"Ava, I'm so fucking nervous. Like, do you think *he's* nervous?" She nods toward the ring. "I wanted to go backstage and see him but the coaches told me no to do that. Apparently it's not good for their focus." She's chewing on one of her long acrylic nails with her other hand and I gently pry it away from her teeth before she does some serious damage.

"I'm sure Eric is fine. He's probably excited, you know? That kind of nervous is good. You heard Rhett. He likes to fight. This is the big time. It's where he wants to be." I wave my hand around the arena, almost laughing out loud at the hypocrisy. Here I am, hyping up the place, when a mere few months ago I would've been the biggest naysayer of anything like this. Funny how quickly you adapt to things.

"You're right, you're right. I think maybe I just need another drink." Shelly smiles tightly at me, her wide eyes still revealing her true nervous feelings before leaping out of her seat in search of alcohol. She needs to move quickly because the lights have started to dim, signaling the fight will be starting soon.

I turn very slightly in my chair, still keeping my torso facing forward. I don't talk loudly but I know my voice is loud enough for him to hear.

"Do you ever get nervous?" I feel Rhett lean in closer to me, my heart thundering again at the proximity.

"Before a fight?" His words are laced with a sensual tone. Or maybe it's just my overheated imagination.

"Yeah."

He doesn't respond right away and I turn more fully in his direction, resting my elbow on the back of my metal chair.

"Not really nervous, no. I actually feel this sense of calm. But it's an energizing calm rather than sedative. Not sure if that makes any sense." He runs a hand through his thick hair and actually seems a little caught off-guard for once. I like it. Too much. His full lips pull upward in an almost shy, subtle smirk, drinking me in.

"That makes sense. I mean, I can't say I've felt it myself, but I think I get what you're saying." I give him a small reassuring smile and open my mouth to say more when I feel

Shelly slide back into the seat next to me. She hands me a vodka soda, nearly spilling it on my dress.

The announcer starts his bit with the audience with a series of crass jokes that I don't find humorous at all. I think even the less-than-proper crowd is ready for the actual fighting to start by the time he finishes his little comedy routine. The place goes nearly black, aside from the orb-like glow that blankets the ring. Silence and suspense hang heavy and expectant in the air.

Finally, the first fighter appears. Eric's opponent. His name is Thorne. Or at least, that's his stage name. I can't imagine that's his birth name. His announcement is met with more boos than cheers, the ground beneath my heels shaking with the power of the crowd. Despite myself, I have to admin that he's surprisingly handsome. Icy blonde spiky hair is sticking out in every direction and you can see how light his blue eyes are even from the floor seating. There is almost something eerie about Thorne, an ancient Nordic Viking in an underground arena, but then again, no sane person just goes willingly go into a death wish like this.

The thought has me squirming in my chair, thinking about Rhett behind me. Realizing he has the same death wish, the same penchant for violence. Maybe even more than any of the others.

When Eric emerges from the opposite corner I think Shelly passes out for a moment on the spot. She's caught between cheering like a maniac and shaking like a leaf. I guess she must really like this guy if she's this worried about him. Shelly doesn't usually stay invested in one guy for too long. I give her a reassuring pat on the knee when she finally manages to sit back down.

To his credit, Eric looks like a natural in the ring. He doesn't have the physique of Rhett, or even of Thorne, but you can tell he's truly loving it. The lights, the drama, the impending danger. This guy is a performer through and through. Just as Rhett had reassured Shelly. I cross my fingers under my thighs that Thorne doesn't knock Eric out in some embarrassingly short amount of time.

The bell rings out and the fight begins. Thorne is jumpy, almost spidery in the wicked movement of his long, strong limbs. He dances around the ring like his feet are on fire. I see Eric's smile waver a bit as a look of confusion crosses over his broad, boyish face. All it takes is one fluid moment for Thorne to get several abdomen jabs in before effortlessly bouncing away. But Eric is a tank. He takes the hits in stride. The blows don't seem to hurt his body as much as his ego.

The fight goes for several rounds, each fighter playing to his respective advantage. Thorne gets way more hits in but Eric throws a few nearly lethal blows. They are taking a break in their respective corners, getting simultaneously chastised and encouraged by their coaching teams. At this point, I can only imagine the insane betting activity going on in the arena with how tight this match-up has become. I'm about to turn to Shelly and ask how she's doing when I notice a warm spotlight swing in my direction.

I blink furiously at the yellow-white light and try to make out what is happening. The heat of the light fans across my skin like an artificial sun. Then I hear the crackling of the arena speakers and a deep, gravelly voice blares out.

"Sweetheart, this fight is for you. Sitting in the front row, you've been damn near distracting me all night." Thorne's voice is laced with exhaustion but he still has his manic energy about him. My eyes dart nervously between the ring and my surroundings but I can't see anything beyond a hazy film with the spotlight still directly on my face. *Is he talking to me?*

"You hear that, arena! We have a man fighting for more than a 'W' tonight. For more than just money!" The announcer raises one of Thorne's arms above his head, his eyes light and wild like an animal's. "He's fighting for some pussy!" The arena goes wild at the obscenity of his words and I can't keep the horrified look off my face. Thankfully the light is swept away, my heart in my throat as I blink through yellow and orange spots peppering my vision before I'm able to actually see in front of my face again.

"Uh, what in the actual fuck was that." Shelly's voice is dead-pan. If this was any other fight, with any other guy, she'd likely be jumping out of her seat with excitement. But it isn't just any fight. And the fighter who made that God-awful proclamation, *the proclamation that's he's fighting for me,* is hellbent on beating Eric. *Beating Eric in my honor?* I feel my skin crawl with confusion and fear, my eyes darting away from the ring and toward any possible exits. Suddenly I want to get out of here. Now.

"God, I have no idea. Maybe his team told him I'm with you? And since you're with Eric this is some sort of mental game he likes to play?" *That had to be it, right?* I'd always assumed all that fake, storyline stuff was just for WWE fights. Not underground boxing rings where the punches are real—

"It's not fake." My train of thought is cut off by Rhett behind me. The severity of his tone makes me sit up straighter, an electric shock of fear snapping up my spine.

"What do you mean it's not fake? I don't even know that guy." I gesture toward the ring as the bell cracks out loudly, signaling that the next round has started.

21

RHETT

J ust my fucking luck. I swear under my breath as I
lean back in my seat, my limbs suddenly rigid and
ready to fight. Of course, right when I'm trying to
make things right with Ava, maybe even see where
something between us could go, she unknowingly captures
the attention of the goddamn Serbian mafia.

Thorne doesn't look like a traditional mafia guy. He
looks like some Nordic warrior: white-blonde hair and
nearly gray eyes. But he is a dangerous motherfucker. The
kind that always wears a smile instead of a scowl. I've known
him for years and I've had my own mix-ups with the Serbian
mob during my earlier years in the ring. They are known for
fixing fights. But that era of fighting and addiction is behind
me. Or at least, I wake up everyday with that resolution
desperately falling from my lips.

And now sitting in front of me, sweet, beautiful Ava is like
a fucking moth to a very, *very* dangerous flame in a place like
this. There are women everywhere in this arena. Women with
long hair and tan skin and big tits, both real and fake. But they

are rougher somehow. They are part of the fabric of this arena as much as I am, as much as the fighters in the ring. They are an integral part of this world. And Ava is anything but.

I don't know if Thorne's ridiculous proclamation is solely based on his attraction to Ava. I mean, I certainly wouldn't blame him if that's the case even if it makes my blood boil. But Thorne has a pattern to his tactics. He's a strategic fucker. Knowing Throne, his decision to call out his proclamation for Ava is probably a toxic combination of both.

Before I can explain to Ava how serious this situation has just become, a woman dressed in a black, slinky bikini crouches down low and whispers in Ava's ear as she hands her a folded piece of paper. *Fuck.* Thorne is acting fast. He either has no idea that I'm sitting directly behind Ava, or has *every* confidence that I am.

If there is one thing I hate more than playing games, it's playing games when I don't know the rules. And what makes it even worse, a pit of anger tightening in my gut, is that an amazing, innocent woman is about the be at that game's center.

I fist my hands at my sides, completely distracted from the fight that has resumed. All I can do is stare at Ava's delicate fingers as she shakily unfolds the small paper. I spot Thorne's name and number. Jesus Christ. *What is this, middle school?* Fat fucking chance that Ava will be calling him tonight. If anything, he's going to get a threatening phone call from *me*.

I lean forward, draping both of my arms on either side of Ava. I look across the ring, staring down Thorne's team of trainers and lackeys. It's hard to make them out through the chaos in the ring, but I want my proximity to Ava known.

Need it known. Even if that's exactly what they're banking on.

"When the fight ends," I feel Ava jump in surprise at my low voice directly in her ear, my hand grazing the fabric of her dress against her arm, "don't make eye contact with anyone. Keep your head down and walk directly in front of me. I'll steer you towards the nearest exit." My words are calm but my tone is deadly serious. I need her to understand how serious this could become.

"Rhett," her voice is breathy and a little frightened, "are you seriously that jealous? I'm really not interested in him. Like at all." I don't miss the hint of cautious satisfaction in her voice, thinking my protective reaction is solely based on male jealousy. It's cute. Just fucking adorable. Too bad it's about to get way worse than just that.

"No, Ava. I'm not jealous." I feel her body bristle, her head facing forward again as I continue. "But I am serious. I'll explain it all when we get in my car." I gave her slender shoulder a reassuring squeeze before leaning back into my seat. If she doesn't walk out right in front of me like I asked, I'll grab her and throw her over my shoulder if that's what it takes to send a signal to Thorne that Ava is 100% off limits for whatever game he's scheming up next.

I imagine for a moment that we will be able to get out of here easily, without any trouble. That I'll have Ava safely in the cab of my truck in no time. But even in the quiet of my own mind, I don't quite believe. Not where the Serbians are concerned.

22

AVA

Rhett's reaction to Thorne's note has my blood strumming through my veins. I don't know him well enough to know if he's truly being serious, but based on the tone of his voice as he spoke harshly and sternly into my ear, he seems to believe Thorne's note is hardly just a flirtatious move. I get the tingling sense that Rhett's trying to warn me but can't say everything he wants to, or needs, until after the fight. Perhaps he's even holding back to keep from scaring me. The thought has me fidgeting in my seat.

Eric and Thorne are at it again, the energy in the arena beating like a living thing as they continue their toe-to-toe fight. Eric and Thorne are so evenly matched but I hate to admit that I think Thorne might have gained the upper edge. His proclamation giving him a wildness, a bravado, whereas Eric's energy appears to be waning. I keep averting my eyes from the sounds of skin against skin and the hard thud of fists impacting bone, unable to watch.

I feel Shelly clutch my forearm in a death grip. It's like she knows the end is near before it actually happens. And just like that, a loud crack breaks out. A heavy body slamming facedown into the mat. The sound seeps into every crevice of the underground arena like water flooding a room. It's over. And Thorne is the winner.

"Shit." I let out a harsh whisper and feel a sense of dread pool in my stomach, mainly for Shelly who is now shaking like a leaf beside me. Eric is laid out flat on the mat, completely cold. Thorne is breathing heavily in his corner, bright red blood trickling from the corner of his mouth. A barely-there but still satisfied smile on his hard, chiseled face. And he's smiling directly at me.

For a moment, the whole arena is held by a pause. Winning bets are definitely placed down the middle tonight with how close the fight has been so I can only imagine how unhappy the losing group is. No one seems to know whether to cheer or boo. Neither of these fighters have a loyal enough following like Rhett. There is just a sense of excited finality without direction or purpose. Almost disbelief.

And then, the movement starts. People begin booing and cheering, yelling out obscenities and rushing toward the ring. Eric is barely up on his feet and being slid to the edge of the ring by three other grown men in matching black pullovers.

I feel Rhett grip my upper arm, my body instantly heating at the contact. "Remember what I said. Meet me at the end of the aisle." He releases me and then starts to move, quickly making his way out of the row of seats behind me. I try to start moving too, but the crowd around us only grows denser and Shelly is nearly frozen in place with fear.

"Shelly, come on. Let's go. We can meet up with Eric as soon as he's done with the medical staff. It will be fine, I promise."

Before I can get her to start moving, I feel a hand grip my waist firmly. My first thought is that it's somehow Rhett but that doesn't make sense since he's been moving in the opposite direction. I turn to see a huge burly man, dressed in all black, with the stoic and bored expression of a club bouncer.

"Thorne is waiting to meet you." His voice is deep, and it rumbles like it's coming directly from his belly. There's an accent to it but I can't place where. My heart starts to race with panic.

"Yeah, um, no thank you." Pretty sure by the expression on his meaty face that was not the appropriate response, but my polite instincts act of their own accord. I need to get out of here. Fast. I stand up on my tiptoes in search of Rhett but I'm even farther back from the aisle now than I was when the fight ended.

"I'm afraid Thorne doesn't take 'no' for an answer. He claimed you as a prize. And he won. Let's go." I feel myself pulled tightly into his enormous side and dragged further from my seat. I try to yell out but my throat is so dry from nerves that no sound comes out. My eyes flash wildly in search of Rhett or Shelly. But the crowd is growing impossibly denser, the amorphous mass of bodies shoving and pushing through the arena. Before I can fight my way free, I feel myself being pulled deeper into the chaos.

23

RHETT

I came to this fight wanting to make up with Ava and see where things could go for us. I rarely come to matches as a spectator, especially ones with hotheaded newbies like Eric in the ring. So it figures that the universe would have something else in store for me since normal and underrated never seem to be my speed. These days, for the first time, I start to wish they were.

Instead, I can no longer see Ava in the crowd. I did manage to see the huge henchman fucker that led her away. He just landed himself at the top of my shit list right next to Thorne. It has been years since I've spent any time with Thorne and I hadn't planned on tonight being our reunion. Guess my plans are about to change.

I make my way outside and around the facility to the back. I know where Thorne and his team would be regrouping before they head out to God knows where. They won't be getting far with Ava in tow. That's for damn sure. That brunette princess is starting to turn into a real headache. I find the metal door that leads to a backstage area and throw it open. I can hear rap music pierced by laughing voices. The smell of sweat, smoke, and alcohol hangs heavily in the air. The door to Thorne's prep room is ajar and I open it the rest of the way.

I take in the scene quickly. Ava is on a black leather couch, her red dress pulled up a bit, showing off most of her thighs. She tries, unsuccessfully, to put a little more distance between herself and Thorne. She has a red cup in hand and one of the bodyguards is staring her down like she's a meal and he hasn't eaten for weeks. There are fresh lines of snow-white cocaine on the table and I hate the fact that I'm momentarily distracted from my purpose in getting Ava out of this place. I see the white lines waiting to be inhaled and clench my fists at my side. It's one thing to resist temptation when it isn't in front of you. It's a whole other beast when it's within reach.

"What the hell! Is that *the* Rhett Jaggar? Well, I'll be damned. It's been fucking years, you bastard." Thorne grins at me like a cheshire cat, his voice dripping with feigned surprise. The whiteness of his teeth and the bright pale gray of his eyes just further emphasizes his evil Nordic look. His cheekbones are so sharp, they seem like they might poke through his pale, sweaty skin.

Ava's eyes widen in both shock and relief and she starts to stand up from the couch, but Thorne clenches his hand on her thigh, essentially stopping her. I zero in on that hand, imagining the feel of his fingers crushing, bone by bone. He's still smiling, but I don't miss the flash of confusion and then understanding that crosses over his face. He chooses not to acknowledge it though.

"You want a line?" He gestures toward the table, his smile growing.

"Ava, let's go." Throne just clenches his grip on her bare thigh even tighter, threatening to bruise.

"Woah, my man, I think there might be a misunderstanding. You did hear me claim this lovely brunette beauty as my prize, did you not? It's actually a move I believe I learned from you." He pulls Ava closer and I hate the look of faint disappointment in her eyes. I'm not the same man I was several years ago. But there's no way for me to try and explain that to her right now. I move further into the room, automatically assuming a fighting stance. Thorne starts to shift his hand up Ava's thigh and underneath the hem of her dress. I notice her squeeze her thighs closer together in response, trying to stop him.

"If you move your hand even one inch higher, I will fucking kill you. I don't care if it's in or out of the ring, you're a dead man. Got it?"

"Whoa!" Thorne laughs, but the humor is laced with acid. He keeps his hand on Ava's thigh, moving it back and forth to taunt me. Then he dips his head forward and inhales the biggest line of coke on the table. His eyes light up and he tosses his head back before leveling his gaze at me again. "God, that's good. Rhett, what happened to you? Are you going all soft for some pussy? You used to share girls all the time. Tell me, is this one as good as she looks?"

24

AVA

"She's a friend. Drop it." Rhett's voice is deathly low, making it far more intimidating than if he'd yelled or screamed at Thorne. I desperately want to get the hell out of here. I hated the terrified, helpless feeling I'd felt ever since that burly man with the accent dragged me through the thickening crowd around the ring and backstage. I've been to my fair share of frat parties, but I've always stayed away from the hard stuff. The cocaine on the table had my heart leaping into my throat when I first saw it, and now here Thorne is practically taunting Rhett with it.

And while I'm desperate and grateful that Rhett is here to hopefully haul me away in one piece, I can't just ignore the comments Throne made about Rhett. I hate picturing Rhett doing drugs and having sex with random women after fights. But I also hate myself for daydreaming that he'd be any different. He's a part of this world. He *is* this world. It doesn't change the traitorous part of my body that still wants him. I can't just pretend that I don't. But I have no idea how to reconcile the genuine glimpses of himself that he's shown me with the accusations that Thorne has just laid bare. But I can deal with those thoughts later. Right now, I need Rhett to get me the hell out of this place. Now.

"Look, Rhett. I'm big on loyalty when it counts, you know that, but that shit doesn't apply to bitches. You're either fucking this girl, or you're not. So which is it?"

"I'm fucking her." Rhett nearly spits the words out, his eyes lethal. He doesn't look at me when he says it. He keeps his focus solely on Thorne and his fists are clenched tightly at his sides. I notice that they are bruised, likely from a recent sparring round in the gym.

"Alright then." Thorne's hand stills on my thigh. "But, you never claimed her in a fight or claimed her publicly. So no hard feelings, yeah?" Thorne sticks out his free hand toward Rhett but Rhett just glares at it and then shifts his gaze to Thorne's other hand, still covering my thigh. Thorne squeezes tighter, taunting Rhett. I almost turn to slap him, my body radiating with anger, but I know that won't end well. At the look of absolute seething anger on Rhett's hard, chiseled face Thorne releases my thigh and I immediately stand up from the couch so fast that I almost fall over in my heels. Rhett catches me by my upper arm and practically lifts me out of the room. Once we are in the hallway, he shifts our positions so that I am standing in front of him with his hand securely on my lower back.

"Do not make eye contact with anyone." He growls in my ear and I nod furiously in agreement. It reminds me of his instructions earlier when the fight was still in action and Thorne had singled me out in the crowd. Back when I just thought Rhett was being jealous. I could have laughed at myself for the irony but nothing in this moment seems very funny.

We finally reach the parking lot without speaking another word, my feet screaming in my high heels. Rhett rounds the front of his truck, keeping eye contact with me the entire way. As he opens the driver's side door, I look over and see him shaking his head in frustration. I pull my phone out of my purse and text Shelly to let her know I'm heading back to our apartment. The fact that I have no missed calls or texts from her makes my stomach drop. Maybe Eric is really hurt. *Why hasn't she called me?* I try to push down my nerves and just focus on Rhett getting me home safely.

Rhett pulls out of the parking lot, rage rolling off of his strong shoulders in waves. He doesn't look me, doesn't make any attempt to cut through the tense silence hanging in the air.

"Thanks for not *sharing* me. Sounds like you and Thorne go way back." My tone is clipped but part of me can't help it. Another rush of adrenaline pulses through me and I start to shiver even though I'm not cold.

"Don't push me, Ava." I notice his hands are shaking on the steering wheel and his jaw is ticking in overdrive. I know I should be nervous. The right thing to do would be to keep my mouth shut and let Rhett drive me home. Avoid poking the bear. *Who am I to judge Rhett's past behavior?* Just because I have a ridiculous crush on someone that isn't even a good choice for me doesn't mean that I can or should dictate how they've lived their life. Plus, he's gotten me out of *three* precarious situations at this point, so the least I can do is shut up and be quiet. But the truth is, I feel wild inside like I need to run or scream or dance. Something, anything, other than just sitting here in silence.

"Take a right." I unbuckle my seat belt and turn to face the window. Rhett keeps driving straight, ignoring me. "Rhett, my apartment is the other way."

"Ava." His voice is so low that I can barely hear it. It's like a vibration in the earth, felt more than heard.

"Where are you taking me?"

"My place."

"I want to go home."

"Yeah, well, I want to be able to sit through a goddamn fight without having to worry about every asshole trying to get in your pants. When are you going to realize this world is no place for someone like you?" He shoots me an angry look. Like he's accusing me of simply existing. Accusing me of having no place to go but Shelly's when my whole world fell apart.

But I also know some of this has been *my* fault. I came to this fight tonight to support Shelly, but in hindsight, I didn't have to. And I probably should never go to an underground fight ever again. But I also have a small, yet growing fascination with this world, and that fascination revolves largely around the asshole sitting next to me. Maybe there's some truth to his whole *daddy issues* theory after all.

We drive the rest of the way to his place in another stretch of painful silence. His hands finally start to relax on the steering wheel as he pulls into a paved stone driveway. I have been glaring out the window for some time and just now start to notice how nice this neighborhood is. There are elegantly landscaped flowers and shrubs along the entrance to the driveway and a series of related, but not perfectly matching, townhomes with dark wood-paneled garage doors. I'm not sure if I feel more uncomfortable or more at home in a place like this.

It reminds me of how I used to live with my dad and his ex-wife. Back in the red brick McMansion with the Volvo and the BMW in the driveway. I have to say I'm surprised that Rhett lives so nicely but I guess all that talk and pressure about the bets placed on his fights results in a seriously pretty penny in his pocket. There is something strange but also alluring at seeing the strong, aggressive Rhett Jaggar living among such order and elegance.

Rhett parks his large black truck outside of one of the wooden garage doors and quickly hops out. I expect him to come and open my car door but he doesn't. Instead, he starts ascending the single flight of stairs to his front door, two at a time. I stare at his broad back, frozen for a moment, before leaping out of the passenger seat.

"Rhett! You're just leaving me in the car?" I follow him inside the elegant townhome and he slams the door so quickly behind me that I swear I feel it rattle on its hinges.

"You. Are. Driving. Me. Crazy, sweetheart." Rhett runs a hand across my stomach, trapping my back against the inside of the door. His mouth locks onto my earlobe and I can't stop the small moan from escaping past my lips.

"You want me?" Rhett whispers roughly in my ear between bites. I can't find enough breath in my lungs to respond.

"Answer me." He growls in my ear as he slips one strong hand under the hem of my dress, lightly gripping my upper thigh where Throne's hand had been.

"Yes! You *know* that." I grasp onto his huge shoulders for support as he moves his hand over my panties, rhythmically rubbing back and forth.

"Always nice to hear, sweetheart." Then his lips are on mine, swallowing my moans as he finally slips his fingers under my panties and rubs them against my slick skin.

"Jesus fucking christ Ava, tell me this is for me." Luckily he doesn't wait for me to respond this time and latches onto my mouth violently, mirroring the movements of his fingers with his lips. I can feel myself building, so close to coming apart when he abruptly pulls his hand away.

"Shit, Rhett!" I bite out harshly, feeling more frustrated than I've ever felt in my life. I move my hand towards my panties, trying to replace his hand with my own.

"No, sweetheart. As much as I'd love to watch you touch yourself, I want all of your pleasure this time." He grabs both of my wrists in one hand and finishes pulling down his black dress pants with the other. I have no idea where he got a condom from, but my eyes nearly bug out of my head as I watch him roll the condom over his full, erect cock. It's so large and already glistening at the top, I let out an embarrassing groan, causing Rhett to chuckle darkly.

He lifts me off the ground and wraps my legs around his waist. He positions me above him and I'm practically panting in anticipation.

"Ava, look at me." Rhett's face is mere inches from mine, his eyes dark and intense, his brows furrowed in earnest frustration. I can see my desperate want mirrored on his face. It's so hot, so intoxicating, I feel my eyes roll back in my head as he lowers me down slowly onto his cock.

"Fuck, baby." Rhett nestles his head into the crook of my neck and starts to move slowly inside of me, each movement seemingly touching everywhere in my body at once.

"Rhett, move." I claw at his back, trying feverishly to move up and down on and fulfill the growing, aching feeling inside of me that's dying for release.

"No baby, I want to feel you." He takes my face in one hand, the other gripping my hip as the length of his body holds me up against the door. I'd always been with vanilla sex kind of guys in bed, maybe in the backseat of a car a few times. I've never felt so wild with the cool wood of the door against my back, my clothes still on but bunched up around my waist, my hair wild and knotted. I whine again, desperate to feel everything that's building inside me.

Finally, Rhett starts to move. Really *move*. I feel my back scrape against the door, my breasts bouncing violently up and down as his fingers dug into my hips, certainly leaving a mark on my skin. Right when I start to feel myself building, he braces both of his hands under my ass and carries us away from the door, not breaking a single point of contact.

He sits down on his leather couch with me still on top of him and I grip the back of the couch for support. Our chests are rising and falling heavily and I can see the fire in his dark eyes. His hands are still holding me beneath my ass as he begins to lift me up and down, creating a pleasurable, mind-altering rhythm. His face starts to blur from my vision, my head tipping back as I do my best to keep up with his movements, thrust for thrust.

"Fuck, Ava, you feel so damn good." His strangled words, my name falling from his lips like a curse and a prayer, throws me over the edge. I feel like all the tension, all the stress of wanting him so badly, the fear of what happened tonight after the fight, builds into a feeling of insane bliss that has me momentarily blacking out as my orgasm takes over. I faintly recognize Rhett still moving inside of me, calling out my name earnestly as he finds his release. He gently lifts me off of his hardness, setting me down on the worn leather couch next to him, my legs limp and sated. He still has one hand firmly on my thigh, as if he still isn't ready to let go of me yet.

Rhett's chest heaves up and down as he tries to recover his breathing. He delicately pulls the fabric of my dress back down over my thighs and straightens my panties as best he can from our seated angle. It's a gesture so gentle and unexpected that I can't help but look up at him, both of us sated and heavy-lidded. He runs a calloused thumb over my bottom lip, our breathing still erratic and ragged.

"Baby." He whispers so quietly I'm not really sure that I'm even supposed to hear it. After a few long moments, I start to straighten and smooth my hair, failing miserably. For the first time since we arrived at his place, I start to feel a little self-conscious as his gaze sears into me, assessing.

"I think...well, I think it's never felt like *that* before." My voice is quiet as I cross my legs, noticing how painful the arches of my feet feel after being in Shelly's insanely high heels through all of *that*. "I think that was my first...official orgasm." I'm not really sure why I say it. I mean, I don't have to admit that. How would he know? Maybe I just want to say it out loud, for me. I've had plenty of sex before but it pales in comparison to what Rhett and I just did together. I expect Rhett to laugh at my embarrassing admission but instead, he looks incredibly proprietary, raking in my body like he's laying claim to something deep and animal inside of me. His face remains serious, a furrow in his handsome brow.

"Won't be your last." A hint of a smirk pulls at his sinfully full lips which I notice are redder from our urgent kissing. I lean up and place my hands on his chest before kissing him chastely. He grabs my hand and pulls me in deeper, breaking our kiss to lift me off the couch and carry me down the hallway, my whole body feeling like a collection of delightfully disconnected joints and limbs.

25

RHETT

I've had sex with my fair share of women. Okay, a fuck lot more than *fair*. Definitely more than I care to admin. But Ava is something else entirely. Her soft skin, the urgency of her moans, the way her body literally *gripped* around me like it was just as desperate as I felt. It felt so fucking good to be inside of her, I almost regretted it the moment I slid in to her ready body, knowing I was going to become dangerously addicted to this brown-haired, golden-eyed girl. Her whimpers, her full breasts moving up and down with her hips, the way she clawed at my shoulders as her eyes rolled back in her head. If that was her first orgasm, the men who'd been with her before were a real waste of fucking space. Women deserve orgasms. And I revel at the thought of giving Ava many, many more.

I look down at her sleeping soundly in my bed, her long hair still damp from a shower and her curvy, slender figure covered in one of my t-shirts. Hell if that isn't a sexy sight. I can't even remember the last time I let a woman sleepover in my bed. Usually, my rules were ironclad: just great sex and a safe ride home.

I want to feel as relaxed as Ava looks in her sleep. Somehow she appears even more innocent than when she's awake with her long lashes swept over her cheeks, her full lips slightly parted. But I know that I will barely be able to get any shut-eye. Tonight was stressful for both of us, but Ava doesn't even know the other stress brewing inside of me. For as long as I can remember, I've never able to isolate my addictive personality. The ring is the only vice where I can channel all of my energy and not crave anything else. That's what I love about how fully it exhausts me, leaving all the turmoil inside of me on the mat.

But the way I want Ava, especially after tonight, isn't healthy. It isn't love, I'm not capable of that. And it's definitely not as fleeting as lust. It's an *addiction*. I know the dreaded sensation like the back of my hand. Which is why I try to only fuck women I have no personal interest in beyond a few nights of fun.

And the woman sleeping in my bed right now is most certainly not that.

I get out of bed and head into the kitchen. It's only 4:00 AM but I know there's no point in me trying to go back to sleep. Between the racing feeling in my veins and years of getting up at the ass crack of dawn for training, I can never sleep in anymore. I start making some coffee and doing my routine of morning pushups. But all I can see are flashes of Ava's terrified face back in Thorne's backstage prepping room and the little white lines of powder on the table. I walk back into my bedroom, quietly, so I don't wake Ava who is still sleeping like a baby. I grab my phone on my nightstand and send a quick text to Leila.

> Rhett: Hey, are you up?

There's a ninety percent chance she is. Two early birds. I know this woman well.

> Leila: Yep, just making coffee. Haven't heard from you in a while.

Her text back is almost immediate.

> Rhett: I know. I've been training a lot.

> Leila: You're going to overwork yourself. When are you retiring so we can relax and hang out like we used to?

I sigh to myself and wonder the same thing. It's not like I can go on fighting like this forever. My goal is to make it to the end of this year's season and then retire: fat and happy. Figuratively speaking of course. I'm at the end of my prime earning years after sustaining so many injuries from years of reckless street fighting before I joined Coach Barry's gym. I need to keep hanging on just a little longer. Reward myself for all the investment, all the training, I've put in and go out on a career high. I'll make sure Coach Barry's pockets are padded as well for all that he's done for me over the years.

> Rhett: I need to see you. Can you meet today?

I pace along the large kitchen island, running a hand through my hair, the dreaded white lines forming in front of my eyes.

> Leila: Of course. Actually, there's a get-together today. You should come with me.

I groan out loud at Leila's response. I hate the get-togethers she's always tries to drag me to and I'd much prefer to just meet with Leila alone. But I'll take what I can get. I'm afraid I don't have much of a choice.

> Rhett: Fine. What time?

Leila: Around 1:00 PM. Meet me at my place first and we can go together?

> Rhett: Sure. See you then.

I quietly walk back to the bedroom and put my phone in its charger on my nightstand before heading into the bathroom to take a shower. A cold one. Then I throw on my jogging sweats and my headphones after setting the alarm in my townhome. By the looks of it, Ava will still be asleep when I get back. Nothing like a freezing morning run to clear my head.

26

AVA

I feel a set of cool, silk sheets under my back as I slowly stretch out my sore limbs. The room is cold and dark and smells faintly like pine. There are blackout curtains over the windows with just a small line of morning light making its way across the hardwood floor. I turn over and find that the rest of the California King sized bed is empty. I sit up on my elbows, feeling slightly disoriented. Then the memories of last night flash through my vision, Rhett's hands and mouth everywhere. I flush at the memory of admitting to Rhett that he'd given me my first actual orgasm. I'd been able to give myself a few over the years, but never anything like *that*. And never from anyone else.

Then the rest of last night's events start crowding my thoughts and I know I need to talk to Shelly ASAP. I hadn't heard from her at all last night and I'm praying that she and Eric are okay. I start sliding my hands around the sheets trying to locate my phone. I hear a buzz from the nightstand and reach over to grab it.

A text flashes across the front of the home screen.

> Leila: Call me later when you're on your way.
> I'm really glad you're coming, Rhett. I've
> missed you. And I've been worried
> about you.

My stomach drops like a lead anchor at sea. I know snooping is wrong but technically I hadn't snooped! I thought the phone on the nightstand was mine when I reached for it. And now I can't stop seeing the name *Leila* in my head mixed with Thorne's words about Rhett's past behavior. His comments about Rhett betting on women and sharing them with other fighters. *I mean, how much do I even know this guy? And now another woman is texting him that she misses him while I'm currently in his bed? What if he's somehow still involved with her?*

I leap out of the bed like it's suddenly on fire and start frantically searching for my phone. I finally find it on the ground, discarded next to my purse, whose contents are scattered around the floor. I'm relieved to see a few missed calls from Shelly and I shoot her a rapid-fire text that I'll call her in five minutes. I need to find my clothes and get the hell out of here before I do something really embarrassing like cry. *How could I l have let my lust get me into this mess?*

I can't find my clothes anywhere and am I forced to accept the fact that they are probably in the bathroom. I take a deep breath and try to remain calm. Rhett isn't my boyfriend. He doesn't owe me anything. I chose, gladly, to sleep with him and I had thoroughly enjoyed it. More like *loved* it. And that's exactly the problem because there is no way I can separate sex like *that* from feelings or at least mutual exclusivity. Call me old-fashioned.

I tiptoe out of the bedroom and down the hallway. The sunlight is streaming in through the windows, showing off the beauty of the living room area. I hadn't been able to see it as well last night but it's modern but not lacking in warmth. I don't know why, but it makes me miss my childhood home again. My childhood home that now belongs to some other family with a dad whose job is real and law-abiding. My eyes sting with tears at the through.

"Hey." Rhett's deep voice catches me by surprise and I let out a little yelp. "Woah, there. You okay?" He doesn't move towards me but his expression looks almost nervous. When I stare back at his frustratingly handsome face, his hair still damp from a shower, all I can see is the text from *Leila*. And that's enough to get me back on track like a splash of cold water to the face.

"Yep! All good. Where are my clothes? I better get going." I aim for casual, landing somewhere near frantic.

"Uh, pretty sure they're on the bathroom counter." I watch him walk over to the room off of the side of the hallway and delicately grab my dress. My cheeks go full pink when he also picks up my panties and my bra. *Why can't I just be a normal adult woman and not get embarrassed by things like this?* The contrast of such a big, strong man gently holding my lavender lace underwear is just...too much for my female hormones to handle.

"Thanks!" I can tell my tone is way too forced but I don't care. It's the best I can manage at the moment. His mouth opens like he's about to say something in response but I'm already slipping into the bathroom to change. I cringe in the mirror at my wild sex hair and smudged under-eye makeup. I wipe under my eyes and rinse out my mouth in the sink before taming my long hair into an acceptable ponytail. I practically jump into my dress and groan at the realization that I'm going to look like such a typical walk of shame heading home in this outfit. *Shit, home!* How am I going to get back to Shelly's? Rhett had driven me here. I send Shelly another text, telling her to come pick me up and drop her my location pin. I don't even know how far Rhett's place is from our apartment but there is no way I'll be letting him drive me home. I'll walk a few blocks if I have to.

"Well, I better be going. Thanks again." I pause in his kitchen and he's looking at me like I've grown two heads. I almost feel sorry for him, the victim of my whiplash, but then I remember its source: him going to have sex with another woman, *Leila*, this afternoon. I toss his T-shirt at him and he deftly catches it, his eyes never leaving me, assessing me with caution. Rhett pushes away from the kitchen counter and starts heading in my direction but stops himself.

"Is someone coming to pick you up? I can give you a ride home." His tone is cautious like he's talking to some crazy chick who might slash his tires or something. That's definitely not my style. But ignoring things that make me uncomfortable and finding creative ways to never see him again alone? Yeah, that's more my speed.

"Nope, all good! Shelly is coming to get me. She needs some girl-time, you know, after all the craziness with Eric last night." My words all smash together as I rush to get them out. Even though I'm already rearing to dart to out the front door, I force myself to say one last thing before I leave. "Thank you again, really, for getting me away from Thorne. I had no idea that they would be like *that*." I pause to compose my thoughts. "I'm still not sure I really understand what happened last night but I know it could have been a lot worse." Even if Rhett is a player who doesn't have a commitment bone in his body, or at least isn't interested in committing to me, he definitely has saved me on more than one occasion. A 'thank you' for that, at least, is more than overdue.

"Don't mention it." His tone is clipped and I can sense a severe shift in his mood. It radiates between us like a physical thing, the tension growing. He runs a hand through his hair before turning to the sink to rinse out his coffee mug, essentially dismissing me. I take the opportunity and head to the front door, leaving without turning back. Once I'm down his front steps I curse out loud at how freaking cold it is! Dressed in my short dark red dress from last night, my only saving grace is that it comes up to my neck and covers my arms but my legs are completely exposed. I hear my phone vibrate in my purse. Shelly.

"Hi! Oh my god, Ava. Last night was hell. I don't know if I can be a fighter's girlfriend! It's just freaking stressful." I grunt in agreement but don't elaborate. Not that I'm anywhere near being Rhett's girlfriend, but even being his lay for the night has me feeling stressed like my world is on fire.

"Is Eric okay?" My teeth are chattering from the cold, making my words come out choppy.

"I mean, yes and no. Like physically he will be fine. But he's really down about losing." I hear the heavy emotion threading in her voice.

"I know, I'm sure it's a tough blow. It was a super close match. And I'm here for you, you know that, but can you please tell me that you are in your car and like less than ten minutes away from the location pin I dropped you? Because I am turning into a cherry red popsicle out here." I make my way down the block so that Rhett can't see me standing outside his lovely townhome like a freaking tramp waiting for a ride.

"Oh, shit! Yes, I'm only five minutes away. Where are you by the way? This part of town looks pretty fancy." I sigh because I thought the same thing when we'd come to this part of town last night. Why does Rhett have to be an insanely talented and sexy fighter *and* have a clean and elegant home? *Why does the idea of him taking care of me send butterflies into my traitorous stomach?*

"Long story. One better told over brunch. With cocktails." Shelly acquiesces to waiting to hear the crazy details of my night and I hang up the phone, shivering to myself, debating exactly how much I'm willing to tell her.

27

RHETT

What the fuck was that? How do I go from finally getting the girl I've been frustrated as hell over for weeks, her own frustration damn near matching mine, to being blown off like some awkward college hook up?

I knew there was good reason why I don't get mixed up with nice, innocent, girlfriend-type girls like Ava. She's probably regretting everything we did last night. All *four* rounds. Realizing she woke up in an underground fighter's bed and not some khaki-wearing finance worker who still talks to his mom probably had her running for the hills.

Normally, I'm relieved when a woman is up and ready to leave the morning after sex. All too often, they get clingy and want to hang around all day, hoping you'll be convinced into taking them out on a date. But with Ava, I would've actually been happy to make her breakfast and try to get to know her a little more. Maybe better understand the things she's been going through recently, the demons that lie past that perfectly pretty veneer. At least pour her a goodman cup of coffee. I rack my brain for any other reasons that I can think of contributing to her sudden shift in behavior other than regret, but I come up empty. And I *know* she enjoyed the sex, I'd made damn sure of it. Couldn't take that from me.

I sip my coffee, trying to more calmly reflect on the events of last night, particularly Thorne's *colorful* mentions of my past behavior. Singling out a ring bunny from the crowd and claiming her as part of a fight prize is something I've done in the past. The *very* distant past, back when I was in my early twenties and had no idea who I was even trying to impress or please, only that I needed to fight to quell the raging fire inside of me. And the ring bunnies were dying for it, came to the fights specifically to be chosen. Nothing like Ava who still doesn't even know the first thing about how the rules of this corrupt world work. I cringe at the memories, but I can't talk them back.

And as for Thorne's comment about me sharing women? Of course I've shared women. But to be fair, they weren't really mine to share in the fist place. They were free agents and they enjoyed themselves. Never bothered me once. I don't give two fucks about ring bunnies either way. Sure, I had my preferences based on what they did in bed and usually how much they were willing to leave me alone afterward, but what did I care if they had sex with other fighters? I've had a few fairly serious relationships in my day, but that usually lead to me getting involved with someone who was as *addicted* as I was, and that never ended well.

I run my hands through my hair to shake away the frustrating thoughts and head back into my now empty bedroom in search of my phone. It smells faintly of vanilla and lavender, Ava's sweet scent still lingering in the air. I see a text from Leila and respond by telling her that I'll get to her house around 12:30 PM. I need to shave and get dressed.

Push the thoughts of Ava and her startling morning reaction out of my mind. When I set the phone down, I realize my hands are shaking. Between how good being with Ava felt and her weirdness this morning, I can't stop fantasizing about the powder. The perfect little white lines blur behind my eyelids, tempting me more than I've felt in months. Thank fuck I'll be able to see Leila today.

—

I grip the steering wheel of my truck and try to focus on my breathing. I really hate going to shit like this. Being able to see Leila alone usually helps with the urges, but a small part of me knows that I have to go to the group events in order to really stay on track. In order to get better and *be* better. I hate feeling like I'm sick and like some dark, twisted part of me will always be sick. It's why I'm so obsessed with the boxing ring. It's the only place where my addiction is my power; my obsession with the fight is what makes me the best. For any other part of my life, that very same trait of mine sends me down a fucking dark and painful path. If I didn't have fighting to keep me in line, I know I'd be in jail or dead. As ironic to some as that may seem on the surface.

Before I call Leila to let her know I'm close to her house, I see Ava's hazel eyes in my memory. I hear her sweet moans in my ear, the taste of her skin under my tongue, and I picture the way she moved her body underneath mine. Like she was made for me. It's a new form of torture, entirely unfair. It's like a drug made from nature, perfectly concocted to be my downfall. Something I can't have. I slam my hand down on the dash so hard that I feel it rattle. I know I shouldn't have gone there. I can't bring myself to regret it but I should. No woman, not even the lovely Ava, is worth what last night is currently doing to me.

I call Leila and pull into her driveway about ten minutes later. The small white house looks in worse shape than the last time I was here, but it's still pleasant and cozy. Welcoming. I make a mental note to come by one weekend and help her repaint the exterior. I park my truck and make my way to the front door. Leila lives more far more modestly than I do. Her salary as a college professor isn't anything flashy but it gets the job done. Every now and then, I try to cover the expense of something for her but she always denies it. It's honestly the least I can do for the countless times she's saved my wretched ass over the years.

"Rhett! Wow, I think you're even bigger if that's possible." Leila laughs gently and gives me a huge hug. The top of her head doesn't even reach my chin. Her light blonde hair is more streaked with gray. She looks bright and healthy for her age, at least ten years younger than she actually is. Her blue eyes are filled with happiness at seeing me, radiating from her small delicate frame.

"Hey, Leila. Good to see you." I tuck her into my side and we make our way into the house. I hear the teapot nearly screaming and already know the drill: pleasantries over steaming tea and then the real talk.

"Well...what's new? How are the matches going?" Leila fixes two porcelain teacups and I always feel like a cartoon giant holding them. It's funny to me, talking to this gentle older woman about my boxing career. She's never been to one of my fights and we both plan to keep it that way. Not sure she could handle seeing me hit, almost like a son.

"Good. Winning a lot of money but I don't think I have too much time left in me. My body is starting to hurt."

"Well any body, even yours, can only take so much,

Rhett. Did you injure something recently?" Leila sets her teacup down as a look of worry crosses over her face.

"Nothing in particular," except all of my ribs, "the fighting just takes a toll after a while."

"I don't doubt it." She smiles warmly at me, her blue eyes crinkling at the corners. "So, how long do you want to do this before we talk about what really brought you here?"

I chuckle and stare down at my tea. Leila may look the part of a sweet sixty-year-old lady but she's been through hell and back. A trip we've both taken too many times.

"Cocaine and women." I don't look at her when I say it, focusing my stare on the steam spiraling from my cup. "Well, one *woman*."

"How much?"

"No cocaine. Yet. But I saw some after a fight. Felt like my skin was crawling, I wanted a line so badly. But the worst is her. She's fucking beautiful and perfect. And I know I shouldn't have gotten with her. It's going to set me off. It was a fucking selfish thing to do." I sigh and slowly flex my hands, feeling every bone and tendon. I don't touch my tea. I never do. The whole tea drinking with Leila is more ceremonial than anything. A way to ease into the hard stuff.

"Do you think you can be...yourself with her?"

I cringe at Leila's question. I need to stop feeling so humiliated during these conversations. I mean it's been years since we started talking about this stuff. But somehow it never makes it easier. Talking about cocaine with a former addict is definitely the closest thing to therapy I've ever let myself have. But Leila has never been a sex addict. For me, the two are inseparable.

"No. Definitely not. She's...innocent. And different from me in every way."

"Have you tried talking with her?

I shake my head, grinding my molars together. I know Leila doesn't mean talking about the weather. She means talking to Ava about *me*, about what I really am. I can't even imagine opening up that way, scaring her even further. Especially after this morning.

"No." I remember the look on Ava's face when she came out of my bedroom, the way she practically sprinted out of my townhouse like she realized she'd waken up next to a goddamn monster. Guess she isn't completely wrong on that one.

"Rhett, at some point it's okay to open up—"

"But not with her." I cut Leila off, my voice acidic. "I won't risk it. I'm already too on edge." I run my palms down my thighs, wiping the sweat on my jeans. I'm already starting to regret today. Maybe I should've just gone to the gym and worked out my frustrations in the ring. Forced Coach to give me enough sparring partners to bruise me for weeks, to let the physical pain take over the mental. To exhaust me.

"Alright, fair. But perhaps we can take it day by day. If she's special, she may understand." Leila keeps her voice gentle as she clears the tea cups and grabs her purse from the counter. "Are you ready to go?"

"Sure." I'm not. I never am. I don't think I ever will be. But I swallow down the fear and frustration, holding the front door open for her as we head out.

28

AVA

I look at the time on my phone and resent the stampede of butterflies in my stomach. My dad's AA meeting is in two hours. I told Shelly everything about last night and about Rhett. Well, *almost* everything. A few sexual details I decided were better kept to myself. Her opinion is that I should keep sleeping with him as long as it feels good. Which I have no doubt it would continue to feel *great*, but I also know that will just make me feel even shittier since I have to admit to myself that I want more from Rhett than just sex. What exactly *more* entails, I'm still not sure, but I know I won't be able to just *hit it and quit it* as Shelly playfully threw out this morning over coffee. I nearly spit mine out.

"When do you think Eric will be out of the hospital?" Apparently, his lung is pretty damaged from the fight. Probably because the whole event lasted so long and Thorne kept pummeling his left side, round after round.

"Probably in a day or two," Shelly stares into her coffee blankly, stirring in some more milk, "I really don't know if I can do this whole dating a fighter thing. I mean, it's just not natural to watch someone you love get beat up like that...for a job!" When she glances up her lips are pulled downward into a frown and there is a deep, worried crease etched across her forehead.

"Um, Shel...did you just say *love*?" Shelly has always been quick to fall in *lust*, but I'm not sure I've ever heard her say the word 'love' before.

"Yeah...I mean, I think I do? I definitely like him more than I've ever liked anyone else." I nod my head slowly at her response but I've heard that line before. Although now is definitely not the best time to bring that fact up.

"That's amazing Shelly, I'm happy for you." And as her best friend, I really am. Even if she's chosen to be in love with a beefy, cocky, currently hospitalized underground fighter. At least I can be sure that whatever confusing feelings I currently have for Rhett, they certainly aren't in the *love* territory. Right now they're more squarely in the *irate* and *sexually frustrated* territories.

"Ugh, it's awful." Her tone is dramatic and I see a glimmer of the Shelly I know and love. "Do you still need a ride to your dad's...meeting today?" Shelly looks at me cautiously, knowing how sensitive the topic of my dad is for me, especially during these past few days.

"Yeah, if you don't mind. I'll go start getting ready. I really am happy for you, Shelly." I give her a light side hug and head back to my bathroom to get dressed. I need a brave face to deal with my dad today.

—

As Shelly turns up the radio in the car, I feel the unwelcome butterflies come clawing back into my stomach. I know I need to go support my dad and that I will regret it if I don't. But seeing him in his hotel room, let alone at an AA meeting, just guts me. The man I used to put up on such a high pedestal is now hardly even a shadow of his former self. I shiver at the thought but am determined to see this one meeting through. It's a starting point, the first step toward repairing our relationship. I hope he will be sincere in his desire to get free of his alcoholism instead of just using sobriety as means to a lighter jail sentence. I try to stuff down the voice inside my head telling me not to trust him too fast.

We pull up to the venue and it's as benign as you can imagine. It looks like some all-purpose nondescript community center. I take a deep breath and open the passenger car door, pausing for a moment before getting out.

"I'll be doing errands, some grocery shopping and whatnot, so you just text me anytime and I'll come right back to pick you up, okay?" Shelly's face is bright and I once again thank my lucky stars for her friendship, even if she gets me into wild situations at times. She's loyal to the death and I'll never be able to thank her enough for it. I give her a tight nod, hoping she can see in my eyes how thankful I am for her, a band wrapping tightly around my throat that threatens tears if I try to speak.

My palms feel clammy as I follow the printed-out placards, directing me towards a standalone building in a courtyard. There is a table set up outside with the de-facto refreshments: cookies, punch, and crackers. The doors to the fancy shed-looking building are open and I can see a few people milling about inside. *What is the protocol for this kind of thing, anyway? Do I sign in and make a name tag?* I try to keep my breathing calm and focus on looking for my dad. I send him a quick text to let him know that I'm here.

> Me: Hey, Dad. I just got here and am walking toward the building past the check-in table.

> Dad: Hi honey! So glad you could make it. I'll meet you by the punch.

I head toward the refreshment table and I see my dad emerge from the building. He looks better. Not like his old self, but definitely not as rough as when I visited him the other day in his room. The progress brings a flutter of hope to my chest.

"Hi, sweetie." He pulls me into a bear hug and kisses my temple. I feel tears prick in the corners of my eyes at the familiarity of his touch.

"Hey, dad. Of course, I'm happy I came." I give him a tight nod and then look around to see what we are supposed to do next. As if he can read my mind, my dad explains what should happen next.

"We will get started in about fifteen minutes, I think. I'm pretty sure we will start out as a big group and then break out into smaller pods. It shouldn't take more than two hours, maybe three tops." He shrugs his shoulders as if apologizing but I just nod in agreement. I said I'd be here and I want to be here to support him. Perhaps this day could actually turn around for the better. I notice my dad fidgeting slightly as we make small talk. Our conversation is full of banal pleasantries, surface-level stuff. He tells me non-details about his current life, how he's been getting healthier, and I tell him non-details about how work is going well and that I'm thinking about heading back to school sooner rather than later. I don't even know if that's necessarily true, but it seems like the right thing to say at the time. I see his eyes light up with joy as I say it.

"Say, honey, do you smell cigarette smoke? I know I shouldn't, but I could really use one of those." My dad starts glancing around, an untouched cup of punch in his shaky hand. I never really knew my dad to smoke, but then again, I never really knew my dad to do a lot of things he's apparently done.

"Um, yeah. I think it's coming from behind the building." We start walking around to the back and I see a large, muscular figure leaning up against the side of the building. His broad back is facing us and clouds of smoke intermittently whirl around his head. A delicate-looking woman, maybe in her late fifties, is standing a few feet from him, smoking a cigarette of her own. I guess cigarettes are the go-to addiction when you're trying to kick another, even worse habit.

"Hey, sorry to bother. Mind If I bum a cigarette off you?" My dad puts his hands in his pockets and sounds like his former charming self. Always adept at getting what he wants. The large man turns around, a lit cigarette hanging from between his full lips.

Then all of the air leaves my lungs in a second. Because the man with the cigarette is Rhett.

29

RHETT

J esus *fucking Christ.* My eyes are playing tricks. That's the only explanation. After years of getting knocked in the head so much, I'm finally starting to lose it. *Am I really seeing Ava standing right in front of me?* I almost pray out loud that I'm imaging things.

She looks just as shocked as I am, and even more mortified if that's even possible. I know this sweet brunette princess isn't an addict, so she must be here supporting someone else. My eyes scan back to the man who asked me for a cigarette and I see a faint resemblance between him and Ava. The shape of their eyes, their coloring. A pit forms in my stomach.

"Oh, do you two know each other?" Leila comes up to stand beside me. The woman is sharper than a whip. I wouldn't be surprised if she's already put the pieces together from our earlier conversation in her kitchen. Neither Ava nor I respond. We just stare at each other, dumbfounded, trying to read the other's expression and failing miserably.

"Here you go." Leila takes a cigarette out of the pack in my pocket and hands it to the middle-aged man with Ava, a warm smile on her face. Typical Leila trying to de-escalate the notably awkward as hell situation.

"Uh, thank you very much." The man takes the cigarette and Leila lights the end until it glows. I watch as he inhales, the similarity in their features growing. I'll bet my right fighting arm this is Ava's dad, and my comment several weeks ago in the locker room about her having daddy issues now comes back to me in a wave of deep regret and shame.

"Ava." I nod at her, my greeting cold and aloof. But what else can I say? If she wasn't already running for the hills from my townhome this morning after what we did last night, this whole AA run-in should really seal the deal.

"Rhett. Hi." Her greeting comes across as more of a question than a statement. I open my mouth to say something else, but a woman calls out over a microphone for everyone to head inside for the session to begin. I feel my nails dig deep into my palms as I clench my hands at my sides, stamping out my cigarette with my boot.

"Well, that's our cue!" Leila smiles at the group and gently claps her hands together before making her way inside. The man I assume is Ava's dad gives me a concerned once-over and a weak cringey smile before heading inside himself. I see Ava look between us, trying to decide what to do. She turns to head behind her father and I make quick work to close the distance between us.

"What in the *fuck* are you doing here?" My voice is a harsh whisper. I can't constrain my emotion, still laced with the annoyance at how she left my home earlier. Dismissing me. Dismissing whatever we were last night. Like she wished it had never happened.

"What am *I* doing here? What about you? Are you an alcoholic?"

"No." And I meant it. I'm not. Alcohol has never been my issue. It was never my addiction of choice.

"Well, then are you here with your...mom? I'm here with my dad." She almost sounds slightly hopeful. Like we might have this one thing in common: parents with addiction issues. I want to laugh bitterly at the irony. I'm definitely not the supporting role here. I'm very much the one with the problem.

"That's not my mom. Her name is Leila. She's my sponsor." We start heading into the room where small talk is dwindling down and people are starting to take their seats in that fucking stupid circle they always make us sit in.

"Oh, *that's* Leila?" Ava looks between me and Leila as if she's putting together the pieces of a puzzle I don't understand. Because I'm sure as fuck that I never mentioned anything about Leila to Ava. But before I can ask her, the coordinator leading the session addresses the group.

"Alright everyone. Please take a seat." The host smiles warmly and gestures for us to choose a chair. I sigh in frustrated resignation. This conversation with Ava is going to have to wait. Doesn't stop a part of me from nearly dragging her ass outside and ditching the session but I see Leila watching me, her pale kind eyes knowing and concerned.

"Okay, thank you everyone. Let's get started." The host sits at the apex of the circle and Ava is almost directly across from me, seated next to her father. Leila taps my thigh in an attempt to comfort me, a small show of support.

"I know we have many family members, sponsors, and supporters here today. We thank you for making the time to be here. As anyone who has struggled with addiction knows, having a support system can make all the difference in a journey to recovery."

I've heard those words so many times, they sound like a

dulled white noise in my head. I actually haven't touched cocaine in years. But I also haven't seen it so close like I had in Thorne's prepping room. The sex addiction issue is more complex to sort out. I feel like I can either fuck only for a fight or abstain altogether. But it's when I start having sex for my own reasons, my own desires outside of the ring, that leads to an uncontrollable urge. And being with Ava may have tipped me off my fucking axis. My eyes flash up to hers before I force myself to look away, to stop thinking about what I might do later, the sex I might seek out and regret with a random woman from a bar.

I don't even realize that it's my turn to speak in the circle. Leila whispers my name lightly and I suddenly notice all eyes are on me. I know the drill. The worst fucking part of this goddamn ceremony. I look at the ground, not daring to look Ava in the face as I speak.

"My name is Rhett. I've been sober for five years. And I'm a cocaine and sex addict."

30

AVA

I feel the color drain from my face. Rhett is still staring at the ground, his elbows on his knees and his head hanging low. He looks like he did between rounds in the ring when he's sitting in his corner as Coach Barry yells harsh advice in his ear. I want to reach out and touch him. But I have no idea what I'd even say. I can't imagine Rhett responding well to even an inkling of pity from me or anyone. My heart breaks staring at this strong man, his jaw tight with emotion, something akin to shame marring his brow.

After everyone in the circle shared their addictions, we break out into small groups. My dad and I are joined by three other pairs and we have a group leader walk us through sharing exercises. Normally, I'd be squirming in my seat at this level of intimacy with strangers, especially since I've never imagined myself and my dad doing attending something like this. But instead, I'm entirely distracted, thinking about Rhett and Leila. I feel like an idiot for jumping to conclusions when I saw those texts on his phone. *But then again, what else was I supposed to think after Thorne's comments?*

I rub my hands down my arms, thinking how hard it must have been for Rhett to keep it together when he came to rescue me from Thorne's crew, all that cocaine on the table. I've never done any hard drugs so I have no idea what that feeling must be like. My biggest addiction is chocolate ice cream, and that hardly warrants regular group therapy.

"Ava, honey. Want to tell me what that was all about earlier?" We have a short break before our next activity and I'm grateful for the fresh air. My dad pours himself another cup of punch that he likely won't drink. Just something to do with his hands is my guess.

"I, um, I know him from work. It's no big deal. Just didn't expect to see him here, obviously." I snort a little. *Who walks into something like this expecting to see the man they just had sex with last night?* But I certainly don't add that level of detail for good reason.

"He seems like trouble, Ava. I have to say, I don't like it one bit." He glares back into the building, no doubt trying to send a fatherly warning in Rhett's direction. I'm positive that Rhett could snap my average-sized dad in half without even breaking a sweat, but that's also another detail better left unsaid. Besides, anyone can come to that conclusion on their own just by looking at Rhett. Even a dad in protective mode over his daughter.

"I barely know him, Dad." Which is both true and also very not true at the same time. "He's a good person though, just clearly has some demons."

"Yeah, I'll say." My dad's tone comes out haughty and the irony isn't lost on me. Rhett may have some serious addiction issues and also happen to be Boston's top underground fighter; certainly not great marks in any dad's book. But he's never lied to me. Never pretended to be something he wasn't and he didn't seem to deceive the people that cared about him the most, like Coach Barry. I can't say the same for my dad. But I restrain myself since I don't want to send my dad into a downward spiral. I came here to support him. I need to see that daughterly duty through.

"Look, honey, if you need a new job I still have plenty of friends that can help." My dad rests his hand protectively on my shoulder. "Okay, maybe not plenty, but a few. I could get you a job working as a legal PA or something. I don't know what exactly you and Shelly are up to these days, but with men like *that* around, I know it can't be much good."

My lips pull into a tight fake smile and I play the part of daddy's little girl. The one who used to trust and depend on him for everything. But I know within myself that I'm not that girl anymore. And in a time when my whole world fell apart, men like Rhett and Coach Barry have shown more faith and confidence in me than my own father. They gave me a chance to prove myself. I don't think I'll ever be able to look back on this mess and be happy that it all happened, but I will be grateful. It forced me to become my own person, something that may have never happened if my dad had been able to successfully keep up the facade that was our life.

"I'll let you know, Dad, thank you. And like I said, I prob-ably won't be working that job at the gym much longer anyway. I'd like to get back to school." These words seem to sooth him for the time being and he gives me a small hug of approval.

After about an hour of another small group exercise, we are dismissed. My dad is smiling and jovial, his social self coming through when he's in groups. I have no idea when his first court hearing will be or what the next steps are with his lawyer, but I figure he'll tell me however much he wants me to know.

"Thank you again, sweetie. I know this isn't an ideal way to spend a Sunday, but it means a lot to me. And I'm doing better. A lot better." He gives me a kiss on the cheek and I pull out my phone to text Shelly to let her know we are done. Right as I'm about to tell her to come pick me up, I hear a deep throat clearing. I turn to see Rhett standing about three feet from me, his hands in the front pockets of his black jeans. My dad is frowning deeply and remains close to my side. *God, I wish the ground would swallow me whole right now.*

"Ava." Rhett nods and then nods once at my dad. My dad just grunts back in acknowledgment.

"Hi." I'm afraid that if I say anything more, my tone will come out breathy and nervous which is exactly how I felt. Rhett looks sinfully hot in his all-black outfit and I can still see the way his muscles moved last night when he was on top of me, beneath me, inside of me...my cheeks start to flush and I avoid looking back at my dad. This has to be ten times worse than any embarrassing teenage moment I've ever had.

"Can we go grab a coffee or something?" Rhett sounds hesitant like he's definitely expecting me to say no.

"Ava, I'm not sure that's such a good idea." My dad steps forward to stand awkwardly between Rhett and me and I roll my eyes in frustration.

"Dad, it's fine. Besides, Rhett can give me a ride home."

"He knows where you live?" My dad's voice notches up a few octaves and I can see his neck turning red and splotchy. A tell-tale sign that he's pissed.

"I can tell him how to get there, Dad. Please, it's no big

deal." I lean up to kiss him on the cheek like I used to as a young girl.

"Fine. Text me when you get home," he stares Rhett down, "and it better be within an hour or two." Rhett nods at my dad's ridiculous threat, a very faint smile tugging at his lips. I seriously want to die from humiliation. My dad wouldn't even stand a chance.

My dad *finally* ambles off toward the parking lot after what feels like the longest awkward silence in history, still looking back over his shoulder once or twice. I cover my face and groan.

"I didn't know you had a personal bodyguard." Rhett smirks at me and I shove him lightly in the shoulder.

"Let's go." I start walking toward the parking lot scanning for his truck, my heart pounding faster with each step, wondering what it is exactly he's planning to say. Why he even decided to ask me to coffee at all after the way I treated him after misunderstanding Leila's texts. After seeing me here and being forced to reveal his secret.

31

RHETT

I already know what I'm going to say to Ava once we get to the coffee shop and she's inevitably drinking some girly latte or whatever that shit is with the floral designs made out of milk. I already know what I'm going to say and that she's definitely *not* going to agree to it. So, I've basically already lost this fight before it's even started which isn't a feeling I like or am used to.

Part of me wants to ask her about her dad. To Learn more about what's really going on there, but I'll restrain myself. After what I'm going to say to Ava, she's likely going to be through with me. For real this time. No point in having her spill her guts about some emotional family shit to a guy she isn't going to want to speak to again.

We don't talk much on the ride over. I choose a place that Leila likes that isn't too far from the AA meeting. It's a quaint, one-off place with large saucers and hipster patrons. I'm not much of a coffee shop guy, but you can't exactly ask a girl out for an afternoon cocktail after running into her at an AA meeting.

"What do you want?" I shove my hands in my front

pockets and watch the way her eyes trail up my forearms to my shoulders. *Fuck,* those honey eyes kill me.

"Mm, a latte would be good. Two percent milk." She rubs her hands down her arms like she's nervous. I'd be nervous also if I thought that what I was about to propose to her even stood a chance in hell.

"I'll go grab us a table." She smiles stiffly at me and I nod back. If she's smart, she'll choose a table close to an exit. After ordering, I wait impatiently as the young guy behind the barista bar with a tie-dye beanie pours frothy milk in the shape of an intricate leaf into the coffee. Seriously, who has time for this shit? I can see a faint look of fear in his eyes when he hands me the mug. I'm definitely not the typical coffee shop patron, clearly. I see his eyes linger on my bruised knuckles. He probably thinks I'm about to rob the place.

"Here." I make my way over to the table and slide the latte to her. She doesn't take a sip right away but she fidgets with the coffee cup handle.

"Jesus, Ava, relax. I've seen you naked. From multiple angles. Don't act like I'm some stranger." I lean back in the chair with a sigh and run my hands through my hair. I hate how stiff and awkward it is between us when only hours ago I had her like warm liquid, moaning between by hands.

"But clearly I *don't* know you, Rhett." Her timidity is replaced with the sass that I love seeing from her and wish she showed more often.

"Sorry, I don't tend to make a habit of telling the women I meet that I'm an addict. I hear it's not the best pickup line." I spit the words out, my tone rough. I don't know if I'm pissed or flirting. When it comes to Ava, it always feels like a combination of both.

"Look," she stares down into her latte and then pins me

with those gorgeous hazel eyes, "I'm sorry I left in such a weird way this morning. I saw the texts from Leila on your phone and I thought she was someone you were...*with*. I didn't mean to see the texts, I grabbed your phone thinking it was mine."

I let out a bark of a laugh at the absurdity of her thinking Leila was some woman I was hooking up with. But there's an edge to it that I feel in my gut, a siren blaring in warning. "And this, Ava, is exactly why I don't let myself get attached to girls like you." I keep my voice low as I rest my forearms on the table.

"Rhett, I promise I wasn't snooping. I'm not like that."

"That's not what I mean."

"Then what do you mean?" Her tone is slightly exasperated and the redness in her cheeks reminds me of the rosiness of her perfect, silky skin after her multiple orgasms last night.

"You're jealous. You thought I was sleeping with another woman. I don't do boyfriend-girlfriend shit. Ever. It's just sex." I let my gaze linger on her face before it drops briefly to the top of her breasts. "Amazing, insanely good sex that I want to have again and again. But still...just sex." I see her face falter and her mouth opens like she wants to protest but I don't let her. "Ava, I care about you more than I care about most women I sleep with. I'm not trying to be an ass. But I'll never be able to care about you the way you'll want me to. The way you deserve. I just...I'm not capable of that." I steeple my hands together and study her face closely. She doesn't respond. Instead, she finally takes a sip of her latte, keeping eye contact with me the entire time. After what seems like forever, she finally speaks.

"So, what do you want to do about," she motions the space between us, "this?"

I clear my throat and feel my blood pound in between my ears. I can't even believe she's given me this opening. I would've bet her perfect ass would already be up and heading out the door when I stated it could only ever be sex between us.

Just fucking say it, and get the rejection over with. A voice in my head blares at me, refusing to delay this torture any longer. *At least then, you'll know she walked away from you and you can be done with this shit.*

"I want," I lick my lower lip, bracing myself for her rejection, "I want you to be my ring bunny."

32

AVA

"**Y**our what?!" There is no way on this Earth that I just heard Rhett properly. He wants me to be his bikini-wearing, ringside watching, friend with benefits? *Um, no freaking thank you.* I am a feminist after all and even at my lowest, I have more respect for myself than prancing around the underground. It just isn't me. I start to stand up from the small cafe table, utterly speechless.

"Wait." Rhett practically growls at me before I can make my dramatic exit. His arm reaches out, his large calloused hand splaying over my mine. I just keep blinking in confusion, his request taking me down a totally different path than how I expected this conversation to go.

I assumed he'd say, *let's just be friends and avoid each other at the gym*, or, *let's have sex one more time as a sexy farewell*, but to be his *ring bunny? What does that even really mean?*

"It's not what you're thinking. I don't want you to change the way you look or the way you dress. I don't want you to change anything." His tone is serious and sincere, a hint of desperation laced in it that has me stopping long enough to hear him out. "I know you have this idea of what you think a ring bunny is, and you're not wrong. But their original purpose is fucking fighters before fights. Sex is good for adrenaline and nerves. It's part of the job." As he's explaining himself, the memory of him on a so-called *business date* with a blonde and leggy Kelsey comes flaring back to me.

"Okay..." My response is more of question.

"The only way for me to...control what I *need*, what I want, is to center it around fighting. I don't want to fuck anyone else. Only you. But it's just sex for my fighting schedule. Nothing more, nothing less. No dates, no promises, no future this or that." He leans back in his chair and then suddenly lets out a dark chuckle.

"Is this all just some joke to you?" I feel a wave of embarrassment crawl up my spine.

"No, no, Jesus. I'm just laughing because I can't believe you're still sitting here. Even if you say 'no', I'm already hard right now knowing I at least had a shot." My eyes involuntarily make their way down his chest, the stupid cafe table blocking my view of seeing anything *further* down. I mentally shake my head at my naughty thoughts and focus back on Rhett's unorthodox request.

"So *if* I agree to this," I lower my voice, emphasizing the 'if' with my tone as I lean in closer, "how exactly does it end?"

Rhett doesn't respond right away. He reaches out and runs a calloused thumb over my cheek, my entire body leaning into his surprising touch of its own volition. Maybe a part of me can actually do this. *Wants* to actually do this. Bank some amazing orgasms and then walk away unscathed. Perhaps, the new independent me doesn't want strings attached and to say 'I love you.' Nothing in my life has played out how I expected it. *Why not add this to the mix?*

"I think this season will be my last," he's still stroking my cheek, his voice somber, "my body can't take it much longer." I clear my throat at the mention of his body and he smirks, a wicked tilt to his mouth.

"So, no other ring bunnies?" My voice is a hoarse whisper, the idea rolling around inside my head. I could do a sex-only relationship but not a polyamorous one. To each their own, but not for me. Clearly I'd already been insanely jealous from a misunderstood text message. No way can I share him, even if this whole thing is just a temporary arrangement. For as long as it lasts, he'd be mine.

"Just you, Ava." I purse my lips together at his response, a small part of me flaring and dying at once hearing those words from his mouth. I toss my head back and forth, pretending to be debating my decision. He can tell I'm toying with him and he gently grabs my thigh under the table.

"My next fight is in two weeks. You think you can wait that long?" His strong hand starts massaging the soft skin of my inner thigh and I squeeze my legs together in response.

"Of course I can." My breathy tone betrays the confidence of my words.

"Oh and one more rule." He gives my thigh a final squeeze before removing his hand.

"What's that?"

"No touching yourself. You only get off with me."

33

AVA

Two weeks isn't a long time. Really, it isn't. I mean, it's half a month. The amount of time it takes to start a new habit. A backpacking stint in Europe. Just two weeks.

But it's starting to feel like *forever.* The tension that has built up in my body between me agreeing to Rhett's insane proposal at the coffee shop to be his ring bunny and the night of his first fight in his final underground series finally ends tonight. I finish applying a light layer of lip gloss and debate for the hundredth time if this is the right outfit for an occasion that has absolutely no precedent in my life. I can't even turn to the Internet for advice on this one.

"Are you sure you don't want me to come with me?" I look at Shelly through my reflection in the mirror as she sits on the edge of my bed with a hot cup of tea between her hands, her blonde hair tied up in a messy bun.

"Yes, I'm sure. I'll be fine, I promise." She offers me a soft smile as I turn away from my full-length mirror and force myself to stop debating my stupid outfit choice. It hardly matters anyway. I know Shelly isn't really ready to go back to another underground fight after Eric's last match with Thorne. Luckily, he is doing a lot better and has been training again in the gym. But I can tell it will be a while before Shelly is ready to see another match again, and I'm not going to let my own nerves force her into an uncomfortable situation.

"You look great by the way." He smile broadens, reminding me of a Cheshire cat, but the expression in her eyes remains tired. "So, what is the deal with you and Rhett Jaggar anyway? Are you two, like, seeing each other?" She wiggles her pale blonde eyebrows at me as she brings her cup of tea to her lips.

"No," I divert my gaze, "not really." I leave my bedroom and head to the kitchen. I need a pregame drink to calm my nerves before I leave for the underground arena.

"And what, exactly, does 'not really' mean, hmm?" Shelly trails close behind, her feistiness returning as she pads after me in her ridiculously fluffy slippers. Shelly loves to talk about all things men and relationships and drama and love. There is no stopping her when she's on a tear. But I'm not ready to tell her about Rhett and my *agreement.* She already has a sour taste in her mouth for typical ring bunnies because she views them as a threat to her relationship with Eric. Which is dumb because despite my initial hesitations about him, he clearly only has eyes for Shelly.

But still, there is no way I can fully explain that me being Rhett's *ring bunny* is a way for Rhett to control his addictions and center every behavior, every choice on his fighting. So, I decide to continue playing coy. For now.

"I mean, I don't know, okay? I'm trying to not overthink something for once. Isn't that what you've been trying to get me to do since, oh I don't know, we met over ten years ago?" Shelly laughs at my response as I make myself a vodka soda with a very healthy pour. It burns on the way down, exactly what I need right now.

"True, true. I hate it when my own amazing advice bites me in the ass."

"What are you going to do tonight?" I glance down at my phone to check the time. I need to be at the arena in an hour. I feel a wave of nerves and excitement slam against my chest. I take another gulp of my drink.

"Oh, you know," Shelly sighs dramatically, waving her hand toward the living room, "probably binge-watch a show on Netflix I've already seen a million times. Something very exciting and very important."

"Are you going to see Eric? Maybe he should come over. You two could order in dinner."

"He had some intense ice bath and muscle therapy treatment with one of the assistant coaches at the gym. It's supposed to help some of his stiffness...from the injuries." Shelly's voice trails off and I can tell she's reimagining Eric's seemingly lifeless body hit the mat. *Time for a topic change.*

"Well, if it were me, I'd probably go for Grey's Anatomy. Unless, you're in a humorous mood then of course, it's The Office." I down the last of my drink and consider making another one. But I don't want to be *too* tipsy when I see him. I want to be completely present. To remember every touch of his large calloused hands against my feverish skin.

"You make a great point. Can't argue with that." Shelly smacks her lips in mock seriousness. "I'll take both options into consideration." She stands up and kisses me on the cheek before heading into the bathroom and turning on the shower.

My phone buzzes and I glance down to see a text, my entire body thrumming with unfettered adrenaline:

Rhett: 30 minutes. Don't be late.

34

AVA

The underground has an entirely different energy tonight. The place is almost violent with activity and everyone seems to be a mixture of excited and on edge. Myself included. When I arrive at the venue, I text Coach Barry. Apparently, he knows the vague details of Rhett and my *agreement* which makes me seriously cringe every time I think about it. But at least it means he won't be setting Rhett up on any more *work dates* with leggy blondes named Kelsey.

"Ava, you look lovely." Coach Barry gives me a chaste kiss on the cheek. "Rhett is in his prepping room, I'll take you there." He offers me a quick closed-lip smile and I feel my cheeks flush. He basically knows he's dropping me off to have sex with his top fighter but I have to remind myself that I willingly, and heartily, agreed to this. Not to mention that I *want* it. Badly. It's part of Rhett's fighting routine, and a new part of me finding my own pleasure. There's nothing to feel ashamed of. Still, I have to repeat the words over and over in my own head to convince myself.

And after everything Rhett had confided in me, the way

his head hung low as he admitted his addictions out loud in that AA circle like a defeated warrior, I do believe Rhett when he says he isn't capable of anything beyond this. The insane physical attraction between us. The tether pulling two opposites toward one another.

Anything more between us could lead to disaster. This agreement is all that we can share. And for the next eight weeks, I'll get the best sex of my life, and then we'll be done. No strings. No promises. No fantasy of more. The old Ava would never have recognized this new Ava in the mirror. And there is something strangely satisfying about that. I feel a smile tilt my lips upward at the shedding of my old self.

Coach Barry and I walk through the maze of corridors that makes up the backstage of the underground arena. I get more looks than I'd like, the leers of other fighters and their entourages glazing over me from head to toe. I feel like everyone *knows* exactly what I'm about to do and with who. I try to keep my gaze focused straight ahead. I certainly do not need another Thorne situation on my hands.

"Do people know this is Rhett's last underground series?" I keep my voice low as we descend a final set of stairs.

"There are rumors, yes. But Rhett hasn't officially come out and confirmed it. Part of me is in denial until he does," Coach Barry laughs fondly, "but I know it's time. That man has put his body through hell and back. He needs to rest." We reach the door to Rhett's prepping room and I can hear low, bass-heavy music spilling out into the hallway from underneath the door.

"The fight starts at 9:00 PM sharp. I'll come get you at 8:30 to take you to your seat." Coach Barry gives me a curt nod before turning to leave. I take a deep breath and knock once on the door. I hear the music lower slightly in volume.

Rhett opens the door. His chest is bare, covered in that sinfully hot smattering of tattoos and faint white scars. He leans against the doorframe and slides one hand around my waist to pull me inside. Then he closes the door to the hallway, his hand not leaving the small of my hip.

"Hi." Rhett's voice is low, gravelly, laced with sensual anticipation.

"Hi." I don't move. I barely even breathe as he takes me in, his eyes drinking me up in a way no man ever has before. I suddenly feel dumb for worrying so much about my outfit.

"Part of me thought you wouldn't come." Rhett removes his hand from my waist and walks over to the black leather couch. The space of his prepping room is dimly lit but organized; mats on the floor, energy drinks laid out in a neat triangle from a sponsor on a table, and a makeshift medical station. He sits down and leans forward, resting his forearms on his spread knees. He glances at the ground briefly before looking back up at me. His gaze is hungry, almost feral, like he's starving. I feel his look mirrored within my own body, in the anticipation that's been thrumming through me these past two agonizing weeks. His eyes are dark, that cut jaw of his jumping like it's an effort for him not to lunge for me. I feel a delicious heat pool in my belly at the desire and urgent need in his expression.

I don't respond. I don't utter a single word. I simply walk over to him, slowly, letting his gaze rake over my body. I stand in front of him, bending over at the waist to rest my palms on the back of the couch behind his shoulders, my face level with his.

"What do you want me to do?" My voice is a shaky whisper, the reality of us here alone, of what we agreed to do, spreading through my limbs like a drug. A new type of high I've never felt before.

"Whatever you want, Ava." His dark eyes glimmer with mischief. I've never been in this kind of control before. Let alone with such an overtly powerful man. The last time we had sex was a follow-on to an argument. Emotions had been running wild and actions had been hasty, erratic. This time feels more deliberate. I'm certainly not some insanely experienced sexual goddess but Rhett's look of raw, carnal desire increases my confidence.

I slide the hem of my dress up higher onto my thighs so that I can straddle him. His gaze lowers to my breasts and I slip down the delicate straps of my dress so he can see more of my cleavage. Rhett doesn't move, doesn't say a word. But I can feel his entire body vibrating, his breathing growing faster, more erratic. His racing heartbeat matching mine.

"Kiss me." I utter the words lightly, my mouth only an inch from his. His eyes flash to mine before he closes the distance between us, wrapping one arm around my waist like a vise and gripping my entire jaw with his other hand. The kiss feels like it sears my entire body, every inch of my skin. His tongue is slow and intentional, more torture than our previous kisses full of rushed desperation. He wants to savor me, to take his time like I'm the most previous thing in the world, and it makes me feel sexier than I've ever felt in my life.

The boldness in me grows and I slowly slide my hand down his bare chest, landing on his growing erection. I palm him, teasingly, over his shorts, a groan escaping from his lips between our kisses.

"Off. Now." Rhett grunts out the words between our lips and I shift slightly to help him slide the shorts down his legs. My eyes grow wide at seeing him naked again. I'm not sure I will ever get used to the sight. My hormones are simply no match for this man.

Rhett pulls me closer to him and uses one hand to drag the top of my dress down even further, the fabric pooling around my waist. He looks up at me with hooded eyes before latching his mouth around one of my exposed nipples, alternating between soft bites and soothing licks. I can feel it all the way down *there,* to my core. I begin to writhe my hips, mirroring the movements of his mouth.

Rhett releases my nipple from his mouth with a soft growl. "Ava, if you keep moving like that I'm not going to last much longer." His voice vibrates against my sensitive skin and it makes the female energy in me smile. I stand up quickly, stepping out of his reach, Rhett's expression like a kid whose candy just got taken away. I smirk at him before slipping my panties down my legs. Without removing my heels, I straddle him again, taking his cock in one hand and resting the other on his shoulder as I brace myself.

"Jesus, Ava. You're killing me." The veins in Rhett's throat protrude, his entire body straining against his desire to be inside of me. I position myself at the top of his cock and start to slide down slowly, the feeling of fullness spreading throughout my entire body.

"Fuck, Ava." Rhett groans into my neck before softly biting my skin. I yelp out in a mixture of pleasure and surprise. We're still for several seconds, feeling each other, our breathing ragged. After a few moments of me adjusting to him inside of me, Rhett starts to move. He lifts my ass in the air before slamming it back down, using his arm around my back as a lever. I hear mewls and moans escape my mouth that sound like they're coming from somewhere outside of my own body. My sense of time and space is reduced to the sounds of us fucking, his grunts in my ear, and my ass hitting the tops of his thighs. I hear myself getting louder, those stars I saw last time coming into view, fluttering behind my eyelids, every fiber in my body connecting with him inside of me. No thoughts, no sense of self-consciousness, no worrying about tomorrow or next week or next year. Only this exact moment exists.

Then, I let go, the feeling like bright, warm light snapping pleasurably through me.

As I come down from my orgasm, I'm aware that Rhett is still moving, even faster, with a desperation further intensified by his raw strength. His head falls back against the couch as he finds his release, his eyes closed tightly and his hands gripping me tightly with pleasure. I slump forward as his hold on me softens, my forehead resting on his sweaty shoulder. We both work to catch our breath, neither of us daring to move away.

"Ava." He says my name like it's a prayer, like I'm something worthy of being worshipped, and I sit up lazily in his lap to meet his eyes. We look at one another but don't say anything more. Everything left unsaid hanging tensely between us.

The room slowly comes back into focus. The reality that Rhett has a fight within a matter of minutes and that our purpose, our time together, is coming to an end. I slowly stand up awkwardly, adjusting my dress, my limbs weak and wobbly as I slide my discarded panties back up my legs and under my dress. I smooth down the fabric and run my fingers through my wayward hair. Rhett reaches for his shorts and stands up from the couch, his hands flexing at his sides.

"Well, good luck tonight." I don't know what else to say. Part of me feels amazing. Powerful, independent. Utterly satisfied. A woman in total control of her own wants, her own pleasure. But the other part of me feels cheap. Like an object. A thing. And I hate that society has made women associate willing and amazing 'just sex' as something demeaning.

Rhett doesn't reply. Instead, he stills for a moment before leaning down and kissing me underneath my ear. The same gentle move he did at the bar after I embarrassed myself trying to get out of yet another tricky situation. He lifts his head back up and we lock eyes. I feel like there's more he wants to say, to express, but he doesn't. I see the strong column of his throat bob once.

Finally he offers me a final nod, essentially excusing me. I take my cue and leave the room without looking back, Coach Barry making his way down from the other end of the hallway just as the door clicks shut behind me.

It's time for the fight.

35

RHETT

My body is buzzing. I haven't felt this good in a long, long time. Ava is fucking perfect. *Too* perfect. I know I should be wary of her actually agreeing to be my 'ring bunny.' Worried that she'll come to regret it, to regret me. She's nothing like the other ring bunnies I've been with and she and I both know that. But having that *agreement* frame our relationship, whatever you want to call it, is my way of keeping my time with her in some sort of box. In a realm within my control instead of out in the open where I know I'll lose it. Fuck it up somehow. Risk hurting her. Seek out drugs, other women...the routine a hellish rollercoaster ride that I'm sick and tired of going on. I just want Ava, exactly like she'd been tonight. Sexy, sweet, in control, and all *mine*. I sure as hell won't take these next eight weeks with her for granted.

My hands are taped and the hood of my silk robe is slung low over my head. I bounce lightly on my toes, feeling the perfect combination of energy and calm. That's the effect sex has before a fight, and with Ava it's on an entirely different level. I've never been attracted to a woman's touch like I am with hers. *Jesus*, the things I'd let that woman do to me. I have to forcibly to block them out, to focus.

I hear my name bellowing out from the audience like a battle cry. I haven't publicly confirmed that this is my last underground fighting series, but some of my true fans have a suspicion. I'm ready to leave the constant pressure, the toll on my mind and my body, but I can't deny how much I love this place. The peace and salvation it's brought to my fucked-up soul. I hop into the ring as easily as breathing, not bothering to pander to the crowd. That has never been my style. Just the art of the fight.

I stare down my opponent, Nico Chavez. He's been making a name for himself and I can sense the pure, unadulterated hunger in his long, lean limbs, the need marking his young handsome face. Something in it reminds me of myself when I was younger, seeking out fights on the streets of Boston. I smirk to myself, knowing his energy and eagerness are the perfect combination for the lack of control I seek out in an opponent.

It's something I've acquired after fighting for so many years. When I step into the ring, I'm in total and complete control; over my body and over my mind. It's my time of salvation. Sadly, I can't say the same for my life outside of this square, roped-in pen. Maybe someday I'll be able to bridge the two.

The bell rings out and every fiber in my being zeroes in on Chavez. Round one will be done in no time.

Within minutes he's on the mat, the round one bell ringing out, barely audible over the roaring cheer of the audience.

"Jesus, Rhett, you're like fucking magic out there." Coach Barry pours water over my head, his voice nearly screaming to be heard in the arena, as I sit in my corner between rounds.

"You writing me a love letter, Coach?" I laugh at his fan-like tone. He sounds like a little kid seeing me fight for the first time.

"I'm serious! It reminds me of when you were younger. Like it's not a job to you anymore. It's like...I don't know, I can't describe it. That Chavez kid has some serious potential though." I see a slight shimmer in his eyes and I want to throw him down on the mat for acting like such a pussy. But I also know that deep down I share a glimmer of the same pride, the same appreciation he has for me reflected back at him ten-fold. For saving my life, for being the first person to stick around. To see my potential and hone it like a weapon, like a work of fine art.

"You're going soft, old man." I through back an electrolyte packet. Coach starts talking to me about technique, giving me tips and tricks I've already gone over in my mind. I start to zone him out, ready for the break to be over, when I spot her.

Ava is sitting front row, her legs crossed like a true lady. But her face is stoic. Almost solemn. She isn't looking at me, giving me full access to just admire her delicate features, the perfect slope of her profile. She seems focused on some point in the center of the ring like she's trying to concentrate. I greedily take her in, the porcelain skin, her pretty naturally pouty lips. Those honey eyes that drive me wild. I wish I could read her mind as well as I can read her body. I want desperately to know how she's feeling in this exact moment, about our arrangement, about what we shared earlier. Above all, I want to know why the hell she even agreed to it in the first place.

"So, you agree right? Jab hard on the left and then back

away and dodge to tire him out before going in for another takedown?" Coach Barry's eyes are alight with excitement and I nod absently, still distracted by Ava. The bell rings out and the familiar sound snaps my focus back to center.

The next few rounds fly by smoothly, my groove perfect, every movement of my limbs flawless like a dance, graceful yet brutal. Exactly as I've been trained.

"Ladies and not-so gentlemen, our winner, our champion, our uncontested favorite, the infamous...Rhett Jaggar!" I hear that familiar announcement ring out like an echo, the crowd rising to its feet. No one expected me to lose this fight, the first in an eight-round series. But I'll hand it to Nico Chavez. The guy has major potential. And he's desperate. If he can channel that shit and combine it with impeccable technique, he'll have a shot at many wins under his belt. All he needs is to gain control of his own power. That had been me ten years ago. It makes that kind of potential easy to spot in others.

"That was some beautiful work, Rhett." Coach's voice is damn near irreverent as we make our way out of the ring. Coach pushes on ahead of me to get through the thickening crowd. Fans paw at me, yelling for autographs. Women scratch and grab at my arms.

"Where is she?" I whisper hoarsely in a low tone to Coach Barry only for him to hear as we finally near the backstage entrance.

"In your prepping room." Coach Barry opens the steel door. My ears feel like I've plunged deep underwater as the chaotic sounds of the arena immediately die away into a low tonal blur. We start walking toward my prepping room when Coach stops me, his hand gripping my bare sweaty shoulder.

"Rhett," he comes around to stand in front of me like he

actually has a chance of stopping me in my path if he wanted to. I almost laugh at the though. But any humor dies on my lips as Coach Barry continues. "She's a good girl...a smart young woman whose been through a lot of shit recently. Don't do something you're going to regret." I run my hand through my sweaty hair and my brows knit in confusion at Coach's sudden protectiveness. Where was this warning side of him earlier when he led Ava to my room?

"What are you trying to say, Coach?" I grit my teeth, keeping my voice low as others pass by us in the backstage hallway.

"Does she know?" Coach Barry rests his hands on his hips like a chastising father. But he doesn't expand on his question.

"Know *what*?"

"Rhett. Does she *know*?" We never talk about my addiction issues out in the open. We just barely reference them, dance around them, watch out for them, and react when it becomes a problem for my fighting schedule. That's the way I like it. The last thing I need is another goddamn sponsor.

"Yes. She knows." I bite out my response and shove past him. I don't like the thought of Coach Barry thinking I'd have Ava with me, in whatever form of a pseudo-relationship this is, without me being completely honest with her. I can be an ass but I'm not a total fucking jerk. Ava is a grown woman. God do I know that. And even though I'm just as surprised as Coach that she's agreed to this with me, she made up her own damn mind with all the facts in front of her. No one forced her to be here.

I reach the door to my prepping room and Coach grabs my arm before I can enter. "She's good for you. If she *knows* and she's still here...she has this effect on you...the effect she had tonight. Then," he pauses, gathering his words, "I'm happy for you, Rhett."

"She's good for my fighting. That's all this is. Don't forget, you're not my fucking father." My words are harsh and part of me immediately regrets them. But whatever match-making, paternal bullshit Coach is pulling when talks about Ava's effect on me is just going to make it that much harder when these eight weeks end. And they *will* end. They have to. I'd rather leave Ava fair and square than keep her in my life and do something so terrible she ends up hating me. I don't think I could live with myself seeing that level of hurt and resentment in her beautiful, honey-hazel eyes.

Coach puts up his hands in mock surrender and I turn away from him, slamming my prepping room door shut behind me.

36

AVA

I've been pacing in Rhett's dressing room when I jump at the sound of the door slamming. Rhett's staring at me, his expression more curious than angry, his strong muscled chest still breathing a bit heavily from the fight.

"Sorry," Rhett clears his throat, the sound like sandpaper, "I didn't mean to slam the door so hard." He smiles at me but the smile doesn't reach his eyes. There's an edge to it, bordering on wariness. Almost like he's nervous seeing me here in his room after the fight. Maybe I *shouldn't* be here? Perhaps this isn't an intended part of the *arrangement*. Only before the fight. I wring my hands together.

"Should I leave? I mean," I let out a hoarse laugh, "I don't know how this works." I rub my palms down my arms nervously, realizing how weird this conversation is. How unprecedented it all feels.

"I don't know how anything works when it comes to you, Ava." Rhett's voice is quiet as he slumps onto the couch, releasing a loud sigh like he's been holding in his breath. He looks sated, a warrior finally at peace. His fighting tonight was...inspiring. There's just no other word for it. Even for someone like me, a person who hates violence and had no appreciation for this world a few months ago, can understand that what Rhett does in the ring is an art form. Not just a physical act of sheer brutality. There's grace and precision in it, something honed over many years of dedication.

"Ava," Rhett leans forward over his strong thighs, his position reminding me of our earlier *activities*, "sit down for a minute." I stop my pacing and take a seat across from him, crossing my legs like I'm in some sort of business meeting. *Perhaps I am in a business meeting?*

"Did I do something wrong?" I feel a flush crawl up over my neck and onto my cheeks. I won't let myself regret or doubt anything we did earlier. It had felt amazing and I wanted it.

"God, no." Rhett pins me with a serious look, his eyes smoldering. "I just...I have to know," he swallows hard, almost stumbling over his own words, "why did you say yes? To this?" He looks down at the ground for a moment, unable to meet my eyes again. "To me?"

I feel a snare in my lungs, like I can't quite catch my breath. For a moment I don't know what to say. And then the honesty spills out of me, unable to be controlled. "Part of me still doesn't know. But my whole life is so different now. *I'm* different now. I've changed and I don't want to care about what people think I should or shouldn't do. I used to be the perfect girl but I was living a life that was a complete lie. My dad—" I cut myself off, not wanting to get into all that right now. "I've never had this kind of...sex before. It makes me feel powerful. Making you come undone, knowing *I* did that to *you*," my voice is a whisper, hanging on by a thread, "I want it. I want you. And I know that it will end. And I'm okay with that." I'm not sure I believe myself but my words ring confident and true, my eyes searing into his tense face, holding nothing back. I slide my hands down my thighs and stand from the chair to start pacing again.

Rhett rises from the couch and crosses the room in three easy strides. He pulls me into a violent kiss, catching me completely off guard. It takes me a minute to return the kiss, finally matching his rhythm and fervor before he breaks away, both of us panting.

"Next Friday? Same time?" Rhett's chest is heaving, his hard erection digging into my stomach. I don't want to have to wait another week. I want him now, here, in this moment. But I know he needs me to walk away, to keep whatever this is between us somehow contained.

I swallow hard past a lump in my throat, digging my nails into my clenched palms to keep myself from reaching for him.

"I'll be here."

37

AVA

The next two weeks pass by in a blur—fast and slow all at once. Rhett's hands, his lips, his body make me feverish between Friday night fights, my entire body buzzing with raw adrenaline. There's something so potent, so intoxicating when it's just Rhett and me in his prepping room, the arena beginning to vibrate with energy in anticipation of violence. It's strange to think how much that turns me on, making our limited time together more sacred, more secluded.

Maybe it's knowing that it won't last forever that drives our desperation. Our kisses often draw blood, followed by sex where we utterly claim each other, fusing our bodies as one. The spent feeling, the heavy breathing, the tender way he tucks my hair behind my ear after we climax. It brings a surreal quiet to my mind that I've never had before, spreading lazily through my limbs. Something this amazing can only be temporary. For the first time in my life, I understand it. I get what it means to be addicted to something so powerful, so thrilling that everything else seems to fade into the background, only serving as the space and time between when I can see him again. When I can feel him again, moving under me, over me, behind me. It isn't not love, I know that. But it's something potent, consuming. Perhaps something even more dangerous than love.

Tonight is the fourth week in the fighting series. Rhett has been moving through the matches fairly easily. From what Coach Barry tells me, it won't start getting more challenging until round six, when more worthy and senior opponents are brought into the ring. But it's hard for me to imagine anyone fighting with the same skill and natural instinct as Rhett.

I towel dry my hair after a shower and hear Shelly making breakfast in the kitchen. She still hasn't returned to the underground, but she and Eric seem to be normal again after his brutal beating by Thorne. He's been back in the gym training, and she stops by to see him and me while I work at the gym between her shifts at the salon. We never really had a formal talk about the fact that I was originally supposed to join her at the salon, working the front desk. Shelly won't pry, but she knows that whatever is going on between Rhett and me, something too strange for me to even understand let alone explain out loud, means that I'm keeping my job at the gym. For the next month at least.

It's the only other place where I can see him. Usually just stolen glances, brushing past each other as he heads into the locker room or as I tally equipment stock for Coach Barry. Usually he ignores me, acting like I blend into the gym environment itself. But other times, I'll catch him staring. A heat in his dark eyes and a tension in his jaw. In those moments he looks strained, on edge. It makes me feel powerful, knowing that I have this effect on him, but I'm also aware that my expression reflects his own. We are both careening towards something, neither of us able or willing to stop it. The fighting series will have to end it for us. Exactly as our arrangement was designed. An escape hatch to prevent a type of havoc I can feel growing in myself, an emotion I've never experienced before.

"You want some eggs?" Shelly starts mixing raw eggs in a bowl, seasoning them with her magic medley. The girl definitely has a better knack for the kitchen than me. Without her, I'd be living off of oatmeal packets and frozen pizza.

"Sure, thanks." I give her a tight-lipped smile, my mind already wandering to tonight's fight. Shelly looks like she wants to ask me something but she stays silent. She works to scramble the eggs and after a few moments she turns to face me.

"So, how's your dad doing?" It isn't the question I expect her to ask and I clear my throat in surprise. *My dad.* The last time I saw him had been at the AA meeting. The same AA meeting where Rhett's admission and request altered the next few months of my life. Aside from the occasional text, I haven't really talked to my dad much. I sigh at the realization that I should probably reach back out.

"I...I'm not sure. I haven't talked to him much," I spin my phone anxiously in my hand, "I should probably call him, right?"

Shelly adds a garnish of chopped chives to our eggs, restaurant-style. *When did she learn to do that?* "Yeah, I'd say so. I mean, I know he's put you through a lot, but I'm sure he's going through it too. He's your family, Ava. Well, along with me of course." She winks at me and slides the plate of steaming eggs my way. They look and smell delicious but my appetite has been less than normal lately, my usual hunger replaced by a tangle of nerves, adrenaline, and hormones. I pick at the eggs before tentatively taking a bite. Shelly eyes me suspiciously.

"Look, you're basically my sister and I'd go to the moon and back for you," Shelly shovels a forkful of eggs in her mouth and swallows, "but if you don't start eating like a normal human being again, you're going to force me to ask you more about whatever the heck is going on between you and Rhett. Because no one gets it, but everyone at the gym knows *something* is up." Her blonde eyebrows shoot up to her forehead, a warning look on her facing indicating she's not backing down this time.

Instead of trying to explain my situation with Rhett to her, a catharsis that would probably be the smarter route to take, I nod affirmatively and shovel a huge bite of scrambled eggs into my mouth.

"Mmm, delicious." I smile at Shelly and she rolls her eyes, knowing I'm being avoidant again, but she can't help a smirk from curving her lips.

"I'm watching you, Ava Young." She squints at me before turning her attention to the rest of her breakfast, essentially ending our conversation. I'll tell Shelly everything at some point, I really will, but not until it's over. Right now, this *thing* is just for Rhett and me. I don't want logic or explanations to take anything away from that. After I clear my plate, to the reluctance of my turbulent stomach, I head into my bedroom to call my dad. I take a deep breath and hit 'dial' before I can change my mind. Pacing the short distance of my bedroom, my dad picks up on the third ring.

"Hey, Dad, how are you?" My tone is high, laced with apprehension.

"Ava, this is Rick Fuller. Your dad's lawyer." The deep, professional voice that comes over the line sounds foreign to me. I feel my back stiffen.

"Oh," I pause, "hi, can I, uh, talk to my dad?"

"Ava, your dad is being held in custody right now. He

couldn't make bail. I'm working with the judge to bring it down to something more reasonable for us to afford." I feel the room spin and I sit down on the edge of my bed. *Being held? Like in an actual jail cell?* My entire body breaks out in goosebumps. It's like I've known on paper that this was coming, that my dad would have to answer for his crimes, but hearing that it's actually happening right now takes the air out of my lungs. I feel a wave of nausea slowly rise from my stomach.

"How," my voice trembles, "how much?"

"Ava..." Rick's voice trails off, almost like I'm a child asking for adult-only information.

"How much, Mr. Fuller?" I put all the calm and power behind my voice that I can muster.

"$1.2 million." His tone is curt, without emotion. I feel bile rise in my throat at the number.

"Oh my god." I have no idea what my father has left financially after this ordeal. My guess is that they took everything when he was arrested. That all of his accounts have been seized. There'd be no way he can come even close to that bail amount.

"Ava, it's all part of the legal process. I assure you I am doing everything within my power to help your father. We will get the bail lowered in due time, and go from there." He may as well have been talking to me about the weather, his tone is so benign despite the gravity of the information. I run my palm down my thigh, my body trembling slightly.

"Can I...see him? Or talk to him?" The thought of seeing him in prison, handcuffed under a table or through a piece of plexiglass guts me. My only reference for visiting someone in jail is what I've seen in movies.

"I can arrange for a meeting, yes. But I will have to ask your father first. I'm going to see him tomorrow to discuss some upcoming trial details. I'll ask him then." It all sounds so matter of fact, so simple, and yet anything but at the same time. I nod and then realize he can't see me, the awkward silence stretching out between us over the phone.

"Thank you." I hang up and let the phone drop to my bed. If it is going to be this difficult for my dad to even make bail, what does that mean for his prospects of not spending the rest of his life in prison? Hot tears pour down my cheeks, but I don't make a sound. I curl up into a ball on the bed, pulling the duvet over top of me, wishing like hell it will swallow me whole.

38

RHETT

Only thirty minutes until Ava will arrive at my door. If we hadn't agreed to constrain this arrangement to pre-fight sex, I'd be completely consumed by this woman. She has no idea how much control, how much power, she has over my body. Over my mind, over every motion coursing through me these past few weeks. Touching her makes me feel more alive than the feeling I get in the ring. It's a wickedly dangerous first for me. Sex before a fight has always been a technicality, a pleasurable one but still with a purpose beyond the sex itself. But sex with Ava is anything but that.

Coach Barry finishes stretching out my right shoulder. "I'll go to get her." I nod at his statement, not wanting to open up the topic of Ava for further discussion. Our "ring bunny" arrangement is somehow working for us. It's the highlight of my week, my sanctuary between the fighting chaos. I'm not open to any outside opinions. It has been tense between Coach and me since I threw out the harsh dig about him not being my father, but we've been through worse. Time is just going to have to wash over that incident, because there's no way in fucking hell I'll be open to some goddamn heart-to-heart bullshit about it. No way I'll ever apologize for anything, any time spent, when it comes to Ava.

I stretch out my hamstrings and my calves, everything tight but thankfully not injured. No doubt, I'll start getting hurt in a week or two. Even when you're the best, this shit still breaks your body down to the bones. Especially since I'd put myself through the wringer without proper training and recovery during the first five years of my fighting career.

About twenty minutes later, I hear the door of my prepping room open and then close. I look up from my padded bench and see Ava standing with her back up against the door, something unsure about her posture. She looks beautiful, as always, but seems off.

"Hi." My voice is cautious, needing to gauge her mood.

"Hey, there." She slurs back at me, tentatively moving further into the room, wobbling slightly in her high heels. I rush over to grab her waist, pinning her against the wall. She lowers her head so I can't see her honey eyes, but I can smell the alcohol on her breath.

"Fuck Ava, are you drunk?" She messily shakes her head to indicate 'no' which is universal drunk speak for 'absolutely trashed.' She tries to straighten her small frame and looks up at me, her gorgeous hazel eyes glassy. I walk her over to the couch, my heart pounding in my chest with concern. I've never seen Ava drunk before. Even the few times I'd seen her at bars, she always stops after the equivalent of two, maybe three drinks. Unlike her friend blonde Shelly, who's surprisingly a tank considering she's even smaller than Ava.

"Ava, talk to me." She looks at me coyly from underneath her lashes, an expression that isn't her.

"We don't talk, Rhett. We have sex." She runs her hand down my bare chest, her nails scraping gently. "So take off my clothes. Make me feel good." She's smiling but it's off. Everything about her is off. This girl is two sheets to the wind. I can't deny my attraction to her body, to her smooth bare legs brushing up against mine. My dick is painfully hard in my shorts, but I'll never fuck her like this. No matter how much she asks for it.

"Ava, no." I push her lightly against the back of the couch so she doesn't tip over and walk to the table to get a water bottle and an electrolyte packet. I hand them to her and she shoves both away lightly, using her hands to pull up the hem of her shit.

"Fuck, Ava. Stop." I pull the fabric of her dress back down over her thighs and place my hands on the back of the couch headrest. She peers up at me.

"Rhett, please. Make me feel good." This time, her voice isn't attempting to be sexy. It's desperate. I feel anger boil up within me, wanting to know what or who got her to this place. And praying to god that it isn't me.

"Ava, tell me what's wrong. Tell me how I can help." I tuck a piece of silky stray hair behind her ear and tip her chin up at me. She doesn't say anything for a few long moments, but I hold her face, waiting it out.

"I think," she inhales a shaky breath, "I think my dad is going to go to prison. For the rest of his life." Her voice cracks on the last words but she doesn't move. She just pierces me with those gorgeous, sad hazel yellow eyes and I feel my other hand instinctively flex on the back of the couch. I want her to tell me a problem that I can fix. Something I can handle. Perhaps a face I can break in. But this? I'm just as helpless as she is.

I graze my thumb across the soft skin of her jaw and kiss

her cheek. Now would be the time to say something like, *it'll all work out*, or, *it'll be okay*, but I can't promise her those things. I knew her dad was an addict of some kind, but I have no idea what he's done. No idea how bad it is.

I sit down next to her and pull her onto my lap. No doubt, she can feel the hardness of my erection digging into her, but she doesn't call attention to it. I tuck her head under my chin and rub her back in slow, small circles. I hear her hiccup a few times and I reach for the water bottle she tossed away earlier.

"Drink this." I unscrew the cap and hand it to her. Thankfully she doesn't protest this time and she downs the bottle greedily. "And this." I hand her the electrolyte packet and watch as her full, pink lips work over the top, sucking the pouch of its contents. A jolt shoots straight to my cock at the sight but I manage to keep myself under control.

After about half an hour of us sitting in silence, her on my lap and me stroking her hair, she pulls away to look at me. "Isn't your fight soon? Rhett we need to—"

"We don't need to do anything." I cut her off. "Stay in here during the fight. I don't want you out in the arena like this. It'll distract me." I run a hand roughly down my face, realizing I need to get my hands tapped soon. I slide Ava from my lap and lay her down on the couch before covering her with a warm blanket from the medical kit. Before I stand back up, she reaches for my face and kisses me so gently it's like torture not to go in for more. This isn't our plan, our agreement. She isn't supposed to get me all worked up about her family issues and her safety and her sadness. All the warning signals go off in my head but I have no choice except to push them aside and deal with all of this after the fight.

"Get some rest." I stand up and text Coach. He's in the doorway a few minutes later.

"Is she ready to head down to the arena?" He keeps his hands in his pockets, his voice a very poor attempt at casual. He must have smelled the alcohol on her as much as I did when he brought her to back my room. Must have been too nervous about my reaction to comment or say anything.

"You and I both know that's not happening tonight." I grab my fighting tape and toss it at him, essentially ending any further discussion. He doesn't nod, he just stares at me like he wants to tell me it's my fault. That I somehow broke this girl sweet girl now laying drunk on my couch. But I didn't. Her own father did. And even if it will end up killing me when I let her go, I'm going to do whatever I can to help her.

39

AVA

I've spent enough time in the underground arena at this point to recognize the differences in cheers from the audience. This one sends vibrations through the floors and up into my bones. I sit up on the couch, my head pounding at my temples. This is the finale cheer, and I can hear Rhett's name being chanted like a battle cry. I rub the heels of my palms over my eyes, disoriented to find myself alone in his prepping room instead of sitting in the front row, where I'm used to the deafening screams of the rough and rowdy fans taking the very wind from my lungs.

I stand up on slightly shaking legs and notice I'm no longer in my high heels. Then it starts to flash back, little scenes like a slideshow. Too many vodka sodas, a sloppy taxi ride, and Coach Barry's concerned face when he walked me down the corridors of the backstage area. I let out a small groan at my embarrassing behavior. *Yes, my dad is not able to afford his insanely high bail and yes, he is probably going to prison for a very, very long time.* But the adult thing to do would have been to get good and drunk, *at home*, rather than in front of my boss and my...well, Rhett.

I find my phone in my purse and squint in confusion at the time. It's nearly midnight. *What the heck?* The fights never go on this long. Right as I'm trying to do the mental math, I hear the door slam hard on its hinges behind me. I turn to see Rhett breathing heavily, his chest covered in sweat and several large gashes peppering on his handsome face. But all of his attention is focused on me, scanning me up and down like he's trying to assess if I'm okay. If I'm hurt. Like I'm the one who's just spent several hours taking a beating under hot stage lights. *He* should be the one getting scanned by a freaking doctor right now. My heart stills at a growing line of dark red blood sliding down the left side of his face.

"Rhett, what—" I don't even know what to ask. I look frantically between Rhett and Coach Barry as he moves into the prepping room behind him and heads straight for the medical kit.

"Did you," I swallow hard, my throat painfully dry, "win?" I could've sworn I heard his name being chanted but my senses are still a bit cloudy with alcohol and sleep. *Could he have lost the fight in round five?*

"Yes." Rhett's words are harshly spoken, a tense glance exchanged between he and Coach Barry. They are clearly holding a lot back compared, silent and terse communication slipping wordlessly between them.

"Well, are you okay?" I start moving closer to him, but the tension snapping in the air stops me.

"Rhett was," Coach Barry busies himself with the medical supplies, laying out gauze and ointment on the table, "distracted."

"Enough." Rhett's tone could cut through steel. He closes the distance between us and rubs the pad of his calloused thumb along my cheek. "You feel okay?" His voice is gruff, laced with an emotion I can't name. I can see the exhaustion under his dark and bruising eyes.

"Rhett, I'm fine...I'm sorry I showed up like that, it's a long story." I nervously tuck my hair behind my ears, self-conscious that Coach is watching us like I might be to blame for Rhett's distractions this evening. "You need stitches." There's a large gash under his right eye that keeps bleeding, the wound looking like it's peeling further open with every passing second.

"Nothing out of the ordinary." He flashes me a sexy wink that looks like it hurts, and squeezes my hand as if to say *'don't worry, it's not your fault'*, which is all the evidence I need to confirm that it very damn well *is* my fault. He heads over to the medical station and Coach Barry starts cleaning his wounds, applying various creams. His movements are methodical but rough, avoiding eye contact. Rhett doesn't even flinch.

"I, uh" my voice wavers as I squat down to pick up my purse, "I should go. Shelly will come and get me." I give the men an awkward strained smile and slip out of the prepping room before anyone can protest. When the door to Rhett's prepping room is safely closed behind me, I lean my head up against it, closing my eyes and counting to ten to beg the alcohol-induced pounding in my head to stop. That's when I hear the yelling.

"You were sloppy as hell out there, Rhett!" Coach Barry's usually calm tone sounds thunderous. "You know I don't give a damn about the money, you've made more for the both of us than we could have ever imagined. I'm worried about your safety, about *you*. You *let* that guy get shots in. I know your moves. You didn't even try to stop it."

I know I should leave. Right now. I should step away from this door and give Rhett and Coach their privacy. I have my phone clenched in my hand, my finger hovering over Shelly's contact name. But I need to hear Rhett's response. I need to know if what Coach is saying is true.

"I won. That's all that fucking matters, Coach. Get off my ass." Rhett's voice is low, teeming with anger.

"I thought she was good for you," Coach Barry pauses, his voice more measured, "and I do think she's good, I really do. You know I respect the hell out of her. But whatever it is you're trying to do, she's getting to you too much. That's why it's always worked better when the women were just...platonic."

"It is platonic." Rhett's voice is a growl and I feel my heart leap into my throat, that word settling into my stomach like a lead weight. *Are we really just platonic? I mean, I guess I know that's the agreement between us but does he not feel anything more?*

Coach Barry laughs, but the humor is hollow. "No son, it's not. You care about that girl so much you don't even know your head from your ass right now. And it's going to get you killed in the ring."

Neither of them speak again for several minutes. I finally text Shelly as I walk quickly down the backstage hallway, asking her to come get me, ending my painful eavesdropping stint. I feel like I've broken my own heart, but I resolve not to break my promise to Rhett. He's a fighter. He needs me healthy and sober before his fights. Not a sloppy, drunk, slurring mess. I want whatever he'll give me, even if it won't ever be enough to fill the growing void in my chest. Being there for Rhett definitely doesn't include drunken stupors over white-collar-crime-committing fathers. And the question of figuring out how to piece myself back together again? How to move forward after it all ends, after *we* end? I'll leave that to figure that out in three weeks. After Rhett's final fight.

40

RHETT

I need to see her. Just to make sure she got home okay. Even with the additional, and admittedly *intentional*, blows in the ring tonight, my body feels like it's radiating on an electric wire. I don't feel tired at all. No sense of that usual post-fight satisfaction or peace within my own body. That's what she brings to me. Ava. She brings me peace. I try to remind myself over and over again that it's simply her body that brings me peace. That it's the mind-blowing sex, the being buried so deep inside of her I'm not even thinking about the upcoming fight, about anything but the feel her clenching around me, driving me higher and higher. But it's more than that. It's her presence. Her smell, her voice, her laugh.

But a drunk Ava with the saddest golden eyes I've ever seen? That shit doesn't bring me peace at all. It fuels a rage that I let my opponent try and squander tonight, practically begged him to beat it out of me but he couldn't. My own instincts in the ring took over, my body eclipsing my mind to win the fight. A win I hardly care about at the moment.

I slowly pull my truck into Ava and Shelly's apartment

complex parking lot. The street lights cast a strange, eerie glow over the place and I curse at the fact that these two girls live in a place like this. I mean, it could be a lot worse. I've lived in a lot worse, but knowing the comfort and security of my townhome on the other side of town makes me feel guilty having Ava live here.

I find a parking spot and am about to hop out of the cab of my truck when I spot a bright streak of red paint that is unnaturally curving around a white car door. I squint but can't quite make out what it is. I check my mirrors and slip a pocket knife from my center console into the palm of my hand. Something irksome settles in between my shoulder blades, lurching tightly in my gut. It's a sense that's saved my life many times, not one that I dismiss lightly.

I step around a few other vehicles carefully, quietly. Then I see the bright red streaks up close, covering a small white sedan. A college girl car. The windows are busted in, the rearview mirror hanging by a cord. In huge, messy red letters that look like they're written in blood it reads, "throw the fight."

"Fuck!" I can't contain my outrage. I know it's Thorne handiwork. Or at least Thorne's men. His fucking goons. Threatening Ava. Attacking her car, her goddamn property, right outside her apartment. Thorne is rumored to be my final match. I hope to God he will be so that I can bury that fucker in the ground where he belongs.

I keep cursing under my breath as I ascend the three flights of stairs to Ava's apartment, two at a time. My guess is that she hasn't already seen her car or she would've called me. But then again, maybe she wouldn't feel like she could. Perhaps she thinks that would be crossing some sort of invisible line...a line that maybe I drew in the sand with my 'ring bunny' request. But right now, it's a line that I find myself crossing willingly. I'll deal with the messiness of what that means later. Right now, I won't be able to focus on shit if I feel that Ava is unsafe.

I find the door to her apartment and knock. Shit, what if Thorne also did something to their apartment? *What if Thorne did something to her?*

I knock louder and harder, the need to see that she's okay and in one piece consuming me. I finally hear the lock in the door slide open and Shelly is standing in the doorway, her blonde hair wispy and in a bun, her eyes wide with shock.

"What the hell man, relax." Shelly tosses me a look like I'm the crazy one. This girl has some balls to stare me down like that. I watch her eyes scan over me, marking all my patches and bandages, the bruising across my face and chest. I grunt in frustration before making an attempt to move into the apartment without touching her.

"Where's Ava?" I'm standing in the middle of the small living room by the time I see her emerge from the hallway, her hair wet and her beautiful face bare. She looks slightly nauseated and freaked out by my being here, but she doesn't look harmed. I keep scanning her up and down, trying to calm my breathing with the assurance that she's fine. That Thorne hasn't touched her. But by the look of surprise on her face, I'm guessing she doesn't know about her car yet.

"Rhett? What are you doing here?" Ava's voice comes out in a rush, her eyes darting between me and Shelly. I turn to see Shelly standing with one hand on her hip and a territorial pissed look on her face. It's enough to almost warrant a broken laugh from my lips, the searing look in her eyes like she might actually try to kick my ass.

"Listen," I run my shaking hand through my hair, trying to keep my anger under control, "you need to pack a bag

and come home with me. It's not safe for you here." Ava
pulls her sweater tighter around herself, her pouty mouth
popping open with confusion and fear.

"What the hell—" Shelly comes to stand closer, posi-
tioning herself protectively between Ava and me. I cut
her off.

"You too. Call Eric. I can drop you off at his place." I
brush Shelly off like a little kid grabbing onto the back of
my shirt. Her expression doesn't give any indication that
she's backing down, but I see her move into the kitchen with
her phone in hand. Hopefully, she's texting Eric a heads up
and not the cops.

"Ava, it's your car. Thorne...tagged it." Tag is definitely
too mild of a description. Totaled, trashed, mutilated is
more accurate. But I don't need to add insult to injury. Not
when Ava's already fair pale is paling at my words, her eyes
widening with concern.

"My car?" Her voice raises a few octaves and she looks
like she's about to move toward the front door and down to
the parking lot, her eyes straying over my shoulders. I close
the distance between us, gripping her chin between my
thumb and finger to focus that terrified gaze on me.

"Ava, not now. I don't know if it's a trap or a way to get
you alone. I just," I exhale heavily, trying to collect myself, "I
need you to be with me. Where I know you're safe. Please."
Me saying the word 'please' is like hell freezing over. And
yet it slips from my lips desperately, without hesitation. I
don't beg, and I definitely don't do desperate pleas. But this
woman is under my fucking skin so deep that I'll say
anything to get her and a duffle back tucked safely into the
cab of my truck.

Ava doesn't reply. She just glances between me and
Shelly again.

"Ava," Shelly's voice is cautious, "it's probably a good idea. Eric said opponents often do stuff like this as a threat. A way to get someone to throw a fight or psyche them out." I want to roll my eyes at Shelly's obvious explanation but I hold my tongue. If Shelly's buy-in will help convince Ava to come with me, I'll take it.

"Is that true?" Ava's eyes turn to mine, her lower lip quivering slightly.

"Yes. It's fucking cowardly as shit. But, it's a tactic." I grab Ava's hand and spin her around to head back down the hallway from which she came. I pull her into a bedroom.

"Start packing, Ava." She closes her fingers tightly around my hand and gingerly pulls me into another bedroom. I guess I'd accidentally gone into Shelly's. She gets out a small duffle bag and starts filling it with items from her dresser. I feel completely out of place in the small room, everything pale lavender and delicate. It smells like her, sweet and floral and perfect. She leaves for a moment and comes back with a travel bag from the bathroom.

"Okay, ready." She looks up at me with nervous eyes, her duffle bag sitting on the edge of the bed. I don't have the right words to comfort her. I never fucking do, especially not now. I pull her into my chest, my hand lightly gripping the back of her head before tilting her face back up to mine. I kiss her fully. Not violently like we've done in the past before fights, but with an all-consuming fervor that neither of us can deny. It's ownership and protection and an apology that she's in this situation because of me. I want to comfort her, to put her at ease, but I also know I'm doing it for me. I *need* it. To feel her warm and tender and unharmed beneath my lips. Her tongue locks with mine, her fingers digging greedily into the back of my head as she stretches up on her toes. When she finally breaks away, we are both breathless, her cheeks flushed a rosy pink.

"Let's go." I give her one last gruff kiss on the temple before tossing her duffle bag over my shoulder. I don't let go of her hand until she's safely tucked into the cab of my truck, my eyes scanning the parking lot every inch of the way.

41

AVA

There is something entirely different about coming to Rhett's apartment this time compared to the last time I was here. As we pull into the driveway, I feel a flush spread from my cheeks down to the front of my chest at the memory of our first time having sex. It was desperate and wild, full of pent-up frustration and unspoken emotions. Only to end in complete awkwardness thanks to my misunderstanding of Leila's texts. But this time, everything feels more deliberate and serious. I don't know how much of Rhett's protectiveness is about me versus just feeling guilty for my car getting damaged by Thorne's men. Either way, the butterflies have swarmed into my stomach, more slowly and more cautiously than before. *How long am I supposed to stay here with him? Is Thorne's threat really that serious?*

Rhett puts his truck in park and grabs my duffle bag with ease from the backseat. When he comes around to the passenger side door, he gives me a look of light-hearted frustration.

"Are you overthinking your car or the fact that you're

moving in with me?" His eyes have a hint of playfulness that I so rarely get to see from him but his face is still serious.

"Moving in with you?!" My voice is a near shriek as my mouth pops open in shock at his words. And even though I'm insanely caught off guard by what he just said, the idea nestles into the very back, dark corners of my mind a little too comfortably.

"Just for the next few weeks, I mean." He brushes off my embarrassing misinterpretation with a quick wink as he slings my duffle bag over his broad shoulders. Once inside, he sets the bag down on the couch in his living room and starts busying himself in the kitchen. Despite my previous nerves at having him barge into my apartment earlier, I feel my stomach growl at the thought of another one of Rhett's home-cooked meals.

"Hungry?" Rhett shoots me a look, his dark eyebrow arched, as he leans against his island with a kitchen towel slung over his shoulder, making him look ten times sexier. *How is that even possible?* Rhett in a boxing ring is already too insanely hot for me to handle but Rhett in the kitchen? I feel myself dangerously close to another free fall zone with him, one that ended in awkwardness and miscommunication the last time.

"Starving." I answer honestly, my stomach in desperate need of sustenance after the few-too-many vodka sodas I'd downed earlier to drown out the thoughts of my dad. Rhett's gaze lingers on my face a moment too long, like he's trying to read every thought in my expression before he finally turns back to the stove. I make my way over to the luxurious kitchen island counter, sitting down on one of the large, masculine barstools.

"So," I attempt to break the silence as Rhett makes quick work of expertly chopping some vegetables, the knife moving like magic, "how bad is it? My car I mean." He looks up at me under his brows but doesn't stop methodically moving his knife across the wooden cutting board.

"It's bad. But nothing that can't be fixed with insurance." He starts mixing the various vegetables in a large pot, the simmering sound so domestic I feel a small crack in my chest at the normalcy of it.

"Right." Then a sense of realization and dread washes over me. *Shit, my insurance! My dad always paid my monthly insurance bill. I don't even know if I've still been covered since his arrest.* "Oh, shit." I say the curse under my breath but it doesn't elude Rhett's notice.

"What?" He looks up from the pot, his dark brows pinching together.

"Uh, nothing. Never mind." I plaster a weak smile on my face, my head suddenly feeling heavy and tired with the oncoming wave of yet another stress, but he doesn't fall for it.

"You're a bad liar, Ava. Tell me." He pulls the kitchen towel from his shoulder and sets it on the counter, my eyes tracking the simple movement, getting lost in the corded veins in his forearms that trail deliciously up his unattainably defined biceps...

"Ava." His voice is stern but laced with male amusement. I snap my gaze up to his, a subtle smirk pulling at the corners of his mouth. Obviously, he caught me checking him out. Great. I sigh deeply and offer him the truth.

"I don't know if I still have insurance. I mean, I know I used to have it but my dad handled all that stuff, and then when he—" I cut myself off realizing I haven't told Rhett anything about my dad. About how my life took a complete one-eighty just a few months ago. Other than seeing him at the AA meeting with me, where my dad was less than cordial, Rhett has no idea about what happened. About the lies my father built, the people he misled for years.

And considering this *thing* between us is ending in a few short weeks, it's likely best to keep it that way. No point in burdening him with it, staining the limited time we have let together. I don't want to see pity in his dark eyes when he looks at me. I'm not sure I can handle that from him.

"Do you want to talk about it?" Rhett's voice is measured, not forceful. I can tell he's letting me set the pace on this topic. The realization makes me want to reach for him. Knowing that if I say 'yes' he will listen but if I say 'no' he won't push me on it.

"Not really." I reach over and pop a piece of raw carrot from his cutting board into my mouth and try to convey my gratitude at him not pushing the topic with my eyes. I don't want my father's drama hanging over me here. In Rhett's home. Where it's just us.

"Fair. But if you need help with your car, just tell me. It's my fault that it's damaged in the first place." He gives me a pointed look as if to say 'don't push me on this' and I simply nod in agreement. I don't need to voice the fact that it would be a cold day in hell before I ever ask Rhett for money. *I'm so deep in new debt at this point, what's a new car in the mix anyway?* The thought weighs heavily in my chest but I push it aside. I have the rest of my life to worry about my new financial situation.

"Where'd you learn to cook so well?" I lean up further on the counter, inadvertently pushing out my breasts a bit and letting my long hair fall over my shoulders. Rhett's growl at the subtle movement is almost imperceptible, but I *feel* it more than I hear it. His gaze nearly searing me as he tracks my body.

"In the kitchen. Where else?" He starts adding more

spices to the pot, the fragrant, delicious smell spreading throughout the space.

"That's not what I meant, Rhett. I *meant*, who taught you?" I reach for another carrot and he gently slaps my hand away.

"I taught myself. If you train like I do, you can't eat like shit. You have to eat real food and it doesn't taste good unless you learn how to cook it right."

"No mother or grandmother who taught you all their top-secret family recipes?" I strive for playful but I can tell the question strikes an uncomfortable chord with Rhett, his dark eyes nearly shuttering.

"No." His response is clipped as stares into the bubbling steel pot on the stove, not offering any further explanation.

"Do you want to talk about it?" My tone is slightly sarcastic and a sexy-as-sin smile curls his lips before he looks back at me.

"Not really."

"Fair." I mirror his response to me and he lets out a deep laugh, the sound reverberating throughout my body, settling deep and warm in my bones. Even though I've had sex with this man several times now, there's something far more intimate about this kind of playfulness and ease in his own kitchen. Like it really is just *us* and not all the stress about the fights and my future and what will happen when it's all over.

"Come try this." He crooks his finger at me and I get up from the kitchen stool to round the center island. He takes a spoonful of steaming liquid from the pot and blows on it lightly before bringing the spoon to my lips. I look up at him as I take the spoon in my mouth, never breaking eye contact. The flavors that explode on my tongue are delicious. An earthy, rich, beef stew with fresh vegetables and herbs. But there's another hunger in my expression too, and I see it mirrored on Rhett's face.

"Food first." Rhett grunts in response to that unspoken need unfurling between us. Although a small part of me flutters with concern at what this might meant for our arrangement since it isn't technically before a fight. I'd woefully failed in that promise earlier, sending Rhett out into the ring, distracted and wound-up. Because of me.

Selfishly my body is screaming *hell yes*, that I won't be able to not crawl on top of him the moment we're done eating. That there's no way I can resist what's been building and crashing and building again between us when we're near one another.

But I also knew that Rhett suffers from addictions, his own inner demons, that I still don't fully understand. Maybe having sex again at his apartment, outside of the confines of before a fight, will tip him over the edge to do something he's going to regret...

"Ava," he sets the spoon down and grabs my chin in his hand, "stop overthinking this. Nothing has changed. There's still the next round of upcoming fights, the agreement, and *us*. You're just here, in my kitchen, eating dinner. Please." His eyes are wary, straining against more that he wants to say. "I want this to feel normal. Even if it's just for tonight." His words are spoken in a low and desperate tone. It's like his mind is racing with all the same thoughts as mine but he's begging one of us to be the first to stop. To just *be*.

I lean up on my toes and kiss him lightly on the lips, the softest I ever have, using my actions instead of my words to promise him that I'll try. To not overthink, to not worry, to just be here with him.

"Let's eat."

42

RHETT

I'm playing with fire. The delicate, feminine, yet powerful all-consuming fire that is Ava.

I know there is depth to this beautiful woman, along with something broken that calls out to me. But that area is off-limits territory. For her and for me. I don't do heart-to-hearts and emotional sharing. Of course, I would've let Ava tell me about her dad if she wanted to because at this point I'm dangerously close to letting this woman do or say whatever the hell she wants around me.

But a large part of me was also relieved that she didn't care to share more. Not because I don't want to learn more about her, but because *I do*. I want to know everything about this girl, her dreams her goals, anyone who's ever hurt her so I can crush them between my fists. And even though she didn't give much away, I know her drunken stupor before my last fight has something to do with whatever shit is going on with her dad. The judgmental ass who looked me up and down at the AA meeting like I was lower than dirt. Not worthy of even having a cup of coffee with his daughter. Not that I entirely disagree with him. Ava is and will always be too good for me which is why I've designed everything about our engagement to let her go. But a wave of male pride builds up in my chest thinking of all that Ava and I have done together...a hell of a lot more than sharing a damn cup of coffee...

I snap my thoughts into focus, pushing away images of her lithe, naked body under mine. The lines are blurring, now more than ever, and after tonight I'll need to rein it back in. Or I'll be at risk of doing something so egregious that she'll hate me forever.

I've learned over the years that sexual addiction is complicated. It's not even recognized formally as an addiction by some groups, unlike my very real and painful history with cocaine. But for me, the sex just leads to my unraveling. To a series of compulsive behaviors: random women, drugs, alcohol, fights outside of the ring, repeat. It's like putting one foot over the edge and then suddenly racing towards the bottom of the mountain with no means of stopping. I never want Ava to feel like she's my tipping point. I never want to ruin the intense and insanely amazing feelings that come from her touch, from her lips, from being buried deep inside of her. Even if it means that it can't last forever. And that eventually, she'll find someone who can treat her right. Someone who is worthy of her. She deserves that. And I'll be damned if I do anything to stand her in way.

But right now, this gorgeous girl is in my kitchen, taking a wooden spoon in her mouth like it's my cock. I try to tamper down the blood rushing from my brain to focus on getting through dinner first. I've barely even touched my meal.

"Mmm, Rhett, this is really freaking good." Ava takes another generous mouthful of stew and unbidden approval spreads across her pretty face. My skills in the kitchen only heightened by her extreme lack of any cooking prowess.

"I'm glad you like it." I finally turn to my food, knowing I need to eat. I still keep a watchful eye on her, relieved that she finally seems relaxed and at peace here after the jarring events of this evening. I'll sleep easier tonight knowing she's with me and not somewhere where Thorne's men can touch her. God, what I'd do to them if they tried.

"What's wrong?" Ava looks up at me, her bowl empty. Clearly she didn't miss the change in my expression at the thought of Thorne.

"Nothing." I shake my head, not wanting to go there. Odds are that he'll attempt a few more threatening tactics before the final fight in three weeks. And I don't want her even more scared tonight. It can wait.

"Well..." Ava looks between the kitchen and the open-air living room that adjoins it. "What should we do now?" She aims for innocent but her body says anything but. I roll my eyes at her and start clearing our plates from the counter.

"Watch a movie." I keep my back to her as I load the dishwasher.

"Watch a movie? I have to say, I can't picture *you* just sitting and watching a movie. It seems so...docile." She laughs at her own comment as I turn back to face her. I can't keep my eyes from trailing down her body. It doesn't matter how many times I've had her. Seen her naked. It was never enough. She's slender but firm and strong, with curves in all the right places. I'm fucking hooked.

Like a drug. The voice pops into my head and I mentally curse at it, wanting that voice far, far away from anything to do with Ava.

"I don't normally watch movies, but I could try one. Tonight." *Just tonight.* I know I'm acting like some bitch-ass boyfriend, cooking her dinner and wanting to sit down and cuddle on the couch. What I really want is to be buried so deep inside of her that we both forget our own names. But I'm trying here to do the right thing.

"Can I choose the movie?" She curls her feet under her bare legs on the couch and pulls a soft, gray blanket over her lap. I don't think I've ever even used that blanket before.

"Sure, as long as it's not some stupid chick-flick bullshit."

"What?" Her voice raises a few octaves in mock outrage. "That's like, all of my choices." I laugh and wipe my hands on the kitchen towel before making my way over to join her.

"What about James Bond or something adventurous?" She asks me the question as I slide in next to her, my hands slowly roaming over her thighs under the blanket. Her breath hitches as her eyes drop to my mouth but I don't lean in to kiss her like I want to. I just stay still, pulling her onto my lap, our faces inches apart.

"James Bond is a classic." My voice is lower, deeper. I watch Ava's delicate throat move as she swallows.

"Rhett..."Her voice trails off but there's a war between desire and fear in her golden eyes. Fear for me. I hate it.

"I'm fine." I run my hand through my hair, resenting that she's so worried about what her proximity might do to me. I know she doesn't understand it fully, sometimes I still grasp at it. And I haven't even had a chance to try and articulate for her what my addictions are like and how they might be different from whatever she's assuming in that pretty head of hers.

"Is this a good idea?" Ava presses on, her voice gentle. "I mean, I promised you I'd be good with only having sex before your fights."

"Who said we're having sex?" I smirk back at her, trying to lighten the mood and she slaps me playfully on the shoulder. We stare at each for a few, long moments, our breath quickening.

"Let me show you that I can control myself. I'll make you feel good. Just you." I dip my head toward Ava's neck, my voice relaying a promise I sure as hell hope I can actually keep.

"Rhett..." She doesn't finish her sentence as my teeth latch onto the soft spot behind her ear, a sexy as hell moan escaping her lips. I move my mouth to cover hers, pulling at her full bottom lip until she's moving her body over mine, straddling my hips on the couch, the blanket wrapped around her waist. The kiss is slow, powerful. We alternate giving the other control. Unlike before my fights, we have all the time in the world. Or at least, we have all of tonight. I'd savor it.

I move my hand up under her shirt, palming her breasts. Without breaking our kiss, I reach behind her and slide one of the couch pillows into a better position.

"Lie down." My tone is commanding but not forceful. I speak the words against her lips, as she slides off of my lap and onto her back, her head resting on the pillow. I start kissing her neck, her collar bone, pulling her shirt up to reveal her sexy pale blue bra. She makes small feminine noises as her hands grip harder into the hair at the back of my head.

I move down lower and glance up at her as I unbuckle her jeans. Her cheeks are flushed, so perfectly roses, her lips parted in anticipation. She looks half sweet, half sex goddess. It's the perfect combination. As I slide the denim down her legs, she wiggles roughly, trying to speed up the process.

"Patience, Ava. It's a virtue." I laugh darkly as I chide her eagerness and she grabs my hair even harder in response. I break our eye contact and focus my attention back on Ava's body. She's writhing on the couch and I use one hand to hold her hips down. I kiss her gently over her lace underwear, earning another garbled plea from her sweet mouth. "Patience." The word is muffled by my mouth over the lace fabric and I start to pull her underwear down slowly, not taking it completely off her legs.

I part her thighs further, settling between her legs and running my tongue through her tender slick skin. Ava bows her back up off the leather couch, groaning out in pleasure. I lick her again, deeper this time, and feel the heat flooding to my cock at her soft folds and sweet moans. I pull my body up a few inches and place both of my palms on either side of her hips, holding her down tighter to intensify the sensation. I can tell that she's building, getting closer with each swipe of my mouth against her heat. She tastes like heaven, and a thought rips through me that I could lay her forever, tasting her.

Finally she comes undone, my fingers joining my mouth in slow, unyielding circles as she yells out mangled phrases that sound like a combination of my name and a whole lot of gibberish in between. I want to keep licking her as she rides out her orgasm but I also want to watch her body come apart beneath me. I lean up on my elbows, watching her beautiful face contort with pleasure until she finally opens her heavy-lidded golden eyes and stares back up at me.

I delicately slide her panties back up over her thighs to her apex and lift her hips to pull them all the way on. Then I sit up and drag her back onto my lap. There's no way in hell she can't feel my raging erection, straining against my jeans. But I won't act on it. God, how I want to. Any man would. But I want to prove to her, prove to myself, that I'm not going to go off the rails. That Ava, the most temptation I've ever been faced with, is worth the effort of restraint. That I can please her without needing my own release. Without spiraling into other temptations and addictions. That seeing her come apart, her beautiful body reach orgasm, is enough. *More* than enough.

"That was," her tone is breathless, almost reverent, her hands still threading softly through my hair, "amazing. I never liked *that* before." She wrinkles her perfect nose and I chuckle in response.

"Best dessert I've ever had." I lick my bottom lip and she nearly squeals in embarrassment, her cheeks flaming.

"You did NOT just say that, Rhett." She hides her face in my shoulder but can't keep the smile from curling her lips. "And for the record, the best dessert is definitely ice cream."

I laugh at the seriousness with which she asserts ice cream as the best dessert even though I can think of a thousand reasons she's wrong. I scoop her up into my arms before she realizes what's happening.

"I might just have some in the freezer." Her arms grip around my neck as I walk us into the kitchen, pulling a carton from the freezer along with two spoons. We don't say anything else when we sit back down on the couch. I pull her onto my lap and she starts playing a James Bond movie on the TV. If we say anything else, we'll risk ruining this moment. We'll risk asking a question that neither of us want the answer to. Because we know this is dangerous. We know that with each moment in each other's arms like this we are making the inevitable end even harder than it already is. But we can't stop. Not yet.

43

AVA

I look at my hair and makeup for what feels like the thousandth time in Shelly's car mirror before forcing myself to take a deep breath and stop procrastinating. I'm sitting in the parking lot of my college's admissions building, warring with myself about whether or not I really want to do this.

Tonight is Rhett's final fight. The biggest match of the eight-week event. The epic and highly betted on battle against none other than Thorne. Just thinking of him, his claim over me during his fight against Eric, and his attack on my car makes a shiver crawl up my spine. Needless to say to the matchup between Rhett and Thorne is a big night for the underground fighting world, especially with more rumors swirling about Rhett's retirement. But for me, tonight just marks the end. Tomorrow morning I'll have to wake up and accept that what Rhett and I have will be over. These whirlwind months of sleeping in Shelly's spare room, working as an assistant at the gym, and having insanely mind-blowing sex that former me could have never even imagined.

Right after my father's arrest, all I wanted was to stay in school, finish my degree, and not be ghosted by all of my college friends. But now, my life feels so different. *I* feel so different. Part of me wonders if I'll even be able to go back to school, or if too much has happened for me to be able to re-assimilate into a shell of my old life. I shake the thought away as it rears its head. It has only been a few months since my life blew up, even though it feels like so much longer. And there is no way that I can keep working at the gym with Rhett retiring. With our arrangement ending. It will just feel like I'm surrounded by memories of his ghost, everything reminding me of him. It's pathetic but I know I won't survive it. Tomorrow I have to be ready to take the first step toward changing everything. Again.

Shelly wishes me luck as I grab my manila packet and head up the small flight of granite steps into the impressive admissions building. I wait patiently for my appointment to be called before being led into a small, cozy office with a plush guest chair. I take a seat and cross and uncross my legs nervously. So far I haven't seen anyone I know but the longer I'm on campus, the more certain running into an old acquaintance will be. It isn't a big university and everyone knows each other. Well, everyone knows *me*, after my father's nightly-news-worthy fiasco, is a better way of putting it. I still haven't heard much from Jacob except a few texts on occasion but I figure it'll be easier to let everyone know I'm coming back once it's official. Right now, I still need to understand what my options for graduating even are with respect to credits and tuition fees.

"Hi, Ava, so nice to see you." A kind-looking woman with pale blue eyes sits at the desk across from me and pulls up my file on her computer. She delicately places a pair of glasses on the bridge of her nose, her eyebrows pinching together as she focuses intently on whatever information is on the screen.

"So, it looks like you may be looking to re-enroll and finish your degree?" She clasps her hands politely, her expression a mix of eagerness and pity. Great, even she knows my story.

"Yes," I clear my throat, "I'd like to better understand what my options are with regard to still graduating on time and tuition fees." She gives me a polite nod and pulls out a course list from her desk drawer, sliding it towards me so that I can read it with her.

"I think you have a few options. If you continue with marketing, you are about a quarter behind but that could be made up with summer classes or taking on one extra class per quarter for the next three sessions." She uses her pen to indicate the courses she's referencing on the sheet of paper between us. "Or, if you've changed interests, say maybe you want to study business, you could apply most of your existing credits and extend your studies by a quarter or two. We have a great internal scholarship program for bright students like yourself within the business school." She offers a tight-lipped smile, her tone subtly implying that I can't really afford *not* to look into a scholarship-enabled transfer into the school's business program since that might be my only way of graduating without a mountain of crippling debt. I've never applied for any aid or loans, something I'm now realizing I've taken entirely for granted.

"Okay, thank you. I'll look into it and think on it." I've never really thought about studying business before, but I also never thought I'd sit front-row at a series of underground boxing fights watching the man I've somehow fallen for for beat another man to a bloody pulp. So, never say never I suppose.

"Fantastic! Here is the information packet," she pulls a large printed pamphlet from under her desk and slides it my way, "and the deadline to enroll is in two weeks, but the sooner the better! With your grades and recommendations, I think you'd be a top candidate for the scholarship. I'd be happy to help you put everything together." Her smile is brighter now, more hopeful. It's nice to have someone so willing to help me, but there is still a strong pang in my chest at the realization that this is really happening. My life is going back. Something I so desperately wanted before is now feeling like a hollow obligation.

I force a bright smile back and take the packet, promising myself that this is the first critical task in putting one foot in front of the other. My dad is more than likely going to prison for many, many years and a college degree will be the best way for me to take care of myself in the longterm. I have always loved school, especially the cama-raderie and university events...I'd somehow find that love again. I'll just need some time. Right?

"Thank you again. I'll be in touch soon after I review the paperwork and application." I gather my things and quickly exit the office, texting Shelly to let her know that I'll be back outside in a few.

—

I'm silent during the drive back and Shelly doesn't push me on it, her natural tendency to badger me with questions thankfully kept at bay. My head feels like it's underwater, swimming with thoughts, with realities that I'm just not ready to face. The past few weeks at Rhett's have been hard to describe. After the first night, things were more tense and formal. Rhett put up walls that were only taken down when we had sex before a fight. I'd catch him looking at me over the kitchen island or meet his dark gaze in the mirror above the double bathroom vanity, his dark eyes looking like he had far more to say than he'd allow himself to express. But he wouldn't open up. And in return, I didn't either. It was like we were both acutely aware of each other's presence at all times, sometimes drawing closer and other times keeping our distance for fear of doing something out of line with rules that didn't even seem to make sense anymore. His touch was becoming more and more like a drug, a high that I could never fulfill my need for, and even I've begun to understand the value of keeping what we have in a box; otherwise it threatens to break *both* us when it falls apart.

Once Shelly parks the car outside our apartment, I haul my duffle bag up the flight of outdoor stairs to her unit. Surprisingly and thankfully, Thorne hasn't attempted anything else after my car before the big fight. Although with tonight being the big event, we are all on high alert. Shelly told me when she picked me up from Rhett's that Rhett had a word with Eric at the gym, asking him to keep an extra pair of eyes out for me anytime I'm not in Rhett's sight. My stomach knots as I set the duffle back bag down in Shelly's spare room, surrounded by my feminine belongings. The image of Rhett being here, demanding I pack quickly, kissing me with an urgency that conveyed his concern, floods back into my memory. Suddenly I want to be back in Rhett's bedroom where everything is large, dark, and masculine just like him. I force myself to go through the motions and admit that this was the plan all along. I'll stay at Shelly's for another week or two after the fight and then move back to campus.

"Which dress should I wear tonight?" I hear Shelly call out from her bedroom. She saunters into my doorway, holding up two impossibly short stresses with will both look amazing on her. She promised she'd come with me to Rhett's final fight tonight and I know it's a big moment for her since it will be her first time back in the underground arena after Eric's near-death experience. He will be joining also of course, both as a spectator and informally as my bodyguard.

"Hey, what's wrong? You look like someone just stole your candy." Shelly sits down on the edge of the bed next to me as I start to reluctantly unpack my duffle bag. I don't respond. I feel like the knot in my throat is the only thing keeping my emotions at bay. Keeping the tears from falling. If I try to open it, the floodgates will rush out. "Ava," Shelly rubs my back gently, "talk to me."

I open my mouth, a shallow sob coming out. "Ugh, Shelly." I put my head in my hands and give in. "I'm just...I'm going to miss him. So much. I didn't think..." My voice trails off and I look at her with tear-stricken eyes. "I didn't think it'd be like this. I thought it would be an adventure, something wild for me to do and then I'd be done, you know? I'd miss my old life. I'd be ready to go back. But I don't miss it all. I feel...I feel so lost." My chest heaves lightly but I keep my composure more intact than I'd expect.

"It's been a wild couple of months, hasn't it?" Shelly strokes my hair, her voice gentle. "But Ava, you love school. And you love going to your university. I promise, it will work out. It's just been a lot of adjustment and back and forth. Rhett..." she looks off into the hallway, clearly trying to find the right words to say, "he's complicated. And intense. I think you always knew this wouldn't be forever. I mean, Rhett isn't the kind of guy you marry or something." She laughs lightly, no malice in her tone. "You want a career, and babies, and all that good stuff that comes from having a college degree and working hard and giving back." She smiles at me before standing and kissing me on the cheek. "I think this has been good for you. All of it. You've grown so much! I mean, you're no longer daddy's little pampered girl. You're like this independent boss who takes risks and figures her shit out. Now it's time to take that new Ava energy back to school, get your degree, and do whatever you want with your life." She pauses a moment before proceeding. "I've always wished I was as smart as you. I was never good with that book smarts stuff." She gives me a brief, wistful smile before standing up and clapping her hands together.

"Okay, enough with the mature, adult talk! We are getting full-on glam and the perfect level of tipsy tonight. This fight is a major event, and we are two VIP ladies!" She shimmies and I laugh at how silly she looks. I wipe at the few stray tears brimming in my eyes and nod in agreement. If tonight is really my last night in this underground fighting world, *and it is*, then I better make sure to enjoy the heck out of it.

44

RHETT

Every final round event has another level of arena energy. It's like my body is somehow tethered to the crowd, more intimately in sync with the excitement and vibration of the audience than during any other fight.

But tonight is even more elevated for me. It's not just my last fight in the series. It's my last fight. *Ever.* It will be the last time I tape up both of my hands with my dark red silk slung low over my head and walk down the dark corridor that ends in blinding lights and roaring fans with nothing separating me from the overwhelming energy but the ropes on all four sides. I am ready. It's been a long time coming. I have no regrets. Well, none about ending my fighting career.

I do have one soon-to-be regret in the form of a living, breathing, impossibly perfect goddess. *Ava.* I know it in my bones that she will be the one that got away. That one woman that men always talk about from their past. I used to think that shit was stupid, childish. But I get it now. I get it so much know it hurts in my chest, as painful as a punch.

And even still, I'd rather let her go than drag her down with me.

My body needs the fighting to end. It's starting to break and crack at my joints, splintering deep within my spine. I look the part of a strong, virulent fighter but my insides can't take anymore beating. The constant abuse. My body needs the fighting to end but my mind has no idea what I'm supposed to do next. *Who* I'm supposed to be next. I still have no clue what my life is going to look like without fighting. It's been my rock, my center, my foundation. The only vice keeping me from all other vices. Ironically, fighting has been my salvation and my safe space. I'm going to have to find a new normal. Not an easy task for a past addict in his early thirties with dangerous proclivities. That'd be a journey for my eyes and my eyes only, and not something I want to burden Ava with. She needs to go back to school, to move on with her dreams, to meet a normal, fucking strait-laced guy with a desk job and good habits. *God, the thought guts me.* I feel my mood start to sour when the door to my prepping room cracks open.

Ava is standing in the doorway, a sweet but seductive smile on her lips. She's wearing a knockout electric blue halter dress, accentuating everyone of her curves in all the right places. Her hair is styled in long, loose waves and her makeup is more prominent than normal. I feel the blood instantly rush to my cock, but force myself not to move toward her. I need to memorize this moment. Take it in exactly as it exists in front of me. Imprint it on my memory. Be able to reference it for years to come. She is so fucking gorgeous.

"Are you nervous?" She slips further into the room, closing the door shut behind her, and I still don't move. My heart rate picks up and I track her every movement with equally lust-filled but wary eyes.

"No." I keep my eyes focused on her, dragging my gaze up and down her body. Memorizing.

"Well I am." She slides her palms up my bare chest, her earlier confidence giving way slightly to the more shy and genuine side of her that I've come to know and adore.

"Why's that?" I slide my hands down her sides, my voice lowering.

"I mean, it's your final fight...it's a big deal. I don't want you to lose." Her honey eyes widen with real concern. I can't keep a quick dark laugh from escaping past my lips.

"I'm not going to lose, Ava." I pull her head gently toward mine, cupping the back of her neck, "but it's nice to know you have so little confidence in me." My tone is teasing and she rolls her eyes in response before a serious expression marks her pretty features.

"Kick Thorne's ass, Rhett." I smile at the sass and determination in her voice. She's sexy as hell when she's giving me orders.

"Oh, I plan on it." I pull her bottom lip with my teeth, forcing myself to take my time, to savor her slowly. But after a few moments, we are already clawing at each other, unable to restrain ourselves. I stand from the couch and back her up until she's flush against the wall, my hands on either side of her head. My gaze is darting wildly between her eyes and her lips and I feel myself racing towards something critical, something life altering, that I can't quite name.

"Don't say anything." Ava's voice is quiet, a near plea, her soft hand grazing my jaw. I don't know how she can read my expression so clearly but I just nod in response, not really sure exactly what I'm agreeing to not saying anyway, but knowing that neither of us wants to ruin *this*. Our final time together. She's been my ring bunny the entire series, although we are way beyond that technicality at this point. She's been my *person*, my *partner*, during these past eight weeks. I know I care about her too much, and a part of me hates to admit that Coach Barry might have been right. But caring about her also means I want what's best for her. And what's best for Ava is definitely *not* me.

"You're overthinking, Rhett." Ava tilts her head at me and I squint my eyes in response, recognizing the teasing in her voice since I'm usually the one always telling *her* that she's overthinking things. I move in closer, my lips moving against hers as I speak.

"Then distract me." She doesn't miss a beat at my request as she palms my cock over my shorts, an animalistic groan clawing from the back of my throat at the friction. I keep my palms on the wall, letting her control me. She takes my heavy cock out of my shorts, gripping it in her hand, stroking it hard just the way I like. She knows my body and exactly how to make me lose my fucking mind. Just like I know hers.

She kisses me gently, matching her tongue with the stroke of her hand until I feel myself building forcefully, too close to coming without being inside of her. I take one hand off the wall and slip it under the hem of her dress, massaging her clit over her panties. Within seconds we are both moaning, sounds of near pain at the mutual delay of our pleasure. I shove her panties to the side and lift her thighs up and around my waist, my fingers digging in to her silky soft skin. She's still holding onto my cock and without breaking eye contact, she guides me to her opening, sinking down slowly, fully, until I'm seated deeply inside of her.

"Christ," my voice is garbled, "your pussy was made for

me, Ava." She doesn't respond with words. Instead, she starts to move, raising herself up slowly over my cock before falling back down. I don't push her or try to control her speed. I let her set the pace, working herself against my hardness to find her pleasure. I feel my thighs quake at the restraint, trying to hold out as long as I can before I start to move. *Really move,* inside of her.

The sounds of our fucking reverberate through the prepping room, her moans in my ear driving me wild, my hips bucking into her as I lose control, one hand on the wall to balance myself as I drive us toward release.

When I come, it's the most powerful release I can remember. I lean my forearms up against the wall for support, my body shuddering with orgasm as Ava moans through her release loudly in my ear, her sex gripping me from the inside, the noise impossibly sexy and uninhibited.

"You're like a drug, Rhett." Ava whispers breathlessly in my ear, her body languid as her slightly sweaty forehead rests against my shoulder.

"Back at you, Ava." I kiss her temple lightly, helping slide her legs back down to the floor. Our gaze is sated as our eyes lock, just staring at one another, memorizing the look on each other's faces as the roaring of the crowd breaks through our sex-induced haze, the floor beneath our feet nearly vibrating with the power of it.

It's time for the fight.

45

AVA

The arena floor feels like the very core of the Earth, rumbling violently like the base of a volcano. There is no denying the elevated sense of energy tonight. It's different, more potent, and equally more dangerous. I allow my senses to take in the sights, the sounds, the smells, and I store them all deep within my memory. This will be the stuff I tell my kids or my grandkids about someday. The adventures of my youth. Shelly is right. I can enjoy this for what it was, for what it has been, and still pursue the professional career goals and dreams I've always had. My life doesn't have to unfold as one straight line from start to finish. These past few months with Rhett have certainly been one heck of a zig-zag that I'll never forget or regret.

"Ava!" Shelly grabs my arm as I find my seat and she pulls me into a tight hug with a squeal. It's so refreshing seeing her back here in the underground as her usual herself instead of as a nervous, deathly pale mess. Eric is already seated and he grunts at me in greeting. He still hasn't grown on me much, but at least he will be keeping an eye out for any of Thorne's men if they try to pull something during the fight. I don't miss the way his eyes scan clear across the ring, his face taut with concentration.

"This is wild!" I whisper-yell at Shelly like we are teenage girls again, sneaking into adult movies or stealing a little bit of alcohol from my dad's liquor cabinet. This whole event feels naughty, just outside the lines of the law, and bursting at the seams with energy. Not to mention the flush-worthy memory of Rhett and me just a few minutes ago, our bodies flush up against the wall, unable to quell our physical attraction to each other anytime it's just the two of us.

I swivel to scan the growing crowd as more and more fans fill the arena. There is a real possibility that the fight could get busted. My heart races at the thought but Rhett has already told me a million times that the cops are usually in on the fights, especially with betting stakes as high as they are tonight. Still, the adrenaline coursing through my veins feels potent and like a force of its own. I can see the same wild expression reflected back at me in Shelly's eyes.

"It's the biggest fight we've ever been to! So, how's the star of the show? Does he seem like he's in a good head space?" Shelly's expression turns serious and I almost roll my eyes at her questioning.

"Are you a Chief Second now?" She jabs me in the shoulder at my sassy response, accusing her of thinking she's basically Coach Barry.

"Well, look at you with all the new lingo." Shelly flips her blonde hair over her shoulder and we both laugh, knowing full well that is *not* the case.

The music starts pounding steadily, a pressure building in the crowded space. I turn around in my seat to see the arena packed full of guests, individuals blurring together into one amorphous mass. It makes me grateful to be up in the front near the ring where we have a little more breathing room. The rumors are really started to swirl that this is Rhett's last fight night and I notice a sea of signs with his name on it, women already screaming his name even though the start time hasn't even been called yet. I don't feel jealousy at seeing all the female fans. I feel something deeper, more painful. Something less selfish. Like I'm letting him go because I have to, *we* have to, and there's already a more than willing throng of women just waiting for him to slip out of my grasp. Not that very many people even knew about us. Especially considering there won't be anything *to know* after tonight.

"Are you, you know, good?" Shelly gives me a gentle nudge and I nod emphatically in return, but I know I'm desperately shoving things down. I'm actually grateful for my classes starting up again soon. They will be a welcome distraction, especially if I get into the business school program. I'll have more than enough to learn to keep me busy and to put this world, put *him*, behind me.

"Anti-ladies and corrupt gentlemen..." The announcer's voice blares out through the arena, low and dramatic. He's dressed in an elegant black suit, his silver hair swept luxuriously to the side. His coiffed style looks so out of place among the brusque, harsh violence.

"Tonight is the night you have all been waiting for, especially the ladies..." The announcer is cut off by a deafening wave of female screams, but his smile and expression reveal that he already knew that was coming, patience spreading over his face. One woman somehow breaks through the surface of the fan noise and can be heard screaming, *"Rhett, put a baby in me!"* so loudly that even I can't help the laugh from bubbling past my lips. Shelly and I throw our heads back in a fit of true, unbridled laughter. Finally, the room settles back down enough for the announcer to continue.

"Tonight, we have the fan-favorite versus the anti-favorite. A rematch many of have been waiting on for years. It will be a ten-round event. Finish placing your bets now. May the best man win!" The crowd goes absolutely insane and I put a hand to my chest, unable to discern my own heartbeat from the roaring that fills every square inch of the arena.

"Without further ado...the famous, the infamous, the best of the best, the bloodiest winner in Boston...Rhett, fucking, Jaggar!" I stand up from my chair, Shelly and I gripping onto each other for support until she starts jumping up and down like a maniac. It's as if Rhett is some rockstar that she's had a crush on for years instead of a fighter that's literally been in her living room on multiple occasions; visits that Shelly hadn't been a fan of one bit at the time. The blonde hypocrite.

"You're going insane!" I yell at her to try and make my voice heard over the arena.

"This IS insane! Don't be a stick in the mud!" She grabs my arm harder, both of us jumping up and down now, my feet protesting in my heels.

Rhett steps out from the long walkway into the ring, the harsh shadows from the overhead spotlights and the silk of his red cape obscuring his face. I stop jumping. I feel like I stop breathing. All of the chaos around me fades to the back of my awareness. My gaze and my body zero in on him as he slips the silk off of his head and reveals himself fully to the crowd. The noise somehow ratchets higher, but it doesn't register. It's just him, and me.

I know it's difficult for him to see my face through the stage lights, but I swear he's looking right at me. His dark gaze searing into mine. I raise my head, wanting to portray strength. Rhett needs to be one-hundred percent focused.

He needs to kick Thorne's ass and have fun doing it. He needs to revel in the last night of his career in the ring. After all the amazing things he's made me feel, the way he's brought my body to pure pleasure that created an entirely new relationship between my mind and my body, I owe him this. I'll give him this. This sense of peace and reassurance at knowing that I'll be fine. I'll be alright after tonight. After it ends. And that I'm here for him one last time.

"Rhett, this floor is yours. Do you have anything you'd like to say to your fans tonight?" The announcer approaches Rhett, shrinking inches in size the closer he gets to Rhett's larger-than-life frame. My heart leaps into my throat. This gesture from the announcer is not standard protocol before a match.

"Good evening, Boston," Rhett's voice rings out deep and sexy over the speakers, the female screams coming back in full force, buoyed by the deeper yells of men shouting out their boyish praises for a man they all imagine themselves to be at one time or another. Shelly doesn't look at me but she grips my hand tighter in her lap, knowing instinctively that I need it.

"I've been fighting in arenas like this for over ten years," Rhett gestures around him toward the fans, his arm muscles rippling under the lights, "and I've been fighting even longer. First on the streets before I found the gym. This place," he pauses, his eyes taking on a far-off look, "has been my sanctuary, my place of peace. A description that most would find...ill-fitting." He smiles sexily and I want to melt into a puddle on the floor. "But, I didn't do it alone. There have been many people, all of you, who have supported me. Some, in ways that I can never repay." His gaze finds mine through the stage lights and I know within my core that he can see me. That he really is looking directly at me, letting me feel the full weight of his gratitude at what the past few weeks between us have meant for him.

"The rumors you've heard are true. Tonight will be my last fight—" Rhett sounds like he wants to continue but the slurry of screams and boos and catcalls force him to pause. Once the noise is finally at a reasonable level again, he raises the microphone back to his lips. "Thank you, truly. I'll win one more for you, Boston." With that, he winks wickedly and hands the microphone back to the announcer, keeping his head down as he makes his way to his corner of the ring. I can feel hot tears streaming down my face but the rest of my body is still and unwavering. I wipe under my waterline, exhaling forcefully to calm my breathing as the crowd continues to go wild. The announcer finds his way back to the center of the ring.

"Alright, alright. I know this is big news, my friends, but we still have a fight to get to..." The announcer smiles wolfishly, clearly getting a thrill out of tonight's hype. "And everyone knows we can't have a fight without a worthy opponent. So, let's give a loud, riotous welcome, to the scrappy, the fearless, the evil, Thorne Montgomery!" This time, the crowd shatters into a series of disparate sounds, clearly more divided between fans and haters. The discordant sound is ugly and anxiety-inducing, bringing a sense of lawlessness to a space that had felt united just moments before during Rhett's announcement.

Thorne makes his way from the dark walkway into the ring, throwing his fists high into the air and dancing jauntily for the crowd. It's hard to tell if he loves the booing more than the cheering, the negative energy seeming to fuel and empower him further. I scowl at the arena, directing only negative energy at the sick man who tried to take advantage of me one night and who had his men deface my car. Trying to threaten Rhett to throw the fight, his *final* fight, through spooking me.

After several more minutes of chaos in the crowd, with Rhett and Thorne prepping in their respective corners with their coaches whispering harshly in their ears, the loud, clear noise of the bell rings out, signaling for the fight to begin. There's no turning back now.

—

Rhett wins the first round, but both fighters are a bit tight, keeping their distance and erring on defense. Thorne looks like he's thrumming with energy, desperate to draw blood. Rhett looks clear-headed, composed, entirely in control. In the ring, they are their traits personified. There's no hiding, nothing less than your truest self taking form in that ring when a win, and your life, are on the line.

Rhett wins the second round too, but Thorne was able to get in a few too many blows, early bruising already peppering Rhett's naturally golden, sweat-slicked skin. They are both breathing heavily, retreating to their corners more bruised and bloodied than they left them.

"Thorne is good." Shelly's tone is laced with disappointment and I can't help but nod in reluctant agreement.

"I know. I hate him."

"Me too."

We sit on the edge of our seats through the next few rounds, watching while both men bring every fiber of themselves with each blow, each punch. Rhett looks conflicted, like he wants to love this final moment but also like his strong body is breaking under the barrage of pressure. He has several years on Thorne. Both men are physically made for this style of fighting, large but agile, lean while still being muscular and powerful. But Rhett has the practiced skill, the right temperament while Thorne is all depraved hunger and youth. It's a fairly equal match-up, as equal as any fighter can be against Rhett, but by the end of round eight, Rhett is up five to three. If he can win the next round, it's all his for the taking. If not, it will go to round ten, and even risk going to a tie.

Thorne moves in quickly, his body launching at the sound of the bell. He pummels into Rhett's side. Even from my seat outside of the ring, I swear I can hear Rhett's ribs breaking.

"Holy shit, ouch!" Shelly yelps next to me, flinching like she's the one in the ring, unable to contain herself.

"Seriously, Shelly? Not helping." I feel my hands begin to shake, my limbs vibrate. I can't seem to control the energy and the nerves flowing through my body. It's like Rhett and I are connected somehow, the more he gets hurt, the more adrenaline and fear that floods through me. But I can't look away, each blow to Rhett's body blazing painfully into my memory, into fear and pain and anger I'll never be able to forget.

Rhett regains himself, anguish covering his face but his body performing expertly on auto-pilot. He rounds on Thorne, getting him in a weak position before jabbing him hard in the jaw, first on the left side, then on the right, blood spewing from Thorne's mouth. Both men stagger back almost dazed. But there is a noticeable shift in energy. Rhett seems like he wants it to be over. Like he's ready for that final fight bell to ring out loud and clear. Thorne looks like the taste of his own blood gives him a shot in the arm. Like he's loving it.

He charges Rhett and kicks his shin so hard that Rhett falls to his knees, giving Thorne the chance to throw a mean uppercut to Rhett's jaw that tosses his head back like a rag doll before he hits the mat with a reverberating thud.

I stand up before I'm even fully aware of what I'm doing. I yell out the word 'no' over and over again but no sound escapes my throat. It's like I don't even exist. Like I'm watching a scene trapped in time instead of something that is playing out right in front of me.

Rhett hasn't lost the match but he's lost the round. The score is now five to four and at this point, it's looking like it might be Thorne's for the taking. Like he really might have a chance. I feel my legs moving underneath me, my arms swaying in sync. I'm standing next to Coach Barry in seconds, my chest heaving unevenly. I tap his shoulder and he jerks around angrily.

"What in the hell, Ava?" Coach grabs my shoulders, his face marred with shock and confusion. I know I shouldn't be here beside the ring. I know that I'm more of a distraction, a liability, and that this goes against all the unspoken rules of the underground. And yes, this violent illegal place does have some *very* serious rules. But I need to see him. Up close. I need to touch Rhett's face, to kiss his lips. I *need* him to end this right now, in this round. I need him to stop breaking his body. I need him to stop breaking my heart.

"Let me see him, Coach. Before round ten." My legs are shaking but I widen my stance to stabilize myself.

"No."

"Yes"

"Ava, please for the love of God, go sit down. Now." Coach Barry looks stressed, his hands on his hips as the announcer calls the round, initiating the break before round ten.

"RHETT!" I peer over Coach Barry's shoulder and yell his name as loudly as I can, my dry throat cracking but still powerful with raw emotion. I see Rhett's strong but tired body lean over the ropes, his dark brows pinched together in confusion and anger.

"Ava?" His voice is both harsh and concerned as he scans me for any signs of injury or harm. I smile up at him, tears threatening in my eyes, as I try to conceal my nerves and my anguish.

"Hi." I start to step up closer to the ring. I hear Coach Barry mutter, *fucking hell*, but he doesn't try to stop my climbing.

"Ava, what are you doing? This isn't a good idea." The ice pack in Rhett's hand goes limp as his gaze tracks me hungrily. I awkwardly slip through the ropes into his corner before grabbing his face in my hands, ignoring some incredibly hostile female screams erupting from the audience at my presence under the lights.

It's just me and Rhett. In his corner.

"Listen to me, Rhett. You are the better fighter here. This is your fight. Your *final* fight. You are going to win this. Right now. There will be no tiebreak." I lean in even closer, my lips brushing up against his. I'll surely be receiving death threats from some female fans after tonight. "You've made me feel...everything. I will never forget it. Not one minute of it." I lock eyes with him and pause before continuing. "Win this fight, Rhett. Please. End this. Right now. For me, for *us*." I'm talking about so much more than this round. I'm talking about the fact that every minute this fight drags on, every minute I have to watch this man take another blow, is another minute of me under his spell. His ring bunny. His good luck charm. Our arrangement. I can't be free of him until he's free of this fight. Even if that freedom threatens to break me.

"God, Ava," Rhett's throat is so dry, the deep gravelly

sound of exhaustion mixing with anguish. "You're fucking special, you know that?" He grabs the back of my head, pulling me closer to him, kissing me like I'm the energy that he needs to finish this. He finally breaks the kiss, my lips salty with his sweat, as Coach Barry taps on the mat, an impatient reminder that our time is running out. "Is this goodbye?" Rhett's eyes are dark and troubled, something like dread and longing lacing through them.

"Yes." I swallow hard past the growing lump in my throat. He goes deathly still, his hands against my cheeks, before he slowly nods at my response, releasing my head from his hands.

"Then I'll finish it." He steps back away from me, his gaze moving determinedly past my face, essentially dismissing me. It hurts but it's necessary. This is it. And he needs absolute laser focus. From this moment on, it isn't about us anymore. From the moment that I confirmed our goodbye, I lost that right. This is about Rhett beating Thorne.

I hop down from the ring, Coach Barry helping me stay upright on my feet in my heels. He looks like he's about to chastise me but I blurt out before he can speak.

"I quit, Coach. I'm going back to school in a week." His expression changes, like he didn't expect those words to come out of my mouth. "I can't thank you enough. I know you don't like me right now, but the job you gave me...it's meant everything to me. I needed it more than you'll ever know." I don't linger around long enough for a response. I walk back to my seat, stoic and calm. The bell rings out and I turn to face the ring, ready to face this head on. Shelly thankfully keeps her mouth shut, clearly dying to ask me *what in the hell* just happened up there. But she knows now isn't the time.

Rhett bounces on his feet, his strong calf muscles raising him high into the air. Thorne appears wary at his renewed energy. But Thorne moves in, always chomping at the bit to make the first move. But Rhett is ready. He captures Thorne's fist in his hand, twisting his forearm painfully and unnaturally. Thorne cries out, the sound seemingly animalistic, supernatural. His face contorts in pain as Rhett jabs his knee into Thorne's side, causing him to buckle. The only thing keeping Thorne upright is Rhett's grip on his fist, still twisting further. A crack breaks out and reverberates in the arena before Thorne finally hits the mat, a writhing mess, and curls into a ball.

Rhett doesn't look at the crowd. He doesn't throw his fist up in the air in victory. He just stares down at the mat, his chest breathing heavily, blood and bruises dotting his impressive torso and chest.

The announcer hops greedily into the ring, grabbing Rhett's heavy wrist in his much smaller hand, and raises it above his head like a kid who just found a treasure.

"Ladies and gentlemen, the winner, the legend...Rhett Jaggar!"

46

AVA (2 MONTHS LATER)

"We've calculated that by moving the revenue model from a one-time licensing payment to a monthly subscription model, we will increase the current user base by 40% by lowering the cost barrier to entry. And we feel confident that we can offer annual and multi-year reduced rates to encourage longer-term commitments." I smile professionally out at the stadium-sized classroom, clicking through the slides in my presentation with ease. I've only practiced it a *million* times. I could give this pitch in my sleep. Since coming back to school, I've thrown myself fully into my coursework. Partly because it hits differently when I'm the one writing my own tuition checks instead of my dad. And partly because I'll do anything and everything to keep my mind off of *him.*

It's been two months. Eight weeks and three days to be exact. I'm not counting, really I'm not, I swear. I've just gotten good at math and quantifying everything since being accepted into the business school's scholarship program. The work is challenging and rewarding. I've met some really cool peers that I enjoy and connect with and surprisingly don't find myself missing my old social circle like I expected to. I really love the scenario-based projects where we take real business cases and reimagine how they can generate more revenue or what new markets they can go after next. It's exciting and thought provoking, always teaching me something new.

But it's still just a glimmer of the adrenaline-induced madness I was deeply and wholly entrenched in just a few months ago.

After my final presentation concludes, I high-five my talented teammates and exit the auditorium classroom.

"Hey, brainiac! You're still coming tonight, right?" Jacob throws his arm casually over my shoulder, a bright smile on his handsome and boyish face. Ever since I've come back to live on campus, he's been the one person from my past reaching out on occasion, inviting me to dinners and parties with his friends. The same friends who *used* to be my friends too until they all ghosted me when I fell from grace. I'm not resentful though. I don't care about that kind of stuff anymore. It used to be so important to me to be popular and to be liked. Now, I just want to feel productive and independent. I won't sacrifice any of that ever again just to fit in.

"Hey! Yeah, I'll be there. I can't stay too late because—"

"Let me guess. Because you have some super big test or important presentation that you're already more than prepared for but you're still going to study more because you're an overachiever?" Jacob grins at me, his arm feeling heavy across my shoulders. "College isn't just about work, you know? Sometimes you have to let loose. Do something crazy." He wiggles his pale brown eyebrows but mind is already somewhere else at the mention of *doing something crazy*. It's seeing the underground arena, the lights and sounds of the boxing ring, *his* strong hands sliding up my thigh under the hem of my dress, desperate hunger in his dark eyes...Jacob has no idea just how *crazy* my life had gotten.

"Hey," Jacob's tone is soft, mildly regretful, "I didn't mean to be rude. I was just teasing. I like that you're a smarty pants." I look up at him and offer a small smile. I don't even care what he said, my mind entirely consumed by my memories. Jacob is harmless. We have a sort-of dating history and a friendship. It's simple and surface-level, all that I have the capacity for right now in my life.

"I'll come over around eight?" I readjust my book bag, putting a little distance between us as I step out from under his arm. Jacob is throwing a big party tonight and it's been the talk of campus all week.

"Hell ya, see you then." He stares at me a moment too long before his usual light-hearted look crosses back over his face and he heads off toward another building for his next class.

—

A few hours later, I'm curling my hair in my small bathroom mirror, missing the slew of hair and beauty products that I used to have at my disposal when living at Shelly's apartment. I hear my phone vibrate and I hate that every time I hear it, I still have a faint glimmer of hope that it will be *him*. I should know by now, and the logical part of my brain does, but I can't quite seem to get my emotions onboard. There's that flutter in my pulse, a breathless 'maybe' on my lips, but it always dies the instant I look at my screen and see that it's not him. When I remind myself for what feels like the thousandth time that it will *never* be him.

When I do glance at my screen, it's a number that I don't

recognize. I slide to answer it anyway, fully expecting a scam call.

"You are receiving a call from an inmate at Massachusetts State Facility for men. Do you accept?"

I swallow hard, my heart thumping loudly between my ears. "Yes." I hear a long beeping tone and then silence.

"Honey? Ava?" My dad's voice comes over the line and I let out a sigh of disbelief. It's been weeks since we last spoke, my only updates coming from his terse and unemotional lawyer.

"Hi, Dad! Are you doing okay?" I don't know what else to ask. *What's the proper phone etiquette for this type of situation?* I wish I could hug him again and see his face.

"Hi, sweetie. I'm good, I am. I'm alright." His voice wavers a bit. "I heard you are back in school and studying business! I am so, so proud of you, Ava." I swallow back tears, breathing in slowly through my nose to calm myself.

"So, what's the latest?"

"Well, my bail is still too high," he lets out a nervous laugh, dripping with bitterness, "but the lawyer worked to get my sentence reduced and I'll be transferred to a more lenient prison. A facility for white-collar crime. So that will be nice." *Nice.* None of this is *nice* but my dad did hurt a lot of people. A lot of families. He has to serve his time. I'm glad to hear a semblance of more positive news at least.

"Can I...come visit you?" I pace my bedroom, laying out a few different tops on my bed. The activity of picking out an outfit for Jacob's party tonight feels trivial and silly considering all of the emotions warring inside of me.

"Yes! Once I am transferred in a few weeks, I can have visitors. I'd love to see you, anytime. I don't have too much going on here." He lets out a real laugh and I follow suit, something like relief bubbling from within me at the sound.

"I'm looking forward to it, Dad."

"So am I. I love you, honey. Stay strong. I'm so proud of you."

"Thank you, Dad. I love you too." We linger quietly on the line for a few moments before hanging up, the phone resting heavily in my palm. But I know it's not a good idea to let myself linger. These past two months I've hardly let myself sit still, sit in any type of silence, for fear of past memories and still-healing pains threatening to take over the progress I've made.

So instead, I throw on some loud pop music and start getting dressed, making myself a strong pregame drink and closing my school books for the evening. Tonight is a party. And I'm going to force myself to enjoy it.

I get to Jacob's around eight. I'm three drinks in and the edges of my vision are slightly smeary but I'm still standing upright. I smile lazily at semi-familiar faces, letting myself fall into the casual and easy-going nature of the crowd.

"Ah, there's my genius beauty in the flesh. Hi, Ava." Jacob pulls me into his side, kissing me on the cheek. I laugh but push him away, a little uncomfortable at his closeness even though we used to casually date. He hands me a recently-poured beer, the white froth sloshing over the edge of the red plastic cup. I take it in my hands as he leads me toward a large, plushy couch that looks like it's seen better days.

"You look pretty." His face is close. Too close. I can smell the beer on his breath and I pull back as far as I can but he just keeps coming closer, crowding my space.

"Jacob, I—"

He cuts me off by planting his lips over mine. I don't respond, my entire body freezing in place. I feel the beer spill from my hands and I jerk to grab it, but Jacob pushes me back down against the couch.

"Jacob. No." I keep my tone loud and clear, my heart rate spiking. He pulls back far enough to see the serious look in my eyes and lifts his hands, palms facing me, as if in mock surrender.

"Fine, prude. Jesus." He gets up from the couch, tossing me a hurt look before getting lost in the growing sea of drunk college students. I run my hands down my legs and stand up in search of water. I chug two full glasses before calling an Uber. No way am I going to stick around and try to force myself to have fun after *that*. I know I've made it perfectly clear to Jacob since coming back that all I want is his friendship. And after tonight, even that's off the table.

I really want to call *him*. I know that despite everything, he would come pick me up if I needed him. Take me away from this place and keep me safe. Maybe even knock out Jacob, not that I'd ask him to. But I've come too far to do that now. I'm making progress, putting one foot in front of the other, each day creating a little more separation between my past and my present.

The last time I'd seen Rhett was in between the ropes, his face sweaty and bruised, his temples red with blood, his eyes full of hunger and longing, replaced quickly by shields of determined focus when we'd said goodbye. Our final farewell.

To obliterate that wouldn't be fair to either of us. And who knows? He's probably already moved on.

47

RHETT (2 MONTHS LATER)

The sounds of punching bags connecting with fists help to calm my edgy mood. But not by much. Never enough these days. It's been two months since my last fight. My final fight. A bitter win. I miss the ring every morning but I know my body couldn't take it anymore. My time in the ring was done. At least that was a farewell I was at peace with.

"Hey, Coach." I amble over to one of the sparring mats, resting my forearms against the ropes. Coach Barry is studying a younger fighter, his moves wild and electric but strangely familiar.

"Nico Chavez. You fought him a few months back. Manic kid but a ton of potential." Coach doesn't look away from the ring as he speaks to me, reading the question in my mind before I could even ask it.

"How old is he?"

"Just turned twenty-four. Been through hell and back though. Acts like he's closer to thirty except when he loses his focus," Coach spits on the ground, "breath between combinations, Chavez! You're not going to beat anyone if you pass out from lack of oxygen!" Coach yells out the instruction before turning fully toward me.

"Aren't you supposed to be on some tropical island somewhere? Picking up women and getting a tan or whatever? This is your retirement. And you've earned the hell out of it. You should enjoy it."

"I enjoy being here."

"Rhett. You must be tired of this."

"It's not that simple." I drag a hand through my hair, a tension lacing through me. "This is all I know."

"Well," Coach rubs his hand over his bald head, "maybe it's time you explore something new. You're still young, by non-fighting standards. You've got enough money to keep you comfortable. That gives you the ability to explore a whole new career."

"Don't say stupid shit like that." I grumble at Coach as he lets out a sigh in mock annoyance but a small smile tugs at the corners of his mouth.

"Well, in that case, you already know that I want you to be a co-owner and head coach here at the gym. I was trying to give you a few months off after your final fight. But you just name your start date."

"Today."

"Seriously, Rhett?" I ignore Coach's surprise, turning my attention to Chavez in the ring.

"Stay longer on the follow-through! You're pulling your fist out of position too early. You're short-circuiting your own impact." Chavez meets my gaze, his expression a mixture of surprise and excitement. Despite his energy and his eagerness, something dark glimmers in his eyes. Something that reminds me of myself ten years ago.

After a beat, he nods at me before turning back to his

sparring partner. He expertly integrates the advice, improving the impact of his punch.

"You can't start today. Start tomorrow." Coach leans back from the ropes but I don't miss the joy in his eyes at seeing me already coaching a young fighter. He turns away from the ring, heading in the direction of his office.

"I'll be here at eight." I call out after his retreating back and he just throws up a hand in acknowledgement. I know he really does think that a bullshit vacation is what's best for me. But I have no interest in doing that. Where would I even go?

It would be completely different if I was going somewhere with *her*. I'd take her somewhere warm, secluded. Do nothing but fuck her senseless and eat five-star dinners for a week. That would be heaven. But men like me don't go to heaven. We stay in boxing gyms where we belong. Surrounded by sweat and blood and the relentless need to channel our violence, to silence our inner demons.

I am excited about becoming a co-owner at the gym and investing some of my winning money back into the place that made me. I've never really thought of myself as a teacher, but boxing is still all that I know. Inside and out. I'm intimately familiar with every detail, every nuance of the sport. If I'm not going to be living between those ropes anymore, then at least I'll be able to get as close as possible by being a coach. It's not about about making a logical or strategic career decision. It's just about doing what lives in my blood.

I head out the front door and shoot Leila a quick text. We've been talking almost daily since my final fight. Since Ava went back to school. Sometimes at night, I wonder if I imagined *her*. Made the whole thing up in my damn head. Like she was just some wet dream apparition, keeping me sane through my final months of fighting, only to leave me feeling hollow and confused as fuck after. I haven't even approached another woman. The thought of having anyone else's hands on me brings a wave of nausea to my gut. The lack of sex definitely has me on edge, but anytime I think about it, I can only picture Ava's gorgeous face and sinfully perfect body. The way her golden eyes would look up at me, lustful and trusting. No one can compare. No one *will ever* fucking compare. I'll just have to hope that time helps me get over it.

I look down at my buzzing phone to see Leila calling me and I swipe to answer.

"Rhett, come over for dinner! I'm so sick of texting. It's just not a real form of communication, you know. Your generation is so screwed up with all this phone stuff." I laugh at her annoyed tone and can't deny that what she's saying is true. I agree to her invitation and hope that my regular meetings with her continue to keep my demons in check.

At the very least, they've been keeping me numb. Able to clamp down any dangerous urges. Getting back into the gym tomorrow for my first day as coach will go further in helping with that too.

48

AVA

My eyes are bleary. The lines of text in my economics book blur together and I rub my eyes with the heel of my hand. I've been studying a ton. Too much. But I need a distraction after Jacob's weird behavior a few days ago at his party. I'm not attracted to him at all, but he has been my friend. I thought we were on the same page. But after my rejection, he's totally boxed me out, taking all of his fair-weather friends with him. That was okay with me, but the quiet stretches in my days have been growing longer, more lonely. It's just studying or Netflix. A short-term band-aid of distractions that will have to do for now.

I close my economics textbook and pour myself a glass of red wine. I cozy up on the couch, hearing the familiar intro sound of Netflix as it comes on the TV at the touch of my remote. I send Shelly a quick text, hoping she has any tidbits of fun or juicy gossip to tell me. Because I'm bored. More than just bored, it's something more hollow growing within me, threatening to swallow me whole. No matter how tired I am or how much I try to wear myself out with my school work, there's still a constant sense of monotone boredom. Like I've achieved a high so great, that I have to live the rest of my life knowing I'll never achieve something like that again. Those adrenaline rushes, the flurry of energy and vibrations that only come from Rhett's world. From Rhett's touch.

I hear my phone buzz and glance down thinking it's Shelly returning my text. Instead, I see a number that I don't recognize. This time I don't hesitate in answering, assuming it may be my dad again, calling collect from prison.

"Hello?"

"Hi, Ava? This is Leila." I hear a soft, gentle female voice on the other end of the phone. My throat leaps into my throat at the mention of her name. *Why is Leila calling me? I haven't talked to Rhett in months. Is something wrong, is he hurt?*

"Um, hi Leila. Yes, this is Ava." I want to ask *about him* because I can't imagine her calling me out of the blue like this with good news, but I hold my tongue. Fear paralyzes me on the couch.

"I hate to bother you like this. I found your number in Rhett's phone. A little intrusive of me, I know." She laughs nervously, her voice still light and feathery. "I know you and Rhett haven't seen each other in some time. I...I don't want to alarm you but Rhett...well, he's not so doing well." The pause is painful. I feel it crack open my chest, a flood of emotion spreading through me as my heart starts to race.

"What," my voice is breathless, "what do you mean not doing so well? Is he alright?"

"I'm afraid not. You know, he's a strong man, but he has his demons. I just worry that he may be letting those demons get the best of him. I just thought—" She cuts herself off by clearing her throat hastily, "I just thought you'd want to know. As someone who was so important to him. *Is* so important to him. Again I really hope I'm not intruding here—"

"Where is he?" I'm already moving quickly towards my front door, pulling on a pair of boots and a sweater. I look around for my keys, scrambling to get my purse in order.

"Well, I'd imagine he's at home. At his townhome." Leila's tone sounds oddly bright despite being laced with concern. Like she's relieved that I appear to be on my way out the door. The fear ratchets higher throughout my body and I force myself to breathe in slowly through my nose so I don't do something stupid like get in a car wreck on the way to Rhett's.

What if he doesn't want to see me? What if he's not alone? I force my thoughts away, unwilling to let the doubt stop me from helping him.

"I'll head there now. Thanks for...for calling me, Leila." She offers a thank you in reply and I hang up the call, quickly locking my front door.

Even if this ends up being irrevocably awkward and heartbreaking, I'll never forgive myself if Rhett is in pain or trouble and I wasn't there when he needed my help.

I have to actively force myself not to speed on the drive over. Which admittedly I don't adhere to very well. When I pull up to Rhett's elegant townhome, I feel my heart constrict at seeing his large black truck parked neatly in the driveway. I take a few deep breaths, resting my forehead against my steering wheel, and count to ten.

I force myself out of the car, my heart and my feet like two separate entities. My legs carry me forward to his door but my chest is like a weight pulling me back. *What am I even going to say when I knock on his door? How will I survive seeing him again?*

I don't let myself pause. I just knock, softly at first and

then harder. I keep my eyes glued to the floor and the air leaves my lungs in one huge gust when the heavy wooden door opens.

"Ava?" Rhett's voice is deep and filled with surprise. His dark brows pinch together and he does that sexy, protective full-body scan to make sure that I'm okay. Like I wouldn't be here on his doorstep if I was.

"Me? I'm fine. Are you alright?" I step forward, reaching my hand out to touch him but I drop it abruptly. I study his face as much as my racing heart will allow and want to cry at how handsome and masculine he looks, nothing like the college boys on campus.

"What?" He grips my forearm lightly, pulling me inside. A mouth-watering smell fills the room and I glance over to see a large pot on the stove. *Great.* Rhett and his irresistible cooking skills are back at it again. Then a pit forms in my stomach at the though that he may be cooking for someone—

"Ava, look at me." He tips my chin up at him, pulling my distracted gaze away from the kitchen. "Why are you here?" His tone is deathly serious and I can't tell if he's worried at my being here or pissed. The thought sends a nervous chill down my spine.

"Leila she—" I stammer out my words, stumbling as my voice shakes, "she told me you were...unwell. She said you had a relapse."

Rhett squints his eyes before responding. "She said that?" He cocks his head, a harsh glimmer in his eyes.

"Well, not in those exact words. But she talked about your demons and made it sound like—"

"Jesus." He drops his hand from my chin and runs a hand through his thick, dark hair.

"What? What's going on?" My level of concern somehow

escalates impossibly higher at his reaction. *What is he not telling me?*

"I didn't have a relapse. I haven't touched cocaine. Not even remotely interested." He looks at me, his voice deep and serious. I swallow hard before asking the question I never want to ask.

"What about—"

"No. Not once." I feel relief swell in me at his brusque response, knowing he's telling me the truth, but it's quickly squandered by the ferocious look on his face, something like painful longing ticking in his jaw. He moves in closer, his strong hands flexing at his sides. He doesn't touch me but he's only a few inches away. "I haven't had a relapse. Leila is...meddling. I haven't had a relapse but I haven't been fine either. Far fucking from it, Ava." His dark eyes are relentless. I finally notice the faint smudges under his eyes, revealing exhaustion on his handsome face.

"Me either." I stare back at him, heat spreading to my chest. "Why didn't you call me?" My voice is faint, barely a whisper. I hate how desperate I sound but I can't help it. Can't hide anything from him.

"Ava, you *made* me say goodbye to you in the ring. We both agreed that this, between us, wouldn't make sense in the real world. I'm not good enough—"

"Stop!" My exclamation is a surprise to my own ears but I don't stop the words from spilling past my lips. "Stop saying that. Stop pretending like that's even remotely true. It's an excuse, Rhett. You *are* good enough for me, for anyone who would be lucky enough to have you, and you know it. You just don't trust yourself. You think there's a chance you might mess this up. There's always that chance! But people choose to take the risk anyway." My eyes are wild as I stare back at him and my inhibitions are gone. I've spent months trying to distract myself from this man. Throwing myself into nameless faces and textbooks, trying to find a semblance of pleasure and enjoyment in anything else, only to find that everything pales in comparison.

"You're not fighting fair, Ava." His voice is gruff. I see a slight flair in his nostrils as he stares down at me, a mixture of anger and passion in his eyes.

"What's that supposed to mean?"

"It means I can't be responsible for breaking your goddamn heart, Ava! I'm not the man women marry. I don't work a desk job and come home at the same time every night. I've never wanted a woman like I want you. You're... God, you've *wrecked* me. But I'd rather live without you than do anything, literally anything, that would hurt you. Why don't you understand that?'

"You're hurting me more, Rhett, by not being with me. Why don't *you* understand *that?*"

Neither of us move. We just stand, inches apart, our chests rising and falling with exertion, our eyes glaring and cheeks flushed. We are on the precipice of something final. Something earth shattering. We both feel it in the air, like the tension might crack at any second but it depends on who will be willing to make the first move.

"I love you." Rhett's voice is deathly low, almost somber like he wishes it wasn't true but can't deny it any longer. Can't go another moment without telling me. It isn't an agreement or a promise. It isn't an apology. It's so much more. It's him baring his soul. *It's everything.*

"Rhett..." tears fill my eyes and I finally close the distance between us, reaching my hand out tentatively to place it on his hard chest. I don't have a chance to finish my sentence, to say the words back to him that we both know I feel in my heart, before his mouth is covering mine. Our teeth clash, our tongues warring only to be soothed by our lips. It's violent and all-consuming. The kiss baring everything we've felt and everything we've denied ourselves over the past two months.

He loves me. Rhett Jaggar, the legend in the ring, the best brawler in Boston, the king of the underground, loves me.

And God help me, I love him too.

49

EPILOGUE: AVA (1 YEAR LATER)

"**O**h my god, Eric, be careful! You're going to pop the balloons!" I hear Shelly whisper-shriek from outside the gym and a smile spreads across my face.

"Rhett..." I look up at him from under my eyelashes, his large warm hand engulfing mine.

"It was *supposed* to be a surprise." He smirks down at me, a sexy five o'clock shadow dotting his jaw.

"Shelly's not the most subtle." I giggle as Rhett guides me into the gym, his hand on my lower back. There are white and pale blue balloons everywhere, and a large sign with the word "Congratulations!" scripted in silver, glittering letters.

"Surprise!" Shelly pops a bottle of champagne when we enter through the front door, liquid spilling all over the gym entryway around her. She pours me a glass as I wrap her into a hug.

"Thank you! Wow, this is so sweet." The gym is filled with fighters and their girlfriends, as well as a few classmates from my business school program. I look over to see

Coach Barry clap Rhett on the back, pulling him gruffly into a hug.

I finally graduated, managing to somehow finish on time with the help of summer classes. I have a few job offers at some exciting companies in Boston, but I know what it felt like leaving this place once before, and I'm definitely not going to do it again.

"Can't wait to have an official Operations Manager running this place." Coach Barry walks over and kisses my cheek. The fatherly gesture reminds me of my dad and I try not to dwell on his obvious absence from this celebration party. I've been seeing him weekly. Despite his lawyer being a real stick-in-the-mud, he did manage to get my dad's sentence lowered to seven years. Which still sounds like a heck of a long time, but considering he was facing twenty-five years to life...seven years is a grateful compromise.

I smile back at Coach Barry, excited for my new role at the gym. Rhett is now a co-owner and head coach, and they've taken on at least eight new fighters over the last year, training the next class of ring winners.

"I'm so excited. The gym is growing so fast, I hope I can handle it all!" I take a sip of my champagne, momentarily distracted by watching Rhett's strong profile as he engages in some discussion with a new, high-potential fighter, Nico Chavez. I can tell that Rhett sees his younger self in Chavez. It's like he feels personally responsible for corralling Chavez's wild, naturally gifted energy into something productive, something powerful in the ring. My heart warms at seeing Rhett in a teacher and leadership role. And I can't deny the sense of selfish relief I feel at knowing he's no longer putting himself in direct danger every Friday night.

"Oh, you know you'll be able to handle it, Ava. You're a

very impressive young lady." Coach's words are warm but there's a slight sad, far-off glimmer in his eyes that I don't quite understand.

"Coach Barry, are you alright?" I rest my hand on his shoulder and he gives me a shrug and a small smile.

"Ah, nothing. I don't want to put a damper on today." He forces a bright smile on his face but continues. "It's just that my daughter...she's a few years younger than you. And she's been getting into some trouble lately. I think her mom wants her to come and stay with me and well," he lets out a hearty and abrupt laugh, "quite frankly I'm terrified. I still picture her as a little girl. I haven't really been around much in the last few years."

I smile at him reassuringly, surprised by his admission. "I didn't know you had a daughter, Coach. I'm happy to spend some time with her. Shelly is good with giving advice too. In fact, she might want to work on taking more of her own advice." We both laugh and look over at Shelly who is making a fool out of herself in a pair of boxing gloves as several fighters shout combinations at her that she fails miserably to mimic.

"I appreciate that, Ava. I really do." He puts his hands in his pockets, glancing tensely between Rhett and me. "You know, I thought at one point that maybe you weren't good for him. For Rhett. But I was wrong, so wrong. You're—"

"It's okay, Coach. I know. At one point, I didn't either. If I was going for him, if we'd work out. But now...now I'm certain. We're very happy."

"Ava," Coach laughs and rubs his hand over his bald head, "it's the most goddamn obvious thing in the world. I've known Rhett for years and I've never seen him as at peace as he's been this past year. With you."

As if on cue, Rhett stalks over to us, wrapping his arm

around my waist and pulling my back to his front. He kisses the top of my head and I can't help the girlish giggle that escapes past my throat.

"Coach, are you trying to steal my girl?" Rhett's voice is a playful growl.

"Only if I had a death wish. Congratulations again, Ava. See you Monday for your first day."

I turn my head up toward Rhett, the top of my hair not even grazing his chin. "Did you know Coach has a daughter?"

"Hmm?" Rhett's nose is buried in my hair, his hand sliding up from my waist to just under my breasts.

"Rhett! We are at a public party."

"All the more reason for us to put on a show."

"Rhett!" I swat playfully at his arm and his dark chuckle sends a pool of heat to my core. "We can't do this here."

"Locker room." Before I can protest, Rhett is pulling me in the direction of the locker room, his broad back leading the way. I let out a laugh until he whips me inside and has me up against the wall, his leg wedged between mine, holding me in place.

"I love you." My voice is sweet, intimate. I know I'll never tire of saying those words to this man.

"I love you more, Ava." His mouth slants over mine, and I lose myself in his touch. My forever fighter. My underground king.

ABOUT THE AUTHOR

My name is Skara Gray and I have always loved to write. My stories are about highly suspenseful and tense relationships between dynamic men and women. Thank you for reading!

www.skaragray.com

skaragrayromance@gmail.com

Wattpad: @skaragray

Instagram: @skaragray

DEAR READERS

Please enjoy a sneak peak of my next fighter romance, *Against The Ropes*! The book is now available for purchase on Amazon.

AGAINST THE ROPES

Nico Chavez doesn't get lucky breaks. He's from the roughest part of Boston and has been dealt a shitty hand. With two younger sisters to care for and no one to help him, he turns to underground fighting to make ends meet. When a match lands him up against Boston's top fighter, Rhett Jaggar, he knows he's got a real shot at fighting full-time.

When Rhett retires from the ring, he takes on Nico as his protégé; the opportunity of a lifetime. After a year of training under the watchful eye of Rhett and the legendary Coach Barry, Nico is ready to enter his biggest fighting circuit yet. And he's determined to make a name for himself and his sisters.

Meredith Barry has been acting out. From drugs to bad boys to skipping class, she's hellbent on making all the wrong choices. When she gets suspended from college for the semester for having drugs on campus, her mother sends her to live with her estranged father—a veteran boxing coach in Boston. Meredith is already angry at the world, but the thought of leaving sunny California to go live with a dad she barely knows has her blood boiling.

When the beautiful redhead sets foot in her dad's boxing gym, all heads turn. Well, all but one. Nico Chavez. The young, wild fighter with potential won't give Meredith the time of day. He has too much at stake for attention-seeking female distractions.

But when someone from Meredith's past comes back to haunt her, Nico may find that the fight for her is one he can't ignore.

CAN BE READ *as a standalone fighter romance, but recommended as a follow-on story to In His Corner.*

52

MEREDITH

"You know, Meredith, if this was your first and only offense, we may be able to agree to a month-long suspension. But you've been in my office nearly once a week this entire semester. I can't give you any more chances." The University Chancellor steeples her fingers on the surface of her desk, a concerned and disappointed look on her softly wrinkled face. "I don't know what's changed for you, Meredith. Your test scores last year were among the top 12.5% of our freshman student body. Your entry essay was a standout. I suggest you do a little self-reflection over the next four months."

My head whips up from staring at her hands on the desk to face the Chancellor directly. "Over the next *four* months?"

"You're suspended, Meredith. Effective immediately. You can come back in the fall. Pending a re-evaluation and absolutely no trouble with the law. Not even a jaywalking ticket."

"But...you can't do that! I mean, I *pay* to be here!" I place my palms on the desk, trying to steady my erratic breathing.

"I'm afraid, Miss Barry, that I can. And to be more accurate, your parents pay for you to be here based on your most recent tuition invoice. Your current credits will remain on file and if you still want to graduate in four years, you'll have the option of taking summer and online classes." The Chancellor leans back in her traditional, straight-back leather chair, watching me closely. "I suggest you focus more on your inner self. Perhaps some therapy sessions would do you good."

"Yeah, easy for you to say." I stand up from my seat, throwing my long, dark red hair behind my shoulders as I sashay angrily toward the office door. What does this woman know about needing therapy.

"I wish you the best, Meredith, I truly do." I don't respond. I need to get the hell out of here, and fast. I'm not about to let some old, ivory-tower Chancellor see any hot tears stream down my face. I'm not sad, I'm frustrated. I'm pissed. At least, that's my internal dialogue and I'm sticking to it. At least anger keeps me in motion.

My mom is going to freaking murder me.

"Woah, Meredith, wait up!" I hear a familiar voice behind me on the university lawn but I keep walking. I need to be alone. Preferably under my sheets in my dorm room where it's dark and quiet and I can be left to think about what the fuck I'm going to do for the next four months. *Four whole months!*

"Hey!" My friend Toni reaches my shoulder and is out of breath by the time she's able to catch up with me. But I don't relent in my pace. "Woah, what is up with you, Red?"

"Don't call me that." I hate that nickname. I've told Toni a million times that I want it to die in high school where it started. Toni and I grew up together, one of the pros and cons of going to a state school in the same place where you grew up. California colleges plus amazing year-round weather made it too hard to leave my childhood state. Even if it means I can't fully recreate my image like I wanted to. I was a little bit of a nerd in high school. Quiet, focused on my grades, shy around boys. I wasn't some loner in the lunchroom, but I definitely wasn't keen on getting attention. The summer before college I made a pact with myself to change that. I didn't want to go into my young adult life as the wallflower or the observer. I followed through on my commitment all of freshman year. I joined a sorority, was involved in academic clubs, went to parties and made more fairweather friends than I can remember.

Too bad sophomore year isn't going nearly as well. In fact, it's an absolute dumpster fire. But Toni doesn't need to know that.

"Look, I just...I think I failed a test and I need some space. Sorry." I keep walking toward my dorm, hoping the lame excuse will get her off my back.

"You? Failing a test? Shit, that *is* bad." Toni sighs and touches my shoulder. "Text me if you need anything. I'll see ya around."

I look down in response to a ping on my phone. I see an official email from the University Chancellor's office. Geez, they waste no time. I open the attachment and it outlines the terms of my suspension, written out in perfectly formal and cordial language that is really just masking a big, giant, "*fuck you, failure*", which honestly would have been an easier pill to swallow.

The Chancellor's words bounce painfully back and forth in mind: *I suggest you focus more on your inner self. Perhaps some therapy sessions would do you good.* If only she freaking knew. My inner self is gone. She's broken. The idea of leaving me alone with my own thoughts for four months is probably the most dangerous sentence she could grant me.

But she doesn't know that. No one does. And no one is going to find out either.

I glance back down at the email, the words blurring and magnifying through my restrained tears. I get to the steps of my dorm building when I notice I'm not the only recipient on the email.

Shit, they sent it to my mother too!

As if on cue, my phone starts to buzz and I outwardly groan in frustration. I can't even have five freaking minutes alone with the news that my life is practically over before my mother is already calling to chastise me even more. If I ignore her call, I will just be delaying the inevitable and the painful. She's relentless. I guess some might say I got that trait from her.

I take a deep breath and hit 'accept.'

"Hi, mom..."

"Meredith Elizabeth Barry! I am getting in my car right now and driving to campus to pick you up. You had better have an explanation for this because I am absolutely livid right now! What am I going to tell your stepfather?" I hear the ding of her Mercedes as she climbs into the driver's seat, already huffing in exasperation. Of course her first thought is about my stepfather. It's like my mother is embarrassed of me whenever I'm less than perfect. Worried it will stain the perfectly polished reputation she's established with her second, and very advantageous, marriage.

"I don't know, Mom, maybe try telling him that I'm a fuck up."

"Meredith! Language! I raised a young lady. What on Earth has gotten into you?"

Part of me wants to tell her. Just say it out loud in plain language, release the weight from my own chest. But she won't believe me. No one will. She already sees me as a failure. Do I really want to risk her branding me as a liar too?

"I'll go pack my things." I grumble into the phone and hang up, angrily wiping the tears from my eyes as I stomp up the stairs to my dorm room.

53

NICO

"Hey, Nico!" I hear Rhett's voice call out behind me. The sweat drips into my eyes as I slam my fists into the cracked leather punching bag, placing one thud perfectly after another.

"Yeah, Coach?" My throat is hoarse. I don't even know how long I've been at this today. Maybe five hours deep already? Time warps when I step into this gym. I never want to leave it.

"Hey, I'm still the 'Coach' around here." Coach Barry comes over to stand beside Rhett, his bald head gleaming under the gym's spotlights. Coach Barry had been Rhett's coach before Rhett retired from the ring earlier this year. And Rhett had been the best of the best. The 'king of the underground' they called him. I'm definitely gunning for his throne. But I know I'm still a hell of a long way from deserving it.

"Why don't you take a rest from the bag and come up into my office to sign some paperwork?" Coach Barry addresses me before he turns to head toward his office. Rhett cocks his eyebrow at me, telling me without words to hurry my ass up. My chest is still heaving slightly from exertion, and every inch of my olive tan skin is covered in sweat as I make my way across the gym floor to Coach's elevated office in a corner of the gym. We call it his watchtower.

"Take a seat, Nico." Coach is seated behind his desk, his glasses perched on his nose. I don't move when I see Ava standing behind him. She's all caramel brown hair, perfect skin, and feminine curves. She looks like a girl from a damn TV commercial.

"Stop." Rhett comes into the office behind me, slapping his hand hard, but not enough to hurt, against the back of my head.

"What? What was that for! I didn't even say anything!" I throw up my hands in mock surrender as Rhett makes his way around the desk.

"Yeah, but you were thinking it." Rhett stalks over to Ava and kisses her possessively, his hand gripping the back of her head. There isn't anyone within miles of this gym who doesn't know that Ava is Rhett's girl. He makes that shit *known*. I'd never go for a girl like that anyway. Girls that pretty and polished make me nervous as hell. Ava isn't simply hot or sexy. She's gorgeous, like something porcelain or whatever. *That* and me just don't mix. Never have. Not sure how Rhett managed to get his way with her but that woman loves him to death. I fidget on my feet, slightly uncomfortable at their overt display of affection.

"Sorry, Nico." Ava gives me a soft smile and pushes Rhett back gently. "I'll leave you all to the contracts. Let me know when we need to start planning travel and staffing details." She flashes me another feminine smile and I just nod awkwardly in response, averting my eyes.

"Are you going to sit down or just keep standing there like a damn statue?" Coach Barry folds his glasses in his hand and I move in quickly toward him, taking the seat across from his desk. "This is a big contract. We're talking a full-on, legit sponsored, no underground tournament. Even the legendary Rhett over here," Coach Barry jerks his thumb at Rhett who is leaning cockily against the wall, "couldn't manage to keep his nose clean long enough to fight in these types of events. There's no drugs, no booze, no prostitutes. And by 'no' I mean the tour will be crawling with that shit but you can't even so much as touch it. Do you understand what I'm telling you?"

I look between Coach and Rhett, nodding fervently. To be honest, I'm not fucking sure I have any clue what he's talking about. I've never left Boston. I've barely left my neighborhood in my twenty-four years of life, except to come to this gym to train. And all that isn't to say that I've been sheltered. Far from it. My younger sisters and I grew up in foster care, bouncing between displaced family members and temporary homes. I started fighting because there was a wild energy inside of me. And I *kept* fighting because I was good at it. And being good at something means you can get paid to do it.

So, no, I don't know the first thing about what traveling the country will be like or how many drugs will really cross my path. But I'm desperate, hungry. Coach Barry could've told me there'd be fucking dragons on the boxing tour and I'd still go. But I keep my mouth shut and just nod.

"Rhett and I will alternate flying in for major fights. We will get you a full-time tour manager who will oversee your day-to-day. We'd come along for the whole tour, but Rhett has Ava who'll be holding down the gym on her own and I have..." Coach Barry trails off as he sighs in something like resignation. "I might have my kid staying with me on and off for a few months so we will just have to be flexible." My brows perk up in surprise, but all the details of what Coach just said start to blur as I stare down at my name, 'Nico Chavez', printed in professional font, waiting for my signature next to a six figure amount that will change the lives of myself and my sisters forever.

"First fight is in six weeks. You've been training for over a year and it's paid off. You're ready for this from a technical fighting perspective." Rhett moves closer to the desk, choosing his words carefully. "But you're still young. Not too young to not be strong enough but not old enough to know the culture, the mental game. If I could teach it to you I would. But it's just one of those things you'll have to figure out on your own. And it's broken great fighters before." Rhett's face is utterly serious. He isn't trying to scare or threaten me. He has shown me over the last year that his intentions with my success are fully genuine. He sees an electricity in me that he wants to cultivate and I couldn't be a more eager student. But, I still have the sense that while we've both been through our fair share of shit in our lives, his is more of the seedier variety while mine is just plain ol' bad luck. Going on this tour and really living the life of a traveling fighter will probably help me better understand Rhett and his past. And hopefully not jeopardize my own future in the process.

"I'm ready." I sign my name as neatly as I can, sliding the contract back toward Coach Barry. My hands are already itching to get back to the bag. Coach Barry smiles at me but there's a lingering exhaustion in his eyes.

"Yeah, son, that's what they all say. The real test will be in a few months when you're really in the thick of it."

54

MEREDITH

I feel my phone ring in my hand but there is no point in answering it. I know my mom and her Mercedes are parked outside of my dorm. I allow myself one more outward groan before I grab my hastily packed bags and fix a look of stone-cold apathy on my face. One I can say I've perfected. Tears won't be getting me anywhere at this point.

"Meredith! My God, I almost crashed driving here I'm so angry with you. I just got off the phone with the Chancellor who detailed for me that you had drugs, DRUGS, on campus! And that they are very confident you were *selling* them! Why on God's green earth would a perfectly spoiled and well-cared for young lady like yourself be selling drugs?" My mom's pale blue eyes nearly bug out of her face, the faint fine lines around her mouth deepening with her emotion. Must be due for a Botox appointment soon.

"Sorry, Mom." I move past her and throw my bags into the trunk of her car before sliding into the front passenger seat and slamming the car door shut. This car ride is going to be hell, may as well get on with it. Besides, the University has only given me 48 hours to get off campus and not a fiber in my body wants to stay here a minute longer. I feel a roil in my stomach at the impending questions and texts from my friends that will no doubt be hurtling my way soon. I'll probably even get kicked out of my sorority, not that I care about that stuff nearly as much as I had freshman year. Too much has happened since then.

My mother slides into the driver's seat and lets out a heavy sigh before turning to face me. "Meredith, I know...I know I've been hard on you and I know I'm not always the sweet, supportive mother. But it's because I love you. I really do love you, you do know that?" Tears spring at the corners of her eyes and I immediately miss her previous show of anger. My mother and I have a tumultuous relationship at best. Anger is easier to deal with. Genuine feelings of regret and disappointment? Yeah, that's just plain torture.

"I know, Mom. I know that you love me." She nods once in response and puts the car in reverse, driving more slowly than I'm sure she drove on her way here. After a few painful minutes of heavy silence, she finally speaks again.

"I called your father." Her voice is quiet, formal. I whip my head from staring out the window.

"You what? Why?" I have barely seen or talked to my father over the last eight years. My parents divorced when I was seven. For a few years I shuffled between houses until my dad up and left me to move to Boston. It was like he wanted to wash himself free of me. I've never been the type to hang on to something that doesn't want to hang on to me. Call it pride I guess. Between a birthday card and a call on Christmas, I consider him a stranger.

"Honey, I'm out of ideas. I've given you every-thing....clothes, trips, tuition to a great University. Maybe you just need a change of scenery or something. Ellis sent her daughter, Amelia, you remember her? From high school? Well her mother sent her to live with her father and it was good for her."

"You just don't want me at home with you and Martin for the next four months. It's fair, really. I don't blame you. But just call it like it is, Mom. I don't mind." I level my gaze with her. My tone isn't angry, it's monotone. Martin and I have never taken to each other. He probably views me as the only thing on his cons list when it came to marrying my mother. We avoid each other and that works for us just fine. There is no way he'll want me back at the breakfast counter after I've already successfully left the house for college.

"Meredith, don't talk badly about Martin. That man has saved this family." I roll my eyes at her dramatic response, having heard this script too many times. "I actually called your Dad a few weeks ago. When you kept getting in trouble for your outfits and for disrupting class. *That* I thought I could still handle. But drugs? Your father has dealt with more in his life than me. He's more...equipped for these types of issues." There's a deep sourness to her tone. Like she's still blaming my dad for behavior that happened over fifteen years ago. All I know about him is that he's some sort of boxing coach. Maybe boxing and drugs go hand in hand. I wouldn't know. And I definitely don't care. I'll never tell anyone about what happened with the drugs they found on campus, least of all my estranged father.

I stare out the window for several long minutes, watching the blur of trees along the highway. The sense that this isn't a discussion but rather a proclamation settles over the interior of the car like dust after a storm. The decision is done. No use in wasting my energy on trying to convince my mom otherwise. I'm tired of picking so many battles.

"I'm assuming there's no point in me disagreeing with this?" I turn toward my mom, my arms crossed over my chest. I can feel a heat in my cheeks but I won't let the tears fall. I clench my teeth tight, physically trapping my emotion down.

"I'm afraid not, Meredith. And if you're going to hate doing it for you, then consider it a favor for me. For your mother who has been worried sick about you. I never had to worry about my sweet Meredith before! You're supposed to go through this kind of phase in high school, not as a young adult starting your life. I simply won't tolerate it. I see no other options." My mother's steely veneer is back in place, our brief heart-to-heart from earlier in the drive effectively over.

"Guess I'm going to Boston then." I pull my ear pods from my purse and close my eyes with my head titled back, my poor attempt at tuning out the rest of this ride and my current, shitty reality.

READ AGAINST THE ROPES, now available on Amazon!

55

ABOUT THE AUTHOR

S kara Gray began writing after her avid love of reading led her to want to create characters and stories of her own. She writes in the mornings, evenings, and weekends, enjoying bringing fresh takes to well-loved tropes with highly dynamic and compelling characters. She regularly releases new works, so be sure to keep an eye out for the next exciting story!

TO FIND out more about Skara Gray or her books, explore the links below:

Amazon Page

Website

Newsletter

Goodreads Page

Wattpad

Instagram